ROOSEVELT'S JUBILEE

A Novel
Revised Edition

Steven M. Wilson

Dedication

To the Men and Women in Blue

About the Author

Steven Wilson is the author of VOYAGE OF THE GRAY WOLVES, ARMADA, BETWEEN THE HUNTERS AND THE HUNTED, PRESIDENT LINCOLN'S SPY and PRESIDENT LINCOLN'S SECRET, published by Kensington Books Publisher, as well as ROOSEVELT'S JUBILEE, and THE ANCIENT BLOOD. He was Assistant Director and Curator of the Abraham Lincoln Library and Museum and Instructor of History for nearly three decades. He developed and presented the web program LINCOLN MOMENTS, contributed to and was the Managing Editor of THE LINCOLN HERALD. He can be reached at authorstevenwilson.com.

The Times of London
A Relic of James II
*An account was given nearly four years ago of discovery at the Scottish College of
two leaden cases, believed to contain the brains of James II and the heart of the
Duchess of Perth.*

CHAPTER 1
THE VICTORIA EMBANKMENTS LONDON, ENGLAND

Madame Tussauds," Edith Roosevelt said, "on Marylebone Road."

"Why in Heaven's Name do you want to go to a wax museum?" Theodore replied.

"The exhibit is Great Romances of the Ages. Oh, please, Theodore? Think of it? Romeo and Juliet, Antony and Cleopatra."

"Theodore and Edith," he teased.

"Promise to take me there, and I shall never ask another thing of you," she said.

"Of course, Edith. Why not? We could use a little adventure."

"Theodore?" Edith Roosevelt said. "Why is that man running?"

A dark form, dashing through the pools of the streetlamps, rushed at them. He wore no hat, and his coattails flapped wildly as he ran.

"Stand aside, Edith," Theodore ordered, stepping in front of her. "Halt!" Theodore demanded.

The man continued running.

"Stop!" Theodore raised his walking stick.

The man tried to stop. "No," he shouted, sliding on the gravel and landing at Theodore's feet.

"Stay back, Edith," Theodore commanded. He pinned the man to the ground with his foot and leaned over him.

"Is he hurt, Theodore? Who is he?" Edith could not see the man's face, but she heard him gasping for air, sobbing.

"Good Lord," Theodore exclaimed. "It's the Prince of Wales."

Albert Edward, The Prince of Wales, face contorted in panic and streaked with dust and tears, looked helplessly at Edith. His coat was ripped, and the knees of his trousers were torn out. He pushed himself up on his elbows. "You must help me," he managed, looking from Theodore to Edith.

Theodore pulled the Prince to his feet and began slapping dust from his coat.

"My dear man," Theodore said. "What has happened? Were you attacked? Can I summon someone?"

The Prince drew a sleeve across his eyes, wiping away his tears. "No. No, you must not," he managed. "You must help me. Please, I beg of you."

"Theodore?" Edith said. "He needs medical attention."

"No. Not me. You must attend to the lady," the Prince of Wales cried. "Can't you see it means humiliation if anyone knows? Will you aid me?"

"All right, man, all right. Of course. You can count on us," Theodore said. "How can we assist you?"

The Prince slumped in relief against Theodore. When he regained his composure, he was ready to talk. "That is the Hotel St. Denis." He pointed at a building with gaslights, filling the windows with a pale glow. It was wedged between two larger structures. "You see it? There."

"Yes, I see it," Theodore said.

"Suite 319," the Prince said. He dropped his hands to his knees, gulped for breath, and then continued. "A friend of mine. In the suite. She is ill. A young lady. Will you go to her?"

"If she is in need of attention," Theodore began, "why ...?"

The Prince grasped Theodore's shoulder. "Please. There is no time. My position. I could not. Please help her."

"All right," Theodore said. "Edith? Will you stay with the Prince, please?"

"No. No," the Prince of Wales said. "I am not injured. My coach is nearby. I will go for assistance."

"You can count on us, Your Majesty," Theodore said.

The Prince nodded. "I won't forget this." He looked from Theodore to Edith. "I promise that I will do everything I can to repay you."

"Nothing of the sort," Theodore waved off the promise.

"Thank you," the Prince of Wales said. "God bless you." He ran off toward his coach, disappearing in the darkness.

Theodore looked at Edith in bewilderment. "Come, my dear. Let us go find what we may find."

"Theodore? What do you have on your sleeve?"

Theodore held his right arm up to the faint light of the streetlamp. The fabric glistened. "Blood," he noted. "From the Prince. We must hurry."

"I don't understand," Edith said, as they descended the stairs down the Embankment and walked across the narrow street to the hotel. "Why did he run away? Why did he not help that poor woman? The Prince of Wales of all people."

"Panic. Sheer panic," Theodore said. "Befuddled and confused. You'd never see an American leader behave in that fashion. I'm not surprised he was ashamed for anyone to see him."

The Hotel St. Denis was unremarkable, a four-story building no more than fifty-feet wide wedged between its more impressive neighbors. There was nothing to indicate it was a hotel except a modest brass plaque to the right of the door. There was no doorman, and the only way to enter was by a pull ringer on the door facing.

"This is a very strange hotel," Edith said.

"Yes," Theodore said, pulling the ringer again. "I imagine it has a select clientele. Princes and whatnot."

"This is certainly not the way I envisioned spending my honeymoon," Edith said.

"Never let it be said that I am a conventional husband."

A young man in a trimly tailored suit answered the door, bid them good evening, and stood aside as they entered. They found themselves in a modest but well decorated lobby. Three men sat reading newspapers, an older couple played chess, and a young man smiled from behind the front desk.

"May I help you?" the man asked.

"Suite 319," Theodore said.

The clerk was discrete. "I'm sorry, but the occupant of that room did not leave instructions to receive guests."

Edith spoke. "Of course, he wouldn't." She moved close to the counter. "But I'm sure Eddie would be more than disappointed if we were turned away."

Theodore caught on. "Yes. Eddie."

The clerk smiled again. "Indeed. Would you prefer a key, or would you like to be announced?"

"A key, if you don't mind," Edith said. "One does like the occasional surprise, doesn't one?"

"Yes," the man said. He fetched a key from the board behind the desk. "You may take the stairs to your right or the lift just beyond."

They started up the stairs when Theodore asked, "Why did you ask for the key?"

"The young lady may not be in any condition to answer the door or be exposed to hotel employees."

"Amazing," Theodore exclaimed. Something else occurred to him. "How could you possibly know to call him Eddie?"

"I read an article in *Colliers*," Edith said. "There is something else as well."

"Something else?" Theodore asked.

"The Prince was completely disheveled when we saw him. Yet, the clerk did not react when we mentioned the room number."

"Perhaps, the room is in the young lady's name," Theodore said.

"We've seen the Prince of Wales once, Theodore; and, yet, we had no difficulty recognizing him. His image is in all the papers. Suppose Cleveland came running through the lobby in the same condition as His Royal Highness?"

"I would have shot him," Roosevelt said, "in the posterior."

"Theodore!"

"Oh, now, Edith, don't be concerned. It's not a vital organ. Even on a Democrat."

"No one saw the Prince," Edith said. "He must have taken another exit."

"That is logical," Theodore said. "He did not want to be recognized."

"Suppose," Edith offered, "he had not been fortunate enough to encounter us? See how he avoided the lobby? He was not seeking help, Theodore; he was fleeing."

They arrived on the third floor, got their bearings, and turned left. It was an intimate space, lit by gas lamps, footsteps muffled by carpet, with the papered walls a wide array of burgundy and gray designs. The hall was L-shaped, with Room 319 at the end of the short leg.

Theodore turned to Edith. "What should we say?"

"What do you mean?"

"We certainly can't trouble this young lady if we don't know what the circumstances are. The Prince was of virtually no help whatsoever."

"Goodness, Theodore," Edith said. "Stand aside." She knocked softly. "The only time I've seen you gripped by indecision is when it concerns protocol."

"Nonsense," Theodore countered, and then added. "Well, perhaps, you're right."

Edith knocked again, peered down the hallway to see if anyone was present, and tried again.

Theodore grasped the doorknob and turned it. The door clicked open. "Hello?" he called softly. "Theodore and Mrs. Roosevelt here." He turned to Edith. "Good Heavens, Edith, I don't even know the woman's name."

"Hello?" Edith called. They moved from the suite entrance into the sitting room. "The Prince of Wales asked us to see to your wellbeing. Miss? Are you all right?"

"Edith," Theodore said, the color drained from his face.

Edith followed his gaze and saw the body of a young woman, soaked in blood, on her back. The dead woman's eyes, partially opened, stared at the sparking chandelier overhead. She was dead.

CHAPTER 2

Theodore," Edith managed. "I feel sick to my stomach."

Theodore approached the body. Kneeling next to the woman, he looked back to Edith. His wife, wide eyes in an alabaster face, sat tightly gripping the arms of the chair. "Edith? How are you feeling? Are you going to vomit?"

"All I see is blood," Edith said. She gathered herself and drew a deep breath. "No. But I'm afraid I can't stand. Give me a moment, will you?" Her eyes glistened. "She's dead, isn't she?"

Theodore nodded. "Yes. Quite dead," he said, studying the wounds across the woman's torso. "She's been stabbed. A dozen times or more."

"Oh, the poor creature."

Theodore stood; his interest drawn to the room. "Someone has ransacked this room. See? There. The drawers in that chest." He moved around the body to an open door that led to a bedroom. "In there." He turned to Edith. "Someone has torn this to pieces."

"Not the Prince," Edith said, rising. "A madman did this." Her strength returned as she studied the scene. "What were they looking for? Money?"

"Perhaps, robbery," Theodore suggested, but considered the scene and agreed with Edith. "A crime of passion, I'm afraid. Look at the poor creature."

Edith stepped around the dead woman's feet, sorting out the confused landscape.

Theodore's hand reached out to stop her. "Edith? Don't."

"I'm quite well, Theodore," she said, turning her husband's concern away. The setting had her full attention. "This is not by the Prince's hand." She was certain of that.

"I don't know, Edith. I believe whoever did this was searching for something or perhaps staged a robbery. Whether this poor girl's fate came as a result of one or the other is a mystery."

Something partially hidden by the woman's body caught her eye. "Theodore? What is that?"

Theodore joined his wife. The corner of an envelope protruded from the folds in the woman's dress. He knelt and gingerly moved the bloody fabric to one side. "This feels uncommonly indecent," he said. "No gentleman takes liberties with a lady, much less one who is dead." He freed an envelope and handed it to Edith. "There's something in it. A letter, I believe."

The edge of the envelope was soaked with blood. Edith opened it and removed a paper. There was writing on one side only. She examined the envelop. It was blank. She returned to the writing.

"'Dearest Eddie,'" Edith read. She looked at Theodore, her eyes filling with tears. "Albert Edward."

Theodore rose. "Albert Edward, Prince of Wales. He may indeed be the monster who murdered her."

"Oh, no, Theodore," Edith said. "That's impossible."

"You don't know that. This is their place of assignation. He approached us on the Embankment, practically mad with distress. It's well-known he has a virtual harem at his disposal. Trust a woman to be lost in romance and ignore the details. The man's coat was stiff with blood. Her blood, I'll wager. He abandoned her, didn't he? Or worse."

"Don't be judgmental, Theodore," Edith said. "It's unbecoming. This is the work of a heinous murderer. I don't believe a member of the royal family is capable of this. Now, shall I continue reading?"

Theodore gave her a chastised look.

Edith took a deep breath. "'Dearest Eddie. How I long to see you, but when you read what I have to tell you, you may never want to see me again. I have been ill-used, my love. A pawn in a horrible game that will cause you, and your family, great harm. Please forgive me, my dear. Our mutual friend has betrayed us both. I care not for harm that comes to me, but I would rather die than to see you in pain.'" Edith looked up, shocked. "'Mutual friend?' Who could that be?"

"The Prince of Wales?" Theodore mused. "Anyone of five thousand souls."

"Of course," Edith replied and returned to the letter. "'I overheard too much, and suspicion has fallen on me. G is suspicious.'" She gave Theodore a questioning look. "Is this a C or G?"

Theodore perched his glass on his forehead and examined the letter. "The writing is atrocious. G. Yes, assuredly, a G."

She continued. "'G is suspicious. You must go away from me. Divorce me from your mind. As for you, I will never forget my love for you, and the time we spent together.'" Blood covered the lower portion of the letter. Edith held it up to the light, hoping to make out the signature. She tilted the letter and said, "'Margaret,' or 'Maryanne.'" She handed the letter to Theodore. "I can't make out the name through the blood." She looked at the body, dressed in white. "She could have been a schoolgirl. Young, and remarkably innocent, I suppose, regardless of her situation." She peered at the body, cocking her head in revelation. "Whoever killed her was right-handed."

"Edith? How can you…?"

"Elementary, my dear Theodore. See the defensive wounds on her right hand and arm? The killer struck, thus," she pantomimed the attack. "Stabbing like so. Right hand across the body."

"Remarkable," Theodore said. "See here, Edith. Any association between this poor woman's death and the royal house could create a scandal that could very well result in the end of the monarchy. We don't know if the Prince has anything to do with this. He may have arrived, found the girl murdered, and been struck insensible by the discovery. No. The best thing we can do is leave the hotel as if nothing has happened, contact the Prince in the morning, and confront him with what we know."

She ventured into another option. "The police, Theodore? Should we not contact them?"

"No. Let the body be discovered."

"Theodore?"

"Trust me, Edith. This is more than murder. This is politics."

"The hotel clerk," Edith reminded Theodore. "He could identify us."

"We'll have to take that chance, I'm afraid. I wish I knew more about the circumstances surrounding this poor girl's death. Somehow, knowing would be comforting."

"We know much more than when we first arrived," Edith said. She held up the letter as proof. "The dead girl and the Prince were involved. That is a certainty."

"What is certain," Theodore said, "is that perception oftentimes overcomes reason. Every newspaper in the land, and every political enemy of the Prince of Wales or Queen Victoria, every anarchist will spin a web of misinformation, lies, and innuendo regarding this horrible incident. The justice this good woman deserves will be denied her, when the vultures arrive."

Edith knew that Theodore was right. "I am frightened, Theodore. Your good name? Once we set out to confront the Prince, when we set foot through that door, we are endangering everything you've worked for. We could be the very pawns the young woman wrote of."

Theodore brushed her concerns aside. "I am perfectly…"

"Theodore," Edith warned him. "This is no time for bravado."

Theodore said, "What you say is true, my dear." He smiled to reassure her. "Edith. There is right, and there is wrong. Regardless of the consequences, we have no choice but to choose the former."

Edith said, "What will we do now, Theodore?"

He thought for a moment before answering. "We will go back through the lobby, making certain to say good night to the front desk clerk. We must be seen, and we must be without a care. We can't let anyone see our distress, Edith. That would convey that something is amiss. Can you do it?"

"Yes."

"Good. We will hail a cab and return to our hotel." He exhaled deeply. "We shall refresh ourselves, study the situation, and develop a plan of action."

"Yes," she agreed, eyes on the dead girl.

Theodore threw his arms around Edith in a bear hug, turning her away from the body. "Now, my dear. Let's be about our business." He led her away and took her small chin in his fingers. "I love you, Edith. We shall overcome this."

They were about to leave when, on impulse, Edith turned to give the girl a last look. "We should say a prayer, Theodore. No one deserves to die without a word to God."

Theodore pulled her away. "In the cab, my dear. For her, and for us as well."

The *Times of London*
AUCTION-SOUTH KENSINGTON
*The Capital family residence, No. 2, Lexhan Gardens, contains a reception room, 10
bedrooms, etc., in good decorative repair, with vacant possession.*

CHAPTER 3
THE LOBBY OF THE ST. DENIS HOTEL LONDON, ENGLAND

Inspector Abberline dropped one corner of his newspaper and scanned the lobby. It was nearly empty. The chess players were gone, and a bellboy and the front desk clerk felt safe enough from the intrusion of customers to banter back and forth.

He dug his watch out of his vest, flipped the cover back, and noted the time. According to the young man at the front desk, two Americans had gone up to Suite 319 just over twenty minutes before the inspector's arrival. They took the staircase instead of the lift. When he had approached the desk clerk to ask the clerk if the two had visited the hotel before, the clerk replied, "I'm sure I have no idea, do I?"

Abberline was tempted to give the man a sharp rap across the bridge of the nose, but he knew it would draw too much attention. He had settled on, "This is police business. Find out, or I'll take you outside and give you a drubbing."

The clerk had appeared unimpressed but said, "Yes, sir. Right away, sir." A few moments after Abberline had returned to his chair, he lowered the paper to find the clerk, who had said, "I'm terribly sorry, sir. No one knows who they are. Americans, that's all. I've never seen them before, sir."

Abberline had retreated behind his newspaper barricade and waited for the Prince to reappear. It was a party; he decided, the Prince and his mistress, the Americans. A quiet little dinner party. He would sit in the lobby and pretend to read *The Morning Post*, and a mutilated copy of the *Illustrated London Times*. His partner, Harvey, was in the alley, watching the servant's entrance in case his Royal Highness chose to avoid the lobby.

It was police work of the most common order. Sit, wait, watch. Boring beyond measure, but he had been ordered to keep a close eye on the Prince of Wales and his activities.

"See that the little squid stays out of trouble," Superintendent Hasselbach had ordered Abberline.

He folded the *Post*, decided against the *Illustrated Times*, and laced his fingers over his chest, closing his eyes so he could watch the lobby through the slits of his eyelids. Hasselbach wanted a report on the Prince and his comings and goings noted. It was a strange request but not outlandish. Men of authority always wanted to know what other men of authority were about. Abberline had no authority or position, but he had common sense enough to keep quiet when his superiors gave instructions.

Abberline saw the Americans descending the stairway, casually, relaxed, the woman's arm looped through the man's. A short visit. A courtesy call. The Prince had received them; pleasantries were exchanged, and the Americans bid the Prince and his mistress farewell. An early night.

He watched them as they approached the desk, said a few words to the clerk, and then moved on.

It was the woman who caught Frederick Abberline's attention. He saw it in her carriage, not the fluid movements of a lady, but tentative steps as if she was being led away. He swung his gaze to the woman's face. Her eyes were swollen, and Abberline noticed when her companion spoke to the clerk, she kept her head turned. She might be trembling, he thought, but it was difficult to tell. She gripped the man's arm tightly, almost as if should she let go, she would fall.

Abberline rose from the chair as the couple passed through the front door. It could be nothing, a drunken exchange. Some unfortunate comments that insulted the Prince of Wales. But as Abberline took the stairs two at a time, he knew it was much more than an exchange of words.

He wouldn't detain the Americans; he could find them when he needed them. The Prince's well-being came first. He made his way up the stairs.

He knocked on the suite door, waited a moment, and slowly opened it. The stench of blood filled the air. He saw the body, looked through the remaining rooms, and satisfied they were empty, and came back to the murdered girl.

She had been butchered, knifed a dozen times or more, and her torn dress was soaked dark with blood, nearly dried. He circled her, calculating how the attack had occurred.

He decided that he had time to determine the circumstances of her death. Only one questioned concerned him now.

Where was the Prince?

Abberline's mind raced through the situation. There were no other exits into the lobby save the staircase and the lift, but the lift was ridiculously slow. The window?

Nonsense. The rotund Prince couldn't climb out the window and make his way down three stories to the street.

The alley, Abberline thought. Harvey?

The Prince had to have made his escape down the servant's stairway and out the tradesmen's entrance into the alley.

Harvey must have seen the Prince. "You'd better have him, you filthy sot," he murmured. Abberline bolted through the door leading to the service stairway and raced down the steps, until he found a doorway leading out into the alley. The air was heavy with the stench of garbage.

"Harvey? Where the bloody hell are you?" He saw the policeman, barely visible in the darkness, leaning against a crate, arms wrapped around his stomach, moaning. He raced over to him. If he'd been stabbed or shot, the poor man's intestines would have spilled onto the dank alley floor. Abberline had seen that sort of thing before.

But not this time.

Abberline smelled raw gin. Harvey twisted around, bleary-eyed, vomit clinging to his beard.

"Freddie?" He tried to straighten. "Hadn't you oughtta be in there?" He glanced in the general direction of the hotel.

Abberline slapped his friend. Harvey, stunned, tried to focus. He hit his partner again, this time with a fist, knocking him into the crate. "Did he come this way?" He grabbed Harvey's collar and jerked him upright. "Did the Prince of Wales come through here?"

Harvey wiped his nose with the back of his hand. It came away with blood. He was stunned by his friend's attack. "Why did you hit me, Freddie?"

"Because you're dead already, and there's nothing I can do to save you. Because there is a girl carved to pieces in a room upstairs."

"What?"

"Albert Edward?" Abberline shouted. He struck Harvey again. He wanted to smash him into pulp on the filthy dirt floor of the lane. Abberline had been carrying Harvey for years with promises that he'd quit drinking, that he'd given up the bottle.

"I went to the temperance meeting, Freddie. Everything is going to be all right. I promise you," Harvey had told Abberline.

Harvey brushed the vomit from the front of his jacket. "The Prince of Wales, Freddie?"

Abberline checked his frustration. "Did you see him?"

"No." Harvey was confused. "Not here. Not tonight." He pawed at his coat for a bottle. He wanted to make everything all right. "Let's have a drink, you and me."

Abberline pushed him away.

Harvey, smiling crookedly, wrestled the bottle out of his coat and held it out to his friend. They would drink, and everything would be fine.

Abberline jerked the bottle out of Harvey's hand and smashed it against the building behind them. "Now listen to me, you drunken fool. Friends or not, if you fail me, I'll have you sacked. Get up to Suite 319. Don't let a soul in. No one. I'll send for the Superintendent. No one's to go into the room. Stay there until Hasselbach arrives. Something terrible has happened, and I've got to go sort it out. Do you understand me? Talk to no one."

Harvey head bobbed out a nod. His hands fumbled to arrange the twisted fabric of his coat.

"That's right, Harvey," Abberline said. "I need you back on the force. You were the best policeman I ever saw. You have a chance again. Now, what did I ask you to do?"

Harvey sorted out the orders. "Go up to 319. No one's to go in. Talk to no one. Only the Superintendent."

"Right," Abberline said. He slapped Harvey on the shoulder. "Off you go." He waited until his friend trotted to the service entrance, and then he ran to the front of the hotel. It was a mistake. He should have stayed with the body and sent for assistance. Harvey can't do it. But he's all I have, Abberline thought.

He spied a cab at the lane's mouth, its driver slumped over in his seat, dozing. Abberline tore off a sheet from his notebook, took the stub of a pencil from his vest pocket, and began to write. When he finished, he pounded the body of the cab.

The driver snapped awake. "You don't have to scare the stuffing's out of me."

Abberline folded the paper and handed it to the cabby. "Take this message to Scotland Yard. Deliver it to Superintendent Hasselbach. For his eyes only."

The man took the note reluctantly. "I trust I'll be amply compensated for my services?"

"If you don't leave just now," Abberline said, "the next services you have will be at Newgate Chapel." The cabby snapped the reins, and his horse took off, increasing its speed from a walk to a canter.

Abberline ran to the cab ahead. The driver had a curry brush out and was stripping hairs from the bristles with a pocketknife.

The driver touched his knife to the brim of his cap. "Evening, sir."

"Did you see a couple come out of the hotel?" Abberline asked. "The man had a mustache. The woman was upset. It's important."

The cabby turned to his horse in thought and began brushing its back. His face brightened. "I did come to think of it. Americans, they were. Lovely couple. Not half an hour ago."

"Yes," Abberline said. He might have made the right decision after all. "Americans. Did they take a cab? Do you know where they went?"

"Well," the cabby said. "They did, and I do. They got in Ernie's cab, and he's the next in the queue, you know. I hear Ernie tell Geraldine, 'Take us to the Russell House, old girl,' and off they go."

"You're sure," Abberline said. "The American went to the Russell House?"

"Geraldine has to know the fare and destination, and she doesn't know that until Ernie tells her. That beast is smarter than her master and more dependable."

The Times of London
At Bow Street, before Mr. Bridge. Lieutenant Colin W. Young, of the 2nd East Surrey
Regiment, stationed at Dover, was charged under the Criminal Law Amendment Act
with the abduction of a girl named Elizabeth Aspey, age 17.

CHAPTER 4
THE DUKE OF LANCASTER'S SUITE, RUSSELL HOUSE, LONDON, ENGLAND

Theodore had dismissed the servants after returning to their suite. Edith sat on a settee, numb, saying nothing. He fixed them both a tumbler of Scotch. He handed one to Edith, who took it without comment. When she realized what it was, she looked at her husband in shock. "But Theodore? This is alcohol."

"I know," Theodore said. He held the glass to the light, watched the liquid sparkle, and then drank. "I took a vow never to touch the accursed stuff after I saw what it did to poor Elliot. But we both need stiff bracing, my dear, so I've set my vow aside for this occasion. Drink only a sip. Your gullet will catch on fire, and it'll land in your stomach like a ton of bricks."

Edith nodded and took a sip. She coughed out a mouthful, and her face turned red. "Water," she gasped, tears streaming from her eyes.

Theodore took the Scotch from her and set it on the end table. He poured a glass of water from a crystal pitcher, wrapped her hand around the glass, and said, "Drink."

A wave of coughing overwhelmed her. She covered her mouth with her hand too late to catch a burp. Edith looked at Theodore in embarrassment.

"Well," he said. "We shall never try that remedy again."

"I feel like I swallowed fire," she said. Her voice was raspy. "How does anyone stand that poison?"

"It's an acquired taste," Theodore said.

Edith wiped tears from her eyes and patted her nose with a silk handkerchief. "What are we to do now, Theodore?"

He sat in a wing chair and gathered himself before speaking. "I shall call on the Prince of Wales tomorrow."

"One does not simply call on royalty, Theodore," Edith pointed out. "There are probably a dozen ministers or lords between us and the Prince."

"My dear," Theodore said, "I am a man of no small means in my country. I'm certain he will see me."

"Theodore," Edith said. "You are a lovely soul and a considerate husband, but you are barely important in America and virtually unknown in England."

Theodore frowned. "Edith, that was uncalled for." He reconsidered. "If perfectly true."

"We have to find an advocate," Edith said. "Someone who can provide access to the Prince."

"You're right," Theodore said. "But as you so effectively put it, I'm practically invisible in Great Britain."

"Wait," Edith said. She went to the desk under the window and rummaged through a pile of invitations. "It was here. I know it's here." She held up a pale blue envelope in triumph. "Got it." She handed it to Theodore. "Your friend, Lord C. Aubrey Turner."

"The naturalist," Theodore confirmed. He opened the envelope and read the invitation. "'Tomorrow evening at 7:00 p.m. at Oak Ridge.' Splendid! Turner knows everyone. We'll ask him to arrange an audience with the Prince." His face fell in alarm. "Oh, dear. I was so enthralled I nearly forgot that young girl. What a cad I am."

Edith took his hand in hers. "Theodore, you're doing everything you can to aid her. I feel terrible for the poor thing. I want justice for her as much as you. We shall go to Lord Turner's estate and seek his advice and assistance. And then, perhaps, the young woman will be at peace."

Theodore was about to respond when he heard a knock at the front door. "Who in Heaven's Name is about this time of night?"

"Theodore?" Edith said. "It might be about the lady."

Theodore nodded, straightened his coat, and opened the door.

CHAPTER 5

Abberline recognized the American from the Hotel St. Denis. He was shorter than Abberline remembered, and stood erect, as if he expected to be obeyed. He could have been military. The low gas lamps on the wall behind Abberline glinted off the man's glasses, obscuring eyes set in a broad, determined face.

"Whom do I have the honor of addressing?" Abberline asked.

"Theodore Roosevelt, my good man." The reply came back without hesitation. "Who is disturbing me at an unreasonable hour?"

"Inspector Frederick Abberline, Metropolitan Police Department." Abberline didn't wait for a response from the American. "May I come in?"

"Come in?" Theodore said. "May I suggest that you send your card around for an appointment at a more appropriate time?"

"You may indeed," Abberline said. But he remained in the doorway.

"Come in, then," Theodore conceded. He stepped aside.

Abberline entered and removed his hat. An attractive lady stood near the settee.

The woman smiled. "Edith Roosevelt." She held out her hand. Americans always played at equality.

He took it. "Abberline, Mrs. Roosevelt."

"What is this about, Inspector?" Roosevelt asked.

Abberline ignored the question. "I won't take much of your time." He removed a pencil and a small notebook from his coat pocket.

Theodore led his wife to the couch. He cradled her hand in his as they sat next to one another.

Abberline wetted the pencil lead with his tongue, preparing to write. The suite was silent, except for the soft click of a table clock.

"You were at the St. Denis Hotel earlier this evening? Were you not?"

"Why do you ask?" Roosevelt said.

"It's a simple question."

"It's late," Edith pointed out. "Could we continue this some other time?"

Abberline let a moment pass before speaking. "It's about something unfortunate, I'm afraid. It's been reported that a couple matching your description was seen in the lobby on the way to Suite 319."

"Nonsense," Theodore said. "A coincidence."

"You weren't there?"

"I cannot answer."

Abberline turned to Edith. "Mrs. Roosevelt, perhaps, you have a different memory of events?"

"Inspector Abberline, my memory exactly matches my husband's. As for our activities, tonight or any night, we are not in the habit of sharing accounts of them with anyone."

Abberline pressed. "Very well. A woman was murdered tonight, Mrs. Roosevelt. Little more than a child. It was a particularly gruesome act. My job is to bring the culprit to justice; and I believed, based on the evidence at hand, you two may have witnessed something to aid me in the investigation." He saw Theodore's face redden, but he couldn't tell if it was from anger or embarrassment. "Mr. Roosevelt, you are a professional man?"

"I'm an attorney," he said, "and politician."

"Oh, they have those in America as well?" Abberline said. "Here on business? Or is it pleasure?"

Theodore bristled. "Our honeymoon. I don't see how…"

"The young lady I described was sent to the Tanner Street Morgue. If the Lord is kind, some mother or sibling will come by and claim the body. I can't do a thing about her, but I can do something about the man who is responsible for her death. I'll leave this with you. You can reach me at A Division, that's Whitehall, or you can go over to Central Office at Scotland Yard. Give the poor girl some justice and yourselves some peace of mind."

"I'm not the sort of fellow who shirks his duty, Inspector," Theodore said.

"I never took you as such, sir. That is why I'm sure you'll permit me to visit you again." Abberline slipped his notebook into his pocket.

"You may indeed. With proper notification," Theodore said. He escorted Abberline to the door. "We intend to stay in the country for another month or so. Then we're off to the continent."

"In that case," Abberline said to Theodore, "I'm sure we'll see each other quite soon."

The *Times of London*
The Admiralty informs us that tests are underway on a device to gather intelligence on enemy fleets. Initial experiments have proven highly successful.

CHAPTER 6

Abberline hailed a cab, showed the driver his badge, and ordered him to proceed to the Hotel St. Denis. He had a chance to think about the Roosevelts in the darkness of the cab and decided they were both very poor liars, but decent folk all the same. It could be they did not want to involve themselves in a murder, particularly, one that involved the royalty. They must have seen the girl's body, Abberline decided; but he wasn't convinced they had seen the Prince. It could have been an intruder, a burglar hoping to snatch up a few trinkets, surprised by the woman. He dismissed the notion as unlikely. Burglars pride themselves on stealth; and, if confronted, they'd likely run than risk an encounter.

Could it be the Prince of Wales? Abberline turned from that thought. There was no possibility the man had done murder. Oh, was that so, Inspector? Is it not in his blood, then? Come on, Abberline, everyone is capable of murder. Even you.

Then tell that to the Superintendent. Say to him, 'By God, it's the Prince of Wales that sliced up that girl. Say that to Hasselbach.'

Abberline chuckled to himself. That's right, you can find humor in anything. Even a girl stuck like a pig. Sure, Hasselbach will be equally delighted. I'm a policeman, he reminded himself. I'm to uphold the law and fight crime. Give me a level playing field, and I don't mind standing toe-to-toe with a superintendent and arguing the merits of a case at Central Office.

But God save me from the Royal family or the Peerage.

"Here we are, sir," the cabby called out.

Abberline jumped out of the cab and tossed the man a shilling. The department paid cabbies a set rate for service to the crown, but it was a measly amount. Abberline added a tip when his finances permitted.

He entered the St. Denis, glanced around the lobby for any sign of Harvey or reinforcements, and by-passed the lift to take the stairs.

There were two men standing outside the closed door of Suite 319. He didn't recognize them, and he was certain they weren't members of the Metropolitan Department.

"What's your business here?" one of them asked. They were street toughs, men who made a living by their fists. They were loyal to the man who paid them.

"My business, indeed," Abberline said, flashing his badge. "Stand aside."

"So?" the other man said, moving to block the door. "You Abberline?"

The inspector felt the ghosts of powerful men looking over his shoulder. "What of it?"

"You're to go down to the alley. One of yours wants a word," the first man said. "He told us to tell you that."

"Do tell? Did he give you a name?"

"He didn't tell us that."

Abberline reached for the doorknob. The tough batted his hand away.

"That's right," Abberline said. "Do that again and see what it gets you."

"Go talk to the bloke," his partner said, trying to keep the peace.

"We'll be here, if you want to talk to us later," the first man said.

The other man reached into his coat pocket slowly. He handed Abberline an envelope. "Read this."

Abberline opened the envelope, unfolded a single sheet of paper, and read. 'These men represent me and are entitled to every consideration.' It was signed Hasselbach.

Abberline handed the document back. "That makes us practically cousins, doesn't it?" he said.

There was nothing he could do. He went to the end of the hall, opened the door to the servant's stairway, and glanced back at the two men. One of them gave him a smug grin. There's no getting in that suite, not with Hasselbach involved. The girl on the Persian carpet. Poor child. I don't know your name, Abberline thought. It's likely that after tonight, no one will. What is complicated will be made simple. What is known will become lost in the dense clouds of deceit. The girl and her death will fade from memory, like the lives of men such as Abberline.

Don't talk nonsense. Don't you see it?

Someone important got to Hasselbach, and now Hasselbach got to Abberline.

Abberline stepped into the alley and called for Harvey. He found the crates his drunken partner had used to support himself. Something glistened in the darkness. He touched his fingertips to it. It was slick. He put his hands to his nose and smelled of it. Blood.

"We couldn't find him either."

Superintendent Hasselbach, cigar jutting from his mouth, materialized out of the gloom; hands jammed in his coat pocket, bowler pushed off his brow. The Superintendent walked up to him as if it was common for the two to meet in an alley. Hasselbach, his manner calm, unhurried. "We looked around for your partner. No luck. Still, Harvey's a bit of a drinker, isn't he? He might have got bored and set out to find a pint. Mightn't he?"

"That's unlikely," Abberline said. "Even for Harvey."

The Superintendent stopped, fished through his pocket, and struck a match. Abberline saw fire glow around Hasselbach's lowered face. Smoke rose into the air. The breath of the devil? No, just a man lighting a cigar.

"Who were the fellows upstairs? The thugs guarding the suite?"

"Chaps I've hired. You know how it is? Got to keep a lid on this. Keep it unofficial, if you will. They did that back before your time, didn't they?"

"I don't know," Abberline said. "I wasn't about before my time."

"Well, they did," Hasselbach said.

Abberline realized what had happened. "The Black Squad's back?"

Hasselbach closed the distance between them. Just a man out for his constitutional. "Now you don't believe in that old wives' tale, do you Inspector? Witches and goblins and the like. The Black Squad, indeed. Things that go bump in the night."

"What about the girl?"

Hasselbach twisted his head as if searching for a memory. "Girl?"

"Don't play with me, Superintendent. It's been a long night."

"Oh, the poor suicide. Dreadful business. Just awful."

"Suicide? Is that what we're calling it? Not murder?"

The Superintendent waved his cigar at Abberline to correct him. "Now, there you have it wrong. I've seen the death certificate. It's all wrapped up as neatly as a Christmas package. Room tidied up, body removed. Windows were thrown open to freshen things up a bit."

"Nothing in the papers, I suppose?"

"With the Queen's Jubilee on the horizon? Why waste valuable space on the last moments of a disturbed woman." Hasselbach examined the blood on the crate next to Abberline. "I wonder where Harvey has gotten off to? Oh Abberline, any luck with those Americans? What are their names?"

"No." Abberline said.

"Who are they?"

"The Roosevelts."

"Jews?" Hasselbach questioned.

"Americans."

Hasselbach nodded. "Jews and Americans. Neither race knows its place. Well, there's no reason for you to bother them again over this business. Go home, get a good night's sleep."

"Very good, Superintendent," Abberline said.

There. All neatly done. You can raise a stink. But it would do no good to question the Superintendent. He would return lies and weave half-truths; and when he was finished, the girl would still be dead, and Abberline would be ostracized.

Even Harvey had known how it was. "Freddie, count to ten, and take a healthy spoonful of the shit they're passing out," he had advised Abberline during one of his few moments of sobriety. "Then go and get the criminals, don't you see?"

Abberline had ignored Harvey.

"I'll be going then, Inspector," Abberline said. He walked toward the mouth of the alley.

"Abberline?" Hasselbach called to him. "A point of interest. What does your father do?" It was the Superintendent's way of reminding Abberline of his place.

"My father died when I was six." I can barely remember him. He smelled of leather, and his hands were laced with scars. "He was a saddle maker."

"Too bad," Hasselbach said. It was a meaningless condolence. "I'm sure he would be most proud of you, if he were alive today. Why don't you stop around the Central Office tomorrow? I'm sure we have a better position for a bright lad like yourself."

The *Times of London*
Almost 50 years have elapsed since the accession of Her Majesty, Queen Victoria to the Throne of England. The effigy seen on the obverse of British coins, which was adopted in 1837, still remains in use.

CHAPTER 7
THE BRIDAL PATH HYDE PARK,
LONDON, ENGLAND

Lord Crittenton had chosen Hampton to ride. Well-disciplined but proud, a fine looking, black gelding with a white face and three white stockings, Hampton responded to Crittenton's hands. He wasn't as intelligent as Marsh or as flashy as Baron; but he was a large horse, which made Crittenton seem more powerful for being able to control him.

The Prince of Wales, awkwardly mounted on some dull little bay, rode beside Crittenton. He seemed just barely able to sit without slouching.

His royal majesty had been unusually quiet this morning, Crittenton noted. They had met at the stables earlier and waited while their groom saddled the horses. They had sat at a table overlooking a broad field, the Prince bidding good morning to those riders who stopped to address him. Crittenton reread Superintendent Hasselbach's latest report, delivered by the Superintendent before the Prince had arrived.

Hasselbach had waited as Crittenton studied the document. Crittenton paused long enough to comment, "That's an abysmal suit, Superintendent."

"I can't afford your tailor," Hasselbach said.

"It doesn't look as if you can afford any tailor." He folded the paper and handed it to Hasselbach. "Have you read the *Times*?"

"I don't waste my time with that filth. A pack of lies."

"Well, of course, it is, my dear fellow," Crittenton had agreed. "But occasionally, even the *Times* happens on a bit of news."

Hasselbach, impassive as usual, replied, "Dugan came ashore at Liverpool."

"I've never been to Liverpool," Crittenton said.

"He's probably in London now. His brothers are with him. That's news enough, isn't it?"

Crittenton had walked away. It was a signal that Hasselbach was dismissed. The Prince would arrive soon.

His Majesty, yawning himself awake, had arrived half an hour late. He tossed a wave toward Crittenton and accepted a glass of champagne from a servant. They set out before anyone else. Other riders hung back out of courtesy to the Prince, their horses walking along the serpentine gravel path.

"My dear Prince," Crittenton remarked, "forgive me, but I sense something troubles you."

The Prince of Wales, until then, his face a mask of good nature, turned dark. He leaned close to Crittenton. "Troubles," he whispered. "Oh, yes, I have troubles. God strike me, but I fear for everything I hold dear."

Crittenton soothed the Prince, "Surely, it can't be as bad as all that?"

The Prince broke into tears, slumping over his saddle. He buried his face in his hands. His mount continued to walk, accustomed to the bridal path.

Crittenton looked over his shoulder. The nearest riders were several hundred yards behind them and interested in each other. "Eddie, get hold of yourself," he commanded. "Straighten up, man, this is unseemly."

The Prince of Wales did as he was ordered, burying a last sob in the crook of his arm. He dug a handkerchief from his sleeve and wiped his face. "I am destroyed. Absolutely destroyed."

Crittenton was accustomed to the performance. It was the Prince's prerogative to sink into despair, waiting for someone to come to his aid. "I will set things right. Have I ever failed you in the past?"

The Prince offered a weak smile. "No, you haven't. You've been a true friend to me. I shall never forget what you've done for me. Truly. But this is different."

Crittenton remembered Hasselbach's account. "Our friend has done it this time. He thinks he's up to his jowls in murder."

Lord Crittenton donned a sympathetic tone. "Why? You must tell me everything. Don't leave anything out. If I'm to help you, I must know everything."

The Prince patted his horse's neck and stared at a group of cricketers on the green.

Crittenton waited an appropriate length of time before speaking. "Your Highness must not prolong the declaration. It would not do for Her Majesty to hear before I do. Your mother, Edward, is aged, but vital."

The Prince of Wales drew a deep breath, preparing himself. "I was to meet an acquaintance of mine. I keep a suite at the Hotel Denis for such occasions."

"It is a discreet house. That is fortunate."

"When I arrived," he hesitated. Tears glistened on the royal cheeks. "I found, to my horror, she had been slain in a most heinous fashion. Cut to ribbons, you see. I was so unnerved, I rushed from the suite and out into the alley." His tone changed to one of indignation. "I nearly stumbled over a drunk. A disgusting fellow." He returned to his account. "I rushed into the night, barely aware of where I was."

"A common occurrence," Crittenton noted.

"What?"

"Under circumstances of great stress, Your Highness," Crittenton explained, "men's senses often flee."

"Exactly. I found myself on the Embankment. Suddenly, I was in the arms of a man. His wife stood at his side. I called for help. I believe I did. I couldn't be associated with this tragedy, of course, so I pleaded for their assistance. The man told me to leave the area. The rest …," he waved an end to his story, "escapes me."

Crittenton dissected the Prince's account. "No one saw you leave the hotel save the drunk and the couple?"

"The drunk was in his cups," the Prince of Wales reminded Crittenton. "He saw nothing."

"No," Crittenton said. "He was a policeman, and he probably saw more than you realize. But he was undoubtedly in his cups as well, so you won that set. Now, for the others. They are the Roosevelts, a politician from a minor American family. They are here on their honeymoon. He has a reputation as a belligerent busybody, and his wife is one of those bookish drones who produce children at an extraordinary rate and grow dowdy in their old age." It occurred to Crittenton that he could have been describing Queen Victoria.

"Well," the Prince of Wales decided, "I certainly don't know them, and I'm sure they didn't recognize me."

"Then we are fortunate," Crittenton said. Hasselbach's report covered the entire evening. Albert Edward was famous for forgetting everything and remembering even less. "I think we can address this matter in a logical and unobtrusive method. Her Majesty will never hear of it. Of that, I can assure you."

"The newspapers won't overlook the murder of a young lady," Albert Edward said. "The vultures will tear at this distasteful incident until they have their fill."

"That," Crittenton pointed out, "has already been addressed. Come to my estate this evening for dinner."

"Lord Crittenton, I am not in the mood for society. The vision of that young lady, splayed across the carpet, has robbed me of my appetite."

"It may be, Your Highness, but I sense it will return to its familiar locale by this evening."

"Lord Crittenton, please," Albert Edward whined, "you must believe me when I tell you …"

"Oh, I do, Your Highness. I can only imagine how unsettled you are by this tragic event. But what the Roosevelts saw, and what they plan to pass on to the proper authorities? Well, leave that to me."

The Prince of Wales was shocked. "Nothing will come of their involvement, will it? I can't see a gentleman speaking ill of another gentleman. Even an American."

"I will make certain that is so, Your Highness." Sometimes, Albert Edward behaved like a dullard. "It is my task to manage such incidents as what bring embarrassment to your Royal Highness. Even this incident should not worry you. How many unfortunates such as this young lady happen every day? Seriously, Eddie, do you imagine the murder of a young girl would compete with accounts of the Queen's Golden Jubilee on the front page of the newspapers, even if the Prince of Wales had been remotely involved?" Crittenton's words were the equivalent of a slap.

"I had nothing to do with her death," the Prince of Wales bristled. "I was the one who found her and went immediately for assistance."

"For which you are to be commended, Your Highness. But you know as well as I that your mother's enemies will use any excuse to tarnish her reputation. These are perilous times. The Irish, the Boers, even members of Her Majesty's own government. I remind, Your Highness, that London seethes with Communists. The Monarchy has never been more in danger."

"You don't expect me to believe my brief encounter with…"

Crittenton turned paternal. "What you and I believe is of no consequence. We are near a new century, Your Highness." It was like a tutor drilling knowledge in the rock-hard skull of a recalcitrant pupil. "Royal houses may become passé. Peoples within countries may arise and demand independence. A strong hand, and a clear vision, are the two elements of a successful government for a new age. There is too much time wasted over acts to sooth the people or debate over Home Rule."

"My dear Lord Crittenton," the Prince of Wales began. He had a point to make but was interrupted by the approach of a young lady and her governess. The governess offered a perfunctory nod, the young lady smiled shyly. As they rode past, the Prince swung in his saddle, keeping them in sight. He turned to Crittenton. "Do you know who that charming creature is? I say, she has the face of an angel. Positively sweet in nature."

Crittenton said, "Her name escapes me, Your Highness, but I shall make inquiries."

"Oh, yes, please do," the Prince of Wales said.

He returned to the earlier subject. "Dinner then. Tomorrow night, if you please," Albert Edward glanced over his shoulder at the girl "I may be otherwise employed."

The Times of London
We have received the following communication through Reuter's Agency: Fire
destroyed an orphanage in Germany. Many dead.

CHAPTER 8
TUFTON STREET, LONDON

W here's Michael?" Benjamin Dugan asked.
Daniel looked over his shoulder, searching the street and a sidewalk packed with people. The serpentine street was caught in the shadow of narrow shops whose windows were stuffed with the trade of an empire. China, French porcelain, ready-made dresses and suits, hats, fabrics, and lace. Older stores, abandoned by prosperity, were plastered with broadsides celebrating the Golden Jubilee. Commerce and patriotism settled in nicely next to one another. An aged street merchant pushed a milk cart, stacked with empty tins over the cobblestones, fighting his way through the crowd.

"I told him to meet us here," Daniel told his brother.

"Do you see him then?" Benjamin snapped in return. He was angry with Daniel for not looking after Michael, and angry with himself for giving the brothers too much credit. He glanced at the old man who shuffled next to him and wondered if bringing August Schiess into this affair was another mistake.

Schiess kept pace with them, but his tiny body shook with each breath. His forehead was glistening with sweat, and his armpits were dark with exertion. He was an ancient man, with sparse white hair, and a frail body of stacked bones, and parchment-like skin. A decade ago, he had been a scholar; but the years had stripped him of the honor, and now he was simply old.

"Roll me a cigarette, will you, Benjamin?" Schiess queried. It had become a tradition, Schiess asked, and Benjamin did. Benjamin Dugan, the giant over six and a half feet tall, was nearly three hundred pounds, with arms as thick as a dray wagon's axle. He had the red hair and beard of a demon, but the agility of a cat.

"You can barely keep up as it is," Benjamin said. "How are you going to draw a breath and smoke at the same time?" There was no malice in his tone. The old man meant too much to him.

Schiess coughed out a laugh, "A wet nurse." He had a habit of making observations under his breath that, if anybody had given them any thought, would have emerged as insults. Benjamin had learned long ago to ignore the barbs.

He rolled a cigarette and handed it to Schiess. "Here you are, you disgusting little man; and you'd better take care not to die before I have need of you."

Schiess smiled at his friend. "There's not a thing I can do about that, and you know it. I'm close enough to death now to shake hands with the Devil." He looked behind them. "We've lost some of our little army."

Benjamin looked over the heads of the crowd. He was right. Daniel had gone looking for Michael, and now the two of them were lost.

"Well, just look about us," Schiess said. He coughed out a plume of smoke. "There are the Houses of Parliament. And there," he pointed ahead with a trembling hand, "is Westminster Abbey."

"I can see, old man."

"The perfect place for those such as us," Schiess said. "Safe in the shadow of the Philistines." A curl of smoke leapt from his cracked lips. "I expected you to be in China by now."

Benjamin laid a hand on Schiess's shoulder to stop him and looked for his brothers. He had talked about it, going to the Eastern Land. Finding sanctuary amongst the fragile temples and diminutive women with dark eyes. Benjamin, safe from the Coal Police and the bobbies. Benjamin in Cathay.

"Did you know," Schiess continued, "that China's greatest admiral sailed the ocean seas in a vessel that was over four hundred feet in length?"

Benjamin's interest was in Daniel and Michael. "I don't care for water."

Schiess's trembling hand brought the cigarette from his lips. "You should broaden your mind, Benjamin."

"Come," Benjamin ordered. They walked onto Deans Yard and stopped. He got his bearings. "There to the left is Victoria Street. To the right is Whitehall. They come together," he formed a V with his hands, "thus. Under the streets are the sewers. The sewers may be our salvation."

Schiess tossed the butt away and motioned for another cigarette. "In the sewers are rats. I hate the filthy bastards. Let us avoid the sewers at all costs."

Benjamin pulled out the paper and tobacco bag. "Do you eat these bloody things, you silly, old man?"

Schiess ignored the question. "What makes you think you can do it? Arrogance? You have that all right. Skill, yes, but you've a great deal of confidence in your own ability. You know there must have been a score of explosions in the city over the last two years. Two on the underground railway, and somebody tried to blow up the *Times* office. Imagine that? Gower Street, Westminster Hall, and if it hadn't been for a bit of bad luck, some misguided soul would have brought down Nelson's Column with sixteen sticks of dynamite." He drew on his cigarette and exhaled. "Not to mention some of your lads tossing the blasted stuff into carriages."

"I'll go after this business is over." Benjamin meant China.

Schiess concentrated on the ash that fell from the cigarette; he saw another time and place. "Before I took to the drink, I was a professor of rhetoric. But you know that, don't you? I spent years making my way through books, manuscripts, letters, and documents."

"You've turned maudlin, Schiess," Benjamin said.

The observation surprised Schiess. "I have? Well, I shouldn't be faulted for it. I'm old and tired."

Benjamin heard Daniel and Michael running up. Before he could say anything, Daniel, the impatient one, said, "He was talking to some silly child." He glared at his brother. "He's no more than a child himself, and he wants to waste time talking to another child."

"I was just talking to her," Michael said to Benjamin. Far too gentle for his own sake, Michael, the kindly one. He did not understand the harshness of the world around him. Michael the one most dangerous because of his innocence. "She was standing there all alone, and I felt sorry for her. I know what it means to be alone."

"Listen to me," Benjamin said, tired of excuses. "There's just us. We brothers. You want a child-whore, there's plenty to be had."

Michael's face fell. Benjamin knew Michael was just beyond a boy, in mind, body, and manner. He drifted through the world in the wake of his older brothers. God help the lad if he set out on his own.

"I don't want …"

"Want. Need. It makes no matter to me, boy. We've come here to do a job and leave again with our heads firmly attached to our necks. There is no time. Don't you understand? The game is the thing now, nothing else. You've got to know that. If your member itches, take it in hand."

"She wasn't a whore. Just a child."

"Child," Daniel spat.

"I understand, Benjamin. I won't let you down. I promise," Michael reassured his brother.

Benjamin nodded. He had raised his younger brothers, until he was forced to escape Ireland and the English law. Daniel was close enough, but there was a secretive nature about him, a coating of distrust that came away in your hands like an oily film. It was Michael who was his favorite. Poor simple Michael, who tried desperately to understand the way of the world but was condemned to be a boy.

Daniel, the schemer, Michael the child, and Schiess whom he trusted but who stank of death. His companions in retribution. And he, his mother's favorite, the man who foresaw fragments of impending events and claimed to reassemble them into visions of the future. Not in years. He had given that up, seeing the years as foolishness and his mother's babbled hopes for him as the last stages of the fever killed her.

It was the reality of things that he was about, not some conjectured glimpse into what may be. Here in London. Not China, or America, or the barren lands of home. Here. He had an army mortally wounded by its own frailties.

Yet, it could still be done.

"Shall we continue, Benjamin," Schiess asked. "Or do you want to stare off into nothing for the remainder of the day?"

Benjamin shot Schiess a hateful look. "If I roll you another cigarette, little man, will you keep your gob shut?"

Schiess's mouth crinkled in a smile. "And a drink, Benjamin. Give me the two, and I'm yours."

Daniel pointed out the obvious. "Can we not get out of the street?"

"That's the first contribution you've made to this endeavor," Benjamin said. "Let's stroll down to Westminster Bridge."

CHAPTER 9
OAK RIDGE, LORD TURNER'S ESTATE

Neither spoke for some time as the carriage rolled through London's crowded streets and entered the English countryside. A few words about the passing scenery, a comment on the weather, but nothing of substance. They had too much on their minds. The Russell House had provided a driver and cabriolet, and the elegant little vehicle seemed to glide over the cobblestone streets. After traveling some distance, Theodore burst into recollection. "I was most impressed by the vastness of the West," he said. "A man could not but be overwhelmed. It was beautiful and harsh. Unforgiving and majestic. I will take you there, Edith. We will travel the American West together."

Edith suspected her husband was trying to be cheerful for her sake, hoping to keep her from thinking of the events of the previous night. But I don't need you to protect me, Edith wanted to say. I'm sorry I'm not Alice. I do not have her allure or vibrancy. Still, I am in the shadow of your late wife. But you see, Theodore, I am my own person.

"I'm certain he has the Prince of Wales' ear," Theodore said.

Edith was confused, "What?"

Theodore lowered his voice, "Lord Turner. He and I have communicated for nearly ten years. His letters are fascinating. The foremost naturalist of his day. Well, Darwin aside."

"Yes," Edith said. "I know that."

"You do?" Theodore said.

"Theodore, my reading is not limited to the arts or history," Edith chided him playfully.

"I read as well," Theodore replied.

Edith laughed. She had almost forgotten the reason for their visit, "Then we must consider this discussion a draw, for we are both well-read."

Theodore slid next to her and kissed her cheek. "My dear, I declare you the victor, and me under your spell."

The carriage turned onto Oak Ridge's drive from the main road, passing between two stone columns on either side of the gate. Edith leaned closer to Theodore, taking his hand in hers.

"Once more, into the breech," she said with a smile.

The cabriolet swung around the driveway circle, joining a line of carriages depositing guests at the manor house entrance. Edith marveled at the building. It was more magnificent than anything she had seen, a fortress of power and wealth. Two stories high, thick columns were equally spaced along the facade, and between each set were arrayed six sets of windows. They gleamed with invitation; echoing an array of lamps leading from the driveway to the front door that sparkled in the descending darkness.

It was romantic and surreal, a storybook scene of elegance. Edith was swept away by her surroundings. It was a wonderland of beautiful people, gleaming lights, and a castle. "I have never seen such splendor," she managed.

"For heaven's sake, Edith," Theodore said. "Control yourself."

She looked at him, almost speechless. "How can such a world exist?"

Theodore folded his arms together in annoyance. He'd been surveying the surroundings as well. "No man ought to have that much money." The cabriolet eased forward, nearing the entrance. "Now see here, Edith. We must approach this thing with the utmost caution. Stealth is the key. I've bagged more than my share of bull moose using the exact same strategy."

Music drifted from the house, faint, and delicate. Voices, high with expectation, and excitement, mingled with laughter, competed with the music.

"Just coming up now, your lordship," the driver called.

Edith touched her husband's arm. "Theodore? Did you mean what you said about caution?"

"Not a bit of it."

The cabriolet stopped in front of the portico. The driver remained seated, controlling the horse as a footman opened the door and stood back. Theodore was out first, extending his hand to assist Edith. She joined him, and another footman with a lantern approached. He, nor the first man, spoke. A man with gray hair, and neatly trimmed mustache, stepped forward. "Good evening. Welcome to Oak Ridge. I am Mr. Hugh. May I have your invitation, please?" His tone was distant, cold, but very efficient. Theodore handed the man the invitation. Mr. Hugh gestured to the man with the lantern. "Will you follow Charles, please?"

They did as they were asked, walking up the broad staircase and into the doorway.

Edith whispered to Theodore. "I think I've just been introduced to that remarkable English reserve I've heard so much about." Thirty feet overhead, three electric-gas crystal chandeliers showered the hall with light.

As they entered the grand hallway, they fell into a line that led to the receiving station.

Theodore stood on his tiptoes. Edith, aghast, pulled his arm. "Theodore, for Heaven's Sake, what are you doing? Behave."

"I just saw Turner," Theodore nodded to the head of the line. A portly man, whose bushy white eyebrows appeared ready to fly away, chatted briefly with each guest before sending them to the ballroom to be announced. He was dressed in superbly tailored eveningwear, accenting his ample waist and drooping shoulders. The somber black front encased a gleaming white shirtfront broken by the sweep of a watch chain across his midriff. His collar and bowtie glowed under the soft light of wall sconces. A statuesque woman, many years younger, stood next to him.

"That's Lady Turner," Theodore explained. "Twenty years his junior, with more money than Croesus."

They made their way alone the line until Theodore found himself facing Turner.

"Why," Turner exclaimed. "My dear Mr. Roosevelt. And this must be his lovely wife, Edith." He turned to the woman next to him. "Look, Lady Turner, here is my friend from America, Theodore Roosevelt, and his wife. Just married, isn't that right, Mr. Roosevelt?"

"Indeed," Theodore said. "It's a pleasure to finally meet you, Lord Turner. And you, Lady Turner."

Turner brushed the compliment into the air. "Nonsense, my boy. We won't have that sort of formality from one scientist to another."

Lady Turner arched an eyebrow. "My dear, we mustn't hold up the line."

"Lord Turner?" Theodore said. "May we have a word with you? In private, if you don't mind?"

"What's that?" Turner said. "Why, of course." He smiled at Edith and led Theodore away from the line. "Now, what is it, young man? What can I help you with?"

"A most unusual request, Lord Turner, but one of the utmost importance. It is critical that I secure a private audience with the Prince of Wales."

"The Prince of Wales? Albert Edward?" Turner asked, surprised. "My dear boy, what is it?"

Theodore hesitated and glanced at Edith. "I'm sorry to say, I cannot divulge the reason, sir; but I give you my word as a gentleman that it is of great importance."

Turner managed a thoughtful, "Eh." He glanced at the receiving line and caught the glare of his impatient wife. He clapped Theodore on the shoulder. "That's good enough for me, sir. I've got just the man for you. You can trust him, as you trust me." He called a servant over. "Matthews, kindly take Mr. and Mrs. Roosevelt to the library, will you?"

Matthews said, "Of course, Lord Turner." To Theodore and Edith, he said, "If you please?”

He led them to a doorway, secreted under a staircase, and into a room surrounded by floor to ceiling bookcases, broken only by a single window, and another door. The Lord’s library, Edith realized, was a surprisingly modest effort for a man who was considered in some circles to be the equal of any scientist in the world. Theodore was stunned.

“I have died and gone to Heaven,” he managed, mesmerized.

“Thank you, Matthews,” Edith said. “That will be all.” When the servant left, she turned to Theodore. “Don’t stand there with your agape. Can we trust Lord Turner?”

“Turner?” Theodore said. “Yes. Yes, he said he would help us. He says he knows someone. Look? Is that the Rubaiyat?”

There was a soft knock at the door, and Turner appeared. “Ah, here we are. Safe and sound. Splendid. Now, you asked me about an audience with the Prince of Wales, and here is just the man to help you.”

Lord Crittenton entered the library with a smile. “Good evening,” he said. “A pleasure to meet you.”

CHAPTER 10

Turner left them alone. Crittenton walked to a liquor cabinet. "I trust Lord Turner would not begrudge us refreshment." He poured himself a drink and turned to Edith. "Mrs. Roosevelt?"

"No, thank you."

"Mr. Roosevelt? Something from the good Lord's cabinet?"

"No, nothing," Theodore replied.

Crittenton held his glass up, the crystal glimmering under the light of a gas outlet on the wall. "Then I shall be the scoundrel in the room. We might as well be comfortable." He walked around a large desk near the window. "Please," he gestured to a set of wing-backed chairs.

When they were seated, Theodore began. "We have the most delicate situation to discuss, Lord Crittenton."

"Mr. Roosevelt?" Crittenton advised the American. "I am a minister to Her Royal Highness Queen Victoria. I'm certain that I have encountered every conceivable delicate situation there is. Pray continue."

Theodore began the story, speaking slowly, deliberately, occasionally glancing at Edith for confirmation. It couldn't have taken more than five minutes, and the library, except for Theodore's voice, was as silent as a tomb.

Edith watched Lord Crittenton absorb the information, his eyelids soft, nearly closed, his mouth unmoving, one finger stroking the glass he held in his hand. The ideal politician, stolid, seemingly indifferent, but capturing every word.

Theodore told him everything, discovering the poor girl's body, the visit from the policeman, everything, except about the letter.

When Theodore finished, Lord Crittenton nodded, took a drink, and stood. Looking down into the glass, he said, "And you've told no one else of this, this incident?"

"Not a soul," Theodore said. "This man, Abberline, a policeman, is the only one to broach the subject to us."

"But you neither denied nor confirmed the story to him?"

"Correct, Your Lordship," Theodore said. He decided to reveal everything.

"There is something else."

Lord Crittenton said, "Something else? What else might there be?"

Theodore looked at Edith.

"A letter," she said. "I found it on the girl's body. In the pocket of her dress."

"A letter?" Crittenton said. "How extraordinary."

"I didn't think to bring it," Theodore said.

"I did," Edith said. She pulled the folded envelope from her pocket. "I didn't feel right leaving it. I know it was silly, but it seemed too important, even to abandon for an evening."

Crittenton walked to Edith, holding out his hand. "If you would be so kind?"

Edith handed him the letter.

As he unfolded it and began to read, Theodore said, "I'm sure the Prince is a man of character; and if I could but have a few minutes with him to state the case, I know he would come around. It would simply be a matter of his speaking to the proper authorities and clearing his name. Of course, now that you know the story, perhaps, you could speak to him."

Crittenton finished the letter, returned it to the envelope, and handed it back to Edith. "Yes, but while that may certainly be true, speaking to the authorities directly, I think it best you address this matter to the Prince. You have already been introduced, in a sense, by your encounter. Frankly, you hold a cache that I do not possess." He smiled at Edith, returning to another element of the situation. "But we don't know who committed this horrendous act?"

Edith was surprised by the question but, moreover, his tone, as if he was mildly disappointed in them. She didn't know what else to say except, "Yes."

"Fate favors the fortunate, Mr. Roosevelt, as I'm sure you know from your study of history. I am sure, also, you're aware of history's foibles. A misplaced lance, and a king dies; a ship strays off course, and a colony is founded. An ill-considered word, and a dynasty falls. You have chosen the right path in not divulging what you know to anyone." Crittenton rolled the liquid about in the glass, and then resumed. "I shall contact His Highness this very evening. Unfortunately, you must bear this burden for yet another day. You can expect a message from me tomorrow setting the time and place for a meeting. Because of the nature of this event, it would be best not to meet at the palace."

Theodore agreed, "Yes. It seems appropriate."

"Well," Crittenton said, "I suppose it would be boorish to suggest we return to Lord and Lady Turner's celebration and behave as if this meeting had never transpired, but so be it."

Theodore and Edith rose.

"What do you think the Prince will do?" Edith asked Crittenton.

"Do?" Crittenton said. "Why, I think he will protest at first; he is human, you know, and then I think he will see his duty and do everything he can to aid in the capture of the young lady's murderer. He is a proper gentleman, after all."

Theodore glanced at Edith. "There, you see, Edith. I knew he would come around. Lord Crittenton, I can't thank you enough for coming to our assistance."

"Think nothing of it, Mr. Roosevelt," Crittenton said. "I believe Providence brought us together, and Justice will see us through this endeavor. I shall borrow a few pieces of Lord Turner's stationary and draft a letter to His Majesty. I suggest you return to the festivities."

"Certainly," Theodore said.

Crittenton watched them leave, walked to the desk, and took a seat. He sighed deeply, found a sheet of paper, an envelope, and took a gold tipped pen from the tray on the desk. Flipping open the cover of the ink well, Crittenton dipped the pen into the ink. "A letter?" He spoke to himself as he wrote. "For Heaven's Sake, it was a simple plan. Is there anything else that could go awry?" The pen scratched across the paper. When he finished, he blew delicately on the ink, drying it. Well, it was a modest effort, bringing right all the things that had gone wrong. They needed a few days only, and they could be had by silencing the two Americans. Newlyweds, Turner had told him, so the bloom was not yet off the rose. That was in his favor, even if the rest of the bloody mess wasn't.

Crittenton would send two messages but neither to the Prince of Wales. One would go to Chambliss, and he would be the one to put this thing right. And the other would be to the two Americans who still believed in honor and charity.

He shook his head in disbelief. "A letter? Who knew the silly thing could write?"

The Times of London
Famous comedian O. P. Langdon has announced his retirement from the stage. Mr. Langdon's antics have contributed to the abundance of mirth recently noted in the city's population.

CHAPTER 11
SCOTLAND YARD

Inspector Frederick Abberline sat in Hasselbach's cramped headquarters at Central Office. It was late, he was tired, and he was certain Harvey was dead. He didn't know how, and he didn't know if Harvey had finally drunk himself to death or if the man's fate had something to do with Hasselbach. And the Black Squad.

The police superintendent locked his fingers together on his desk. "What was that?"

"The Prince of Wales?" Abberline reminded Hasselbach. "I take it, I'm no longer to shadow him?"

"You see, Abberline, you do begin to understand the nature of things."

"And Harvey?" he asked Hasselbach.

"He was a drunk," Hasselbach pointed out.

This time, Abberline kept his words to a minimum. "'Was?'"

"You know what I mean." Hasselbach said.

"Who were those two men?"

"They never existed. You understand what I'm saying, don't you? Abberline, we've got enough crime in this wretched city without worrying about the suicide of one filthy, little tart. We had an incident last night, and some whore died. It happens every day. You know the times, Abberline."

"I know the times," Abberline confirmed without conviction.

Hasselbach rose, checked to make sure his office door was closed, and leaned over Abberline so that whatever he had to say would go no farther. "Now, you listen to me, you pissy little saddler's boy, if you don't clear your mind of this business, you'll walk Drury Lane and Catherine Street every night until you die. You'll never be able to get the stench of offal and gin out of your nostrils. Hades never had it so bad, and you'll be up to your neck in it. You know it to be true, Abberline. Puss covered bodies, toothless hags offering themselves to you." Hasselbach took his chair. He examined his cigar, saw that it still had life, and coaxed a pall of smoke from it. "You know, Inspector Abberline, Warrant Number 43519." The tone was pleasant;

the storm had passed. "I'm a cordial fellow. I've found it the best manner to adapt. Do unto others, you know." He smiled at Abberline. "Stay close to the truth as it's fed to you, and you'll go straight up the ranks. If not? Why, it's a dangerous city. Keep that in mind, won't you, Frederick. That's a good fellow. Dismissed."

"Yes, sir."

Abberline walked down the steps, the dark recesses of the staircase thick with foreboding, through the booking room, and into the sunlight. He was used to the Superintendent's deceit, and the man had threatened him before. But this was different.

It might be the Americans, he thought. They were a complication, and Hasselbach detested complications mucking up things. It's your job to keep things simple, Hasselbach had ordered a double row of inspectors drawn up for assembly. Supervisors, bundled against one wall to avoid being mistaken for inspectors, nodded in concurrence. Keep the crime scene tidied up; one supervisor had suggested, hoping to win Hasselbach's favor. The Superintendent had been impressed. "Just so," he had agreed.

Wagging tails, tidy crime scenes, a missing cop, bungling Americans, and the Royal Family.

Abberline stopped near the wrought iron gate that surrounded the office and watched a beer wagon pass. The Roosevelt's claimed to know nothing. They were the worst liars Abberline had ever encountered.

So, Abberline thought, I have a tidy case. If it were any tidier, it would be virtually invisible. He felt someone behind him. Abberline turned and saw Christy, his thin body hidden in a crumbled suit.

"Inspector Abberline? Inspector? A word?"

"No," He walked out the gate.

"Give us a moment, will you, Inspector? At least have the common decency to slow down."

"Go away, Christy," Abberline called over his shoulder. "I've got too much on my mind to waste my time on you."

Christy had a child's face almost waiflike, except for the grime-encrusted wrinkles around his eyes. He was a cripple and ill, some sickness or other. A little squealer, bits of information for sale. A mouse scurrying across the floor. Here and gone. He caught up to Abberline. "Why have you gone so cold-hearted for? I'm not asking to borrow a quid, am I?"

"I'm busy, Christy."

"Well, of course, you are," Christy said, sliding to one side to catch Abberline's attention. "Who said you weren't? Not I. Won't hear of anyone saying such a thing." He scudded to Abberline's left. "I'm here with a gift, Mr. Abberline. Just for you. No one else."

"I don't have any money," Abberline said. They continued down the street, Abberline walking at a steady pace, Christy bouncing back and forth, a terrier seeking attention.

"I don't want money," Christy protested, hurt. "At least not much. Oh, show a little kindness, won't you, Mr. Abberline. Me poor mother is ill."

"Your mother is dead."

Christy cried, "Blimey! It's worse than I thought."

Abberline stopped, suppressing a smile. "You little shit. What is it?"

Christy beamed with triumph. "This'll make you champion of the Fenian Squad."

"I'm not on the Fenian Squad anymore," Abberline said. "I've been reassigned."

Christy was shocked. "But that can't be. I don't trust a soul with that bloodthirsty band but you. You can't be."

Abberline continued walking. "You'd better find a bloke that can help. I'm no longer chasing Fenians."

"Wait. Wait. Wait." Christy caught up to him. "I'll tell you, and you can pay me later. A contract, but you don't have to sign nothing. A handshake. That's what it will be."

Abberline hesitated. The little fellow was a pest, but he'd been a good informant. He had an irritating way of winning Abberline's favor, even when the inspector was angry with him.

"All right," Abberline said. "I don't have the money now, but I'll pay you later."

"Two bob," Christy said.

"I said I'd listen, you little thief. I didn't say I'd stand here and let you rob me. Out with it, before I change my mind."

"It's three brothers," Christy said. "The Dugans. Anarchists. Dynamite patriots."

"Three brothers," Abberline said, hiding his interest. If he were too enthusiastic, he'd have to pay more.

"Here in London. The oldest, Benjamin, is the most dangerous. A killer."

"How do you know?"

The question stung Christy's pride. "I can't go about betraying a fellow's confidence. Let's just say that people hear things, and what they hear comes right to me. And I give it to you."

"Give?"

"In a manner of speaking."

"Why are they here?" Abberline asked.

Christy's face fell. "Well, that's the rub, isn't it?"

Abberline was convinced that was all the information he had. "Go and get me something else. Something worth a shilling or two."

Christy looked toward the Yard. "That constable's trying to get your attention."

Abberline watched the blue uniform race toward them. "How do you know he's not after you?"

"And you have so little confidence in me; you don't think I can tell when a peeler wants to pinch me?" Christy said. "No. He's yours, and I'm off for home."

The constable stopped and threw a hasty salute. He was a new man, and uncertain of protocol. "Beggin' your pardon, sir. But Sergeant Malloy sent me to fetch you. They've come across a body near the Commercial Docks."

"Right," Abberline said, signaling a cab. He kept the body on the Thames at arm's length as the cab carried him from the sturdy elegance of Central Office at Scotland Yard to the grimy decay of the docks. One murder at a time.

When they arrived, he gave the cabby a chit for his troubles, and prepared himself. Bodies, late of the Thames, were generally slimy lumps that smelled to High Heaven.

A bobby, posted at the stairs, holding a torch to keep the approaching night at bay, nodded a welcome to him. Abberline descended the stone steps of the Embankment that kept the filthy water of the Thames River out of the filthy streets of London and walked around the rotting carcass of a half-sunken lighter. He saw a modest crowd of inspectors and constables gathered on the gravel beach, a few feet from the water's edge. Torches were stuck in the gravel, their wavering flames throwing dancing shadows on the ground.

Abberline was accustomed to bodies. Sometimes, they were drained of blood; and except for the wound that killed them, they could have been carved from marble by a semi-talented sculptor. It was the sight of the dead who had lain for too long, stewing in the hot summer sun or washed ashore in a mass of bloated tissue: that was the worst kind.

And the children. God, how he hated to come upon the little beasts. He had stood over them; a rescuer come just too late to be of any help. Raped, clothes ripped aside. Little bodies, covered with filth. Discarded by London, abandoned by the Devil, and overlooked by God. The sight of violence done to children darkened his soul, so that he half expected there would be no light left to guide him to Heaven.

Abberline walked around the barrel of pitch lying on its side. A pair of legs jutted out of the dull, black mass. He knew the trousers. The pitch was littered with twigs, bits of straw, and the unidentified refuge of the river, anything that came close enough to be sucked into its oily grasp.

The gravel crunched under Abberline's boots. It was the only sound he heard.

Inspector Mackie, a red-bearded Scot, who was so anxious to be at the center of any circumstance that would advance him, handed Abberline Harvey's badge. "They jammed him into the barrel and tossed him into the Thames." He squinted into the distance, measuring the river. "A couple of miles upstream." He thought to add, with a trace of arrogance, "I know the river."

Harvey's left boot was missing, and his shriveled foot stuck out of a tattered sock. The whole place stank of dead fish and mold, and the only relief from that stench was the sharp odor of pitch.

Abberline examined the badge. He'd have to hand it over to the Superintendent, and someone would write a paragraph to be inserted deep in the body of the *Times*. One of the illustrated papers would probably create a lurid wood-engraving of the scene. But no one cared.

"They made a mess of things; those what killed him," Mackie said.

Abberline rubbed his thumb over the badge in thought. "What?"

"The chaps that do this sort of thing for a living know better. When they send them down, they stay down."

Abberline understood. "Is this all?" He held up the badge.

"All from his trouser pockets. Two pence, three. I'll give that to the undertaker. Everything else is under pitch."

"How was he killed?" Abberline asked and regretted it. He'd find out soon enough. You're an inspector, he told himself; you need to know how. Yes, the man meant so much to you. Fuck off.

"It was the pitch, wasn't it?" Mackie said. "They up ended the poor soul and stuffed him into the barrel. He drowned in the stuff." He walked back from the body for another point of view. "Makes no sense. Why torture the bloke before killing him? Why not just shove a knife in his gut and be done with it?"

Abberline slipped Harvey's badge into his pocket. "The Black Squad's back."

"I fished a woman out one day. Her husband did her in." Mackie realized what Abberline had said and shot him a look of disbelief. "Not you, too?"

"You don't believe it?"

"I've never believed it. It's nonsense," he scoffed, "Black Squad."

"I suppose you're right," Abberline said. It did sound too melodramatic.

"I blame the papers for that rubbish," Mackie said. "They're always stirring things up."

"You're probably right."

The two watched as a handcart was maneuvered down the rough beach and aligned next to the body. Two workers removed an axe and sledgehammer. They planned to break the barrel apart, freeing the pitch and body.

"He was a fine policeman when he started out," Mackie said.

"If you say so," Abberline said. "I never knew him then."

The Times of London

Villas (first class) for SALE, for occupation or investment. Ten bedrooms, located on a lovely lot. Ideal for a lady and gentleman who desire to entertain. The very best

CHAPTER 12
RUSSELL HOUSE

Edith watched Theodore pull open a drawer and take out a box. They had barely entered the suite when he raced to the desk. He opened the box lid and turned to her.

"Good Lord, Theodore," she exclaimed. "It's a pistol."

"It is indeed. I bought it before I left America. Lovely, isn't it? It's a Colt in thirty-eight caliber. I bought it and sixty rounds."

"Why in the world would you bring that gun with us on our honeymoon?"

He gave her a disappointed look. "I didn't bring it on our honeymoon. I brought it with us."

"On our honeymoon," she insisted. "I don't like those things. Suppose it had accidently gone off and killed someone? I am terribly disappointed in you, Theodore."

Theodore set the box on the desk, took Edith's hand, and led her to a chair. When she sat down, he spoke. "I know how to handle a firearm. I was raised with those most useful instruments. I haven't killed anyone yet." He patted her hand. "Accidentally."

Edith pulled her hands away. "Don't be condescending, Theodore." She stood, walking to the window. "Oh, how I hate to wait."

"We have Lord Crittenton's word," Theodore reminded her.

"Yes, I know. Theodore?" she said. "You don't think it inappropriate to inquire of him, do you? Lord Crittenton? A reminder of our concerns, perhaps?"

"Edith?" Theodore began. "Oh, very well. I can't say I blame you." He took paper and an envelope from the desk and wrote. "A simple inquiry," he said. "Nothing more." He signed his name, addressed the envelope, and slipped the paper inside. "There." He kissed Edith on the cheek. "Signed, sealed, and shortly to be delivered."

"Shall I ring for a servant?"

"Absolutely not," Theodore replied. "I will take this to the front desk and make certain to see it on its way. By God, these English will see how Americans take things in hand. No dilly-dallying for us." He kissed her again.

"Theodore?" Edith said. "Be careful."

"My dear, I'm going to the front desk, not up the Amazon. You have the pistol. Use it to defend yourself if necessary." He winked at her. "But don't shoot me when I return."

He made his way quickly down the stairs to the front desk. A desk clerk behind the counter approached him.

"Yes, sir?"

"This must be delivered to Lord Crittenton at once," Theodore said.

"Oh, Mr. Roosevelt? We've just received a message for you, from Lord Crittenton himself."

"Splendid," Theodore said, taking the message from the clerk. He tore it open and read the message. St. Martins-in-the-Field at one o'clock this afternoon, the note read. "Perfect."

The young man struck the call bell, and a bellboy appeared. "Yes, sir?"

"Randolph, stand by for a reply."

"Right you are," Theodore said. "Best to acknowledge my recipe of the message. Please convey to His Lordship that Mr. Roosevelt has received his instructions and will follow them to the letter."

The desk clerk's eyebrow arched a quarter of an inch. "Perhaps," he suggested. "Mr. Roosevelt would prefer to put that in writing?"

"Oh, well, of course," Theodore said, taking a pencil and paper from the clerk. When he finished, he slipped the paper into an envelope and scribbled Crittenton across it. "You know, in America," Theodore told the young man, "we use   Mr. Bell's telephone instrument for speedy communication."

"In England, one does not relegate important messages to a machine," the young man said coolly, handing the letter to the bellboy.

Theodore stopped Randolph before he had a chance to leave and gave him a pound note. "Randolph, is it? Get the message to Lord Crittenton in a timely manner, and you'll get another pound in reward."

"For two quid, I'd deliver it to Satan, sir, and wait for the reply," Randolph said.

Theodore beamed. He was a good judge of character. "Off you go then."

Randolph touched his fingertips to his pillbox hat and left. He passed the concierge, tossed Burt, the doorman, a quick wave, and ran out onto the nearly deserted street. There was a cab queue just up the street. The hotel didn't want them hanging at the front door like a bunch of beggars, but he didn't need a cab just now. Just ahead was a livery that had a man on duty in case any of the swells at the hotel took a fancy to go for a drive. It was a grimy little shop, but his uncle owned it; and that's where Randolph told the man with the white streak in his hair to wait.

The front door of the livery stable was propped open. Old Dan, the night manager, lay folded in a pile of hay, asleep.

The man with the white streak sat on a carriage step, watching him. "You've got something for me?" he asked in a deep voice. He was a big man, with a scarred face. One of the scars ran in a swoop from his cheekbone to his hairline, disappearing into the white streak that spoiled a thatch of black hair.

Randolph stopped a short distance from the man. He waved the letter. "From Mr. Roosevelt himself, Mr. Chamblis."

Chamblis took the message and read it. "You didn't see a copper hanging about, did you? Name of Abberline?"

"Abberline?" Randolph said. "No. But if I do, you'll be the first to know."

The man silently removed several bills from his pocket, peeled off a one-pound note, and gave it to Randolph. "A fortnight's wages for you, isn't it?"

Randolph reconsidered, asking for more. "Not nearly, Mr. Chamblis."

Chamblis said, "Yes, but it's more than you'd thought you'd get, but not as much as you hoped for." His hand shot out and grabbed Randolph by the collar. "You know not to say anything? You know what will happen if you do?"

"I ain't no squealer. I don't tell the bobbies nothing."

Chamblis released the boy. "You're a credit to youth everywhere. Go on now. Run home." He pulled a bulldog pipe out of his pocket, stuck it in his mouth, and lit it. He tore the envelope open and read the note. "See here, mother," he smiled. "Your boy's going to church."

The Times of London
The Times is honored to present a series of installments entitled PARNELLISM and CRIME, for the edification of its readers. These articles will investigate the recent increase in unlawful activities of the Irish race in this city.

CHAPTER 13
THE HOUSE OF LORDS, PARLIAMENT

Would the animals, two by two, enter Noah's ark? No, sir. Liberals, Conservatives, Radical, Whigs, Home Rule, and Nationalists, never two by two. Say, rather, they bray and kick, jostle and jump with the water rising, and Noah wringing his hands. The House of Lords, and not a handful of superior minds among them. Burke was mistaken. Dying was easy; politics was hard. But Crittenton's distaste for Parliament was sublime. "I should have been an actor, if not for my calling to the House," he had remarked to a friend. "I do truly appreciate the adoration of the crowd, even if they don't understand a word I say."

"My Lords," Crittenton said, his eyes sweeping the skeptical faces of his opponents in the House of Lords, "we near the end of a century as an empire unsurpassed by any that came before. Great Britain is great indeed, for it controls the seas and a vast portion of the lands. Our strength is our unity. Our power lies in our determination to bring English civilization to the world. We are given power by the Almighty over the lesser peoples of the world."

Several members on both sides mumbled, "Here, here," and slapped their thighs.

Crittenton continued, "It is the destiny of the White, Anglo-Saxon, Protestant occupants of the United Kingdom to protect those races unprepared to manage themselves or their lands. I speak now of that island laying off our western shores. Of a people who cannot control their violent nature. How does anyone suppose that the Irish, a vulgar and crude race, can govern themselves? That is the height of naivety. Irish Home Rule? The Irish cannot rule their own tempers without our guidance. Leave it to us, their betters, to decide for this poor, misguided race."

Lord Warren, the Old Lion, a Nationalist, stood and addressed the Lord Speaker with a nod to Crittenton. "Will the gentleman yield for a clarification?"
Members of the House looked at Crittenton in anticipation. The request might signal the beginning of a battle between the two enemies.

"Lord Warren," Crittenton replied, his voice betraying nothing but good will, "I wonder if you would be so good to tell me, will this be a short clarification or a long clarification?"

Warren said, "My dear Lord Crittenton, I'm afraid the days when I could claim anything of length have long passed."

The House chuckled at the response.

"It is a naturally occurring condition, even among the august members of the House of Lords. Pray continue," commanded Crittenton.

"Does the Conservative Party," Warren's voice boomed over the heads of the members like the low rumble of a distant storm, "truly believe the Prime Minister intends to carve the empire into disparage pieces? Naivety, indeed. Infuse power, I say. Strengthen this empire to which Lord Crittenton refers. We, as a nation, relinquish nothing. We, as a nation, ensure cooperation. Seek, peace. Strive to introduce a logical means for the two peoples, and indeed, we are two peoples, to co-exist. Do not fear the motion. Embrace it." He sat down.

"Noble words, My Lords," Crittenton said. "Yet again, my learnered friend teaches us that the pen is mightier than the sword. Prime Minister Gladstone has made his position on Home Rule abundantly clear. But gentlemen," he raised a doubt, "he wants the Irish to rule themselves. It should also be abundantly clear to this body that, as a people, the Irish have neither the ability nor experience to build and govern a country. A country? Nay, say a province. But even that taxes them. Then, suppose they could govern a village? No, My Lords. It has been proved for years they cannot, in any sense, be trusted with their own future or the violent present. Despite the Prime Minister's contention, or Mr. Parnell's urging to release the Irish, to do so is to commit that troubled island to a wave of death and destruction the likes of which this Empire had not seen since that debacle in Afghanistan."

Warren stood. He was an old fox, sniffing the air for scents. "The Queen does not wish it?"

"The people do not wish it," Crittenton returned. "If Disraeli were alive again today, and he and I never agreed on a single issue save the miserable state of the Royal Post," laughter stuttered throughout the chamber, "he and I would lock arms and march to Buckingham Palace, making a common show of our resistance to the Queen on the issue of Home Rule."

"But he is dead," Warren countered, "and gone off to his Jewish God…" He never got a chance to complete his point.

"Who commends Disraeli for keeping English authority over Irish anarchy?" Crittenton pushed the issue. "Among the Irish are barbarians who kill our diplomats, toss dynamite at civilians, and plot to overthrow the government. Were we to erect a wall around that island like Hadrian's against the Scots, it would not stop the killing. They would turn on themselves, killing innocent along with guilty. Then they would export their venomous hatred to all points of the globe."

"Come now, Lord Crittenton," Warren said, "I believe rhetoric has overcome reason."

Crittenton chose to ignore Warren's quip. He paused to reinforce the importance of his words. "Despite my dire warnings, I am convinced that the issue of Home Rule will be defeated, without violence. I must respectfully inform my colleague, however. I shall advise the Queen not to include a contingent of Fenian revolutionaries in her Golden Jubilee celebrations. Their sartorial taste is always in doubt." He stilled an objection from Warren.

"My dear Lords, let us leave the Irish for a bit and revisit the elemental but the seedier aspects of London life," Crittenton said, "that was once resolved but are now revealed once again." The other members sat on their benches, like ponderous sea lions scattered along a stony beach. "Lord Ashley and later Lord Shaftesbury were instrumental in passing the Labouring Classes Acts and succeeding acts to control the lower classes of London."

Warren rose, but Crittenton cut him off. "Yes, I know the acts were for the benefit of Her Majesty's subjects, but better still, they kept the mobs at bay. Anarchy, in any form, from any source, weakens the Empire. The latest Act, just two years passed, addresses the unsanitary conditions under which these people live. Pay heed. Parliament had to address the people's needs, because the people could not. Parliament will care for the Irish, because the Irish cannot. Home Rule, my friends, will not stop at home. The Irish, unchecked, will bring their brand of malice to the slums of England's cities and spread it liberally over the dissatisfied like manure on a fertile field." He let the image linger and was pleased that Warren and his camp made no effort to respond.

"I, for one," he continued, "will fight to my death to prevent such a pestilence from engulfing the Empire. I am the Monarchy's staunchest friend. I will, by any measure necessary, protect the royal house and the empire."

The Times of London
The Queen's Jubilee
The Duke and Duchess of Connaught arrived in Marseille this morning from India
by the steam packet Sutle.

CHAPTER 14

A knifeboard bus passed, its interior and top deck crammed with clerks and office workers. An advertisement on its side read *Scientific Dress Cutting— 272 Regent Circus*. Edith watched from the Hansom cab as the bus passengers laughed and spoke to one another with the familiarity that comes from common experiences. They looked so light-hearted, squeezed shoulder to shoulder in the lumbering vehicle. Only the fare-taker, stationed at the back steps, looked glum. He had a right to be, he was excluded from the comradeship.

"There, see that," Theodore gestured out the window. "They're called hokey-pokey stalls."

Edith saw a tattered tarp thrown over uprights on a handcart. A plump man wearing a straw hat lounged at the rear of the cart. It was the ragged bunch of children besieging the man who captured Edith's attention. They were clothed in cast-offs of oversized coats and hats, stained, and covered in grime. But it made no difference. Each child was lost in the pure delight of a cup of ice cream. The treat covered their mouths and dripped down their chins onto their clothes. A moment of delight in a world of misery. They would soon return to a dusty street hemmed in by dull buildings caked by coal smoke, buildings that ran from horizon to horizon. These children of suffering would go no farther than this poor, sordid universe.

"Theodore," she said, "don't you think it odd we are to meet at St. Martins-in-the-Field?"

"Not at all, Edith. It's brilliant, positively brilliant. Out of the way, so to speak. Completely unexpected."

"Oh," she said, not entirely sure why she agreed with Theodore.

"Think of it. Our acquaintance comes in through some rear entrance, we chat in an anteroom, some out of the way location, and off he goes without attracting attention."

"I suppose you're right."

The Hansom slowed, and Edith saw people rush by the vehicle. She heard shouts in the distance. The cabby's face appeared at her window. He pulled his cap off. "I'm sorry, your lordships, but there's some sort of foolishness going on up ahead."

"What do you mean?" Theodore asked.

"It's one of those labor rallies. Everyone wants an honest day's pay, you see, but give them a job, and nobody wants to work." He looked at them in embarrassment. "The truth is the streets are so clogged up; I can't get you to your destination. It's a fine day when I have to advise a fare to walk."

"So be it," Theodore announced and stepped out of the cab. "Come, Edith, we'll continue on foot."

Edith joined her husband. They heard the hollow sound of cheers echoing off the storefronts. More people, mostly men and boys, raced down the street.

Theodore pulled a handful of change from his pocket and held it out to the driver. "How much?"

"Oh, no, sir. The job wasn't done."

"Nonsense. Take what's fair."

The cabby looked over the coins. "The rate's a shilling a mile up Charing Cross." He selected the amount.

"Take another for your trouble," Theodore said.

Edith was drawn to the sound of the crowd. "I hear drums, Theodore. Do you hear that?"

"Now," Theodore asked the cabby, "how would one get to the church from here?"

"Go straight down the street, your lordship. If you'll kindly step a bit this way." Theodore did as he was asked. "There's the steeple, just above the roof there. Mind your step. There's a small army of men building stands for the Jubilee on every square inch of ground along the street." He leaned close to Theodore. "Didn't want the missus to hear, your lordship, but certain of the ladies' roost on the steps of the National Gallery looking for companionship, if you know what I mean, so you might want to avoid that spectacle if possible."

"Yes, indeed," Theodore confirmed. "My thanks to you."

Edith heard shouting in the distance, and the sharp clatter of horse's hooves on street stones. She felt adrift in a sea of confusion, and the chaos was increasing as she and Theodore set out. As the street opened a bit, she saw thousands of people jammed in Trafalgar Square.

The National Portrait Gallery lay across the square. In the center, Nelson's monument.

There, gleaming in the mid-day sun, was St. Martins-in-the-Fields. "There? Do you see it?" Theodore asked, taking her arm. "Just a short jaunt."

"Theodore," Edith said as they walked down the street, "this has all the makings of a riot." Several men ran along the other side of the street. She watched them disappear around a bookbinder's shop on the corner.

Theodore dismissed the idea. "No, Edith. Didn't you hear the driver? Just a few communists trying to stir up trouble. That wouldn't happen in America, by God."

"The army's been called out," Edith said.

That got Theodore's attention. "How's that?"

"I heard bugle calls."

"Let us stay close to the shops," Theodore instructed. "We should be at St. Martin's in a moment." They had gone several hundred yards. Ahead on the left was the huge portico and massive columns of the church. A spire, almost too fragile to sit atop its fortress-like box, pierced the sky.

"If I were you folks, I shouldn't go much farther." A short man with a sketch pad was pressed into a doorway of one of the buildings. The man stuck out his hand. "Fenwick," he jabbed at the scene with his pencil. "Lovely, ain't it?"

Over the heads of the crowd, Edith could see a group of men gathered on the base of Nelson's Column. Red flags flashed overhead.

"Quite the event. Quite the event," Fenwick returned to his pad, drawing rapidly. "Twenty thousand, I'd say." He smiled impishly. "Not counting the Metropolitan Police. Sir Charles Warren himself will gather up every bobby in London and lead them here." He looked at Theodore and Edith. "You're not Londoners."

"Americans," Theodore said. "On our way to church."

"Church," Fenwick mused. The idea puzzled him. Something got his attention. "Oh? Do you see there?" He ripped a page from his pad and began sketching frantically on a clean sheet, straining to see over the crowd. "On the far side of the crowd. It's the Grenadier Guards who come to rescue the police."

Edith heard more bugles over the heads of the grounds.

"The Life Guards as well," Fenwick shouted. He was thrilled. "The filthy little bastards, all polished and preened." He shot Edith an apologetic look. "My apologies. Now, the ball's about to begin. If you two are going to church, you'd best be going. Once the army begins clearing the square, it's every rioter for himself."

"What about you?" Edith asked.

Fenwick was shocked. "I'm the press, aren't I? My duty's to be out here and record scenes of mayhem. And I'm well paid for it. Now, on with you. Say your prayers."

"Good luck to you, sir." Theodore took Edith's hand. "Are you ready?"

She nodded.

"Wait a moment," Fenwick stopped them. "Best watch the ebb and flow of the mob. There's an opening. Now go."

Theodore took Edith's hand in his, and they ran. They skirted the edge of a building and, ran up the steps of the church, and dashed into the shadow of the portico. They stopped against one of the columns, catching their breath.

The square was a wild swirl of rioters, fleeing in a dozen directions. Pushing them, crimson uniforms on horseback, and the sun gleaming off highly polished armor. Cavalrymen in dark uniforms swung their sabers above their heads. They were windmills, beating the rioters with the backs of their swords. It was madness. The sound of screams rose. They watched as the crowd disintegrated.

Edith said, "Theodore?" Her voice broke the spell. "The Prince? We must be going."

"Yes," Theodore managed. "Madness. Absolute madness." Collecting himself, he led Edith across the portico to the massive wood doors.

Edith stopped him as he reached for the bronze handle. "What are you going to tell him?"

"The Prince? Everything," Theodore said. He was so straightforward with the answer that it was almost comical. "What we saw, what we know. About that chap, Abberline. The truth."

Edith kissed Theodore. She hoped he could see how much she adored him.

"What do you think?" he began.

"The truth," she nodded. "Yes, by all means."

Theodore gasped at the handle and opened the door. They entered and closed the heavy door behind them. The terror they had just seen disappeared. They were submerged in silence.

"Oh, how beautiful," Edith said. Two rows of walnut pews marched down the central nave to a pulpit that swept from the church floor on a curving staircase. Overhead, the barreled ceiling floated down to rest on painted bronze Doric capitals that sat atop gleaming columns. Balconies were suspended between the columns. Overhead, brass chandeliers hung by slender strands, waiting to be swayed by the hymns of the worshippers. There were no more than a dozen people scattered throughout the pews.

Surely God was present in such a remarkable place, Edith thought. She quickly said a prayer.

"Do you see him? I don't see him," Theodore said. He guided Edith to the base of a column. It towered over her. "Perhaps, Crittenton is here. I want you to wait."

"No," she said. She had no intention of being separated from Theodore.

"Edith. I am only going to go up there." He pointed to a door opposite the pulpit. "You can see me all the way, and I can see you."

"Theodore," Edith was firm. "Let him come to us."

"He can't show himself, my dear. The Prince of Wales? He'll be known straight away. Don't be concerned; it's almost over. Will you wait here, please?"

She relented. "All right. But please be careful."

"I will, Edith." He planted a kiss on her cheek. "For good luck."

Edith watched him move up the aisle. She almost laughed despite the situation. Theodore was clearly in his element.

A noise to her left startled her, and she turned to see a big man almost at her elbow; a white streak ran through his hair. Before she had a chance to say anything, he spoke.

"I'm sorry to give you a scare like that, madam." His voice was soft, inviting, but it did nothing to lessen the menace she felt. "You are, Mrs. Roosevelt? Are you not?"

She hesitated. She was afraid, unable to move. Don't be silly, Edith. You're in a church, and Theodore is a few feet away. There was no harm in answering. "Yes, I am. There is my husband. Did the Prince send you?"

It was his smile that frightened, Edith. "In a manner of speaking, he did." There was no emotion in his eyes, and his smile faded. "Let's be on our way, shall we?"

Something was wrong, terribly wrong. Edith calmed herself. "I'll go and get Theodore? Wait a moment? Will you? He's over there." She tried to stop herself from trembling.

"Don't trouble yourself," the man said.

She felt a knife blade pressed against her side.

She knew if she screamed, Theodore would hear her. Scream. Shout. Do something. As she opened her mouth, arms encircled her like a vice. She struggled. A rag was pressed over her mouth. She tasted something metallic. She couldn't breathe. She tried to fight, but the man's arms were like iron bands trapping her body. She couldn't move. Her body was failing her, and his legs lost all their strength. Edith's mind fought to clear itself, but she felt as if she was on the edge of a deep sleep. Her eyelids were stealing her vision. She sensed other men around her. She was being lifted. She was tumbling over and over. The letter. She had the letter.

She heard the terrifying sound of the crowd outside.

Theodore peered over the pews for the Prince. He should be here. Somebody should be here. If not the Prince of Wales, then a representative. The whole thing was ludicrous, having come for a meeting and not a soul in sight. Crittenton will hear about this and the Prince as well. In the middle of a riot as well. He'd find Abberline and tell him everything. Let the Prince deal with him.

He turned to Edith when he saw the men. They had her.

He was running before he realized it, digging through his pocket for the pistol. "Let her go! Damn you, let her go."

The few people in the church, scattered as he shouted.

The men ignored him. They had the door open, and two of them were carrying Edith's limp body. One man, big, had a white streak through his hair, and the leader turned to face him.

"Stay, Mr. Roosevelt, if you want to see your wife returned unharmed."

Theodore stopped, jerked his pistol out of his coat pocket, and aimed it at the man.

"Let her go, or you're a dead man."

"Now, you don't want to do that, do you?" the man said. "Let's all be civilized about this."

"Bring her back," Theodore demanded. "Now!"

The man shook his head. "Harm me, and you'll return to America a widower."

Theodore lowered the pistol. "What do you want?"

The man with the white streak in his hair said, "Your cooperation. You've been going about making accusations. Not the sort of thing a gentleman does. We can't have that now, can we? You just behave yourself like a good gentleman, keep your opinions to yourself, and all will be well."

"Bring my wife back to me."

"In due time," Chamblis said. "Let's understand each other, shall we? All we ask is your cooperation."

"And you'll return Edith unharmed?"

"You have my word," the man said. "One gentleman to another."

Theodore erupted. "So help me, God, if anything happens to her, I'll hunt you down and kill you like a dog."

"Four hundred square miles, Mr. Roosevelt. And three million citizens. That's London. Hunt all you like. Of course, if you don't do what I say, it won't make any difference."

"I have money," Theodore said. Maybe that was it. Ransom. "I will pay you."

"I've been paid, Mr. Roosevelt," the man said. "Don't follow me. For your wife's sake."

He turned slowly and walked out the door.

Theodore hesitated and then ran after him, bursting into the sunlight. The crowds had fallen back from the Square and into the street in front of the church. Police and soldiers were battling rioters.

Theodore raced to the end of the portico, looking for Edith. There, on the steps. The letter. From the murdered girl. Edith must have dropped it. Theodore picked it up, crushing it in his hand. "Edith?" he screamed.

There were no carriages in sight, no cabs, not even a wagon. They had retreated from the streets. He ran down the steps, two at a time, hoping that someone had seen the men who had taken her.

"Edith?" Not again. Not like this. First Alice. Then his mother. "Edith?"

Someone had to have seen her. They must have. The men carried her from the church. It couldn't have happened without someone noticing.

Theodore stopped at the last step. He knew it was useless. In the middle of a riot. A thousand people. No one had seen her. No one knew what happened.

He'd failed her.

Theodore slipped the revolver into his pocket.

Crittenton. He'd done this. Somehow. Find Crittenton, Theodore told himself. Abberline was involved in this. He'd find them. He'd find Edith.

He saw Abberline come out of the alley on the other side of the street. Theodore raced across the street, dodging rioters and policemen. Abberline. He'd beat the truth out of him.

He'd kill Abberline to get Edith back.

The Times of London
The Queen's Jubilee
*On the eve of the departure for England of those members of the Imperial family
who are to represent the court at the forthcoming Jubilee fetes, the semi-official
North German Gazette devotes a long and prominent article to the occasion.*

CHAPTER 15
LESTER'S ALLEY, OFF ST. MARTIN'S LANE

"Abberline?" Theodore shouted, pushing his way through the crowd. The inspector saw him, started to wave, and then realized something was wrong.

Theodore bowled into Abberline, knocked him off his feet, and sent him tumbling back into the alley. He landed in a surprised heap against a stack of battered pallets. "What the bloody hell is wrong with you?"

Theodore took his stance, fists up. Then he remembered his glasses. He took them off and slipped them into his coat pocket. "Get up," he ordered.

Abberline climbed to his feet. "Too right, I'm getting up. Have you gone mad?"

"Where is Edith?" Theodore shouted.

"How the hell do I know where she is?" Abberline said.

Theodore closed the gap between them, and, before the policeman could react, landed a solid right on his chin.

Abberline, stunned, stumbled back, tripped over a pallet and landed in the dirt. He shook his head and looked around. "Well, here I am again." He felt his jaw, tasted blood, and looked at Theodore. "Right." He stood, but this time had a slat from one of the pallets in his hand. "Mr. Roosevelt, I have no idea what you're talking about, and hitting a policeman is a serious offense. Especially me. I order you to stand down immediately." He brought the slat up, gripping it with both hands.

Theodore was defiant. "That will do you no good, Mr. Abberline. I want answers. Where is she? You had a hand in it. I'll have the story at your expense." He slipped to the left, keeping an eye on the slat, and then bobbed to the right. The man would swing from left to right. Theodore drove his fist into a spot just below Abberline's sternum, but the inspector dodged the blow.

"Stand down, Mr. Roosevelt," Abberline said, side-stepping to the right, keeping his distance from Theodore.

Theodore had him now. The man favored his right. Theodore shifted to the left, bobbed right, and closed the distance. A feint to the left and an uppercut, he thought.

The slat shot out, the butt end driving hard into Theodore's gut, driving the air out of his lungs.

Theodore staggered back His fists fell. He sucked air into his lungs. His legs turned to cloth, and he dropped. He rolled to his side, trying to rise, got to his knees; but he didn't have the strength to climb to his feet. He gasped, fighting to draw a breath.

Theodore watched helplessly as Abberline squatted next to him, resting his chin on the end of the slat.

"Now, when you're able, tell me what has happened," Abberline said calmly.

"Edith," Theodore choked out. "Kidnapped."

"I had nothing to do with Mrs. Roosevelt's abduction, but I have an idea who has." He laid his hand on Theodore's chest. "Breathe slowly, Mr. Roosevelt." He stood and tossed the slat away. "I received a message, from you, to meet at St. Martins-in-the-Field. The riot delayed me. Any better?"

"Yes," Theodore said. "You were not involved?"

"No," Abberline said. "I suspect I would now be dead had I arrived on time."

Theodore nodded. "You're very proficient with lumber," he managed.

Abberline smiled. "Cricket. Speak softly and carry a big stick, I say."

Theodore extended his hand for Abberline to help him to his feet. "I shall keep that in mind." Finally, able to breathe, he told Abberline about Edith's kidnapping.

"How many men?"

"Three. Four, possibly," Theodore said. "Their leader was a big man with a streak of white hair, running so." He passed his hand over his forehead.

"I know the man," Abberline said.

"They have my poor wife," Theodore said. "Please? We must do something."

"Yes," Abberline agreed. "But what, is the question? It appears we are targets as well."

Theodore dug through his pockets. "There is a letter. From the murdered girl." He handed it to Abberline. "Edith dropped it as she was being carried away."

Abberline read it. "This certainly complicates things. 'G?' Who might G be?" He rubbed his chin in appreciation. "Well, we have a conspiracy here, Mr. Roosevelt."

"Lord Crittenton is involved," Theodore said. "Edith and I went to him for assistance, and he betrayed us."

"Crittenton," Abberline said, "is the Prince of Wales' champion. But why go to these measures to protect the Prince? He has merely to offer denials and refute your account. Hasselbach has declared the girl's death a suicide; the papers will report it as such; and the officials will close rank around the Superintendent. There is no evidence the Prince was in the woman's room, except his revelation to you. There's nothing to indicate he had anything to do with her murder. Why complicate this affair by kidnapping your wife? Why involve the Black Squad?"

"Black Squad?" Theodore queried.

"Ancient history," Abberline replied.

A squad of cavalry galloped by the alley's mouth. There were shouts, followed by a scream, and one of the horses returned, without a rider.

"We must be going," Abberline said.

"My hotel is less than a mile from here." Theodore announced.

"No. Not there. Just because they've let you go doesn't mean you've escaped danger. Now or in the future." Abberline started walking deeper into the alley. Theodore followed but had no idea where Abberline was leading him.

Theodore asked, "What is the Black Squad?"

Abberline answered as he walked. "Several years ago, some of the superintendents formed a sort of flying squad. They started out well enough, with good intentions and all, but what happened is always what happens when men are given to believe their cause is righteous. These men, never more than a dozen, considered themselves the only law."

"You mean above the law?"

"No." Abberline was emphatic. "I mean, they subverted the law for their own benefit. The Black Squad, it was said, was to sweep the city of crime. I knew some of the blokes. Good men. But after a while, corruption set in, and the Black Squad existed for the Black Squad's sake. News of their existence became known; Parliament demanded an investigation; and the very men who created the squad returned a report denying its existence. The Black Squad disappeared."

"It is a band of criminals?"

"Criminals," Abberline conceded. "Ex-police, former military. Men who have no allegiance save to themselves. Wealth and power, Mr. Roosevelt."

Theodore nodded, thinking. The church. The big man? He had to be the leader. "Is he one of them, this Black Squad? The man with the lock of white hair?"

Abberline turned on him. "Chamblis?" he confirmed. "Yes. And others."

They walked in silence. The sound of the riot gradually disappearing. "I should have shot him," Theodore muttered.

"You have a revolver?"

"Yes, I have, and I don't want to hear any nonsense about surrendering it."

Abberline dismissed Theodore's concern. "Keep it. I'm sure we'll need it. We have a girl dead, a woman abducted, and the next in line to the crown stuck between the two incidents. What would you have me do? Call up the reserves? We're it. There are some well-placed chaps who'd much rather have us dead than embarrass the royal family." He reconsidered. "Well, me, at least, because my death wouldn't make a ripple."

"They've picked the wrong American to trifle with," Theodore said. "By God, whoever is responsible for this is going to pay."

Abberline patted Theodore on the arm. "Admirable sentiments. Well spoken. Commendable."

"Would you be so kind as to tell me where we're going?" Theodore asked.

"The Three Sisters. Drury Lane," Abberline said. "We need a place to hide, and I need to gather reinforcements. We are both in the shit pile, Mr. Roosevelt."

The Times of London
The Hudson Bay House is pleased to announce the opening of The International Store at 163-5 Regent Street, offering select items from around the world. Special attention is paid to riches from the Near East.

CHAPTER 16
WARDER'S COTTAGE IN THE ENGLISH COUNTRYSIDE

The scent of wood smoke was faint. Edith thought it strange because it was summer and the warm closeness of a fireplace wasn't necessary. A dream, then. She knew she was asleep, or at least in that otherworldly time between sleep and awakening.

Her eyes fluttered open without seeing, closed again because they were too heavy to remain open, and she settled for the darkness. She slept, but for how long was uncertain. Her eyelids parted, and her eyes focused. She was looking at a crude table and chairs. Edith sat up in the bed, heard the rustle of corn shucks in the mattress, and after her mind cleared, looked around.

She was in a tiny, one-room house. The fireplace was to her right, the table and chairs directly in front of her, with a cupboard and shelves on the left. She sat on a small bed that was covered by a sheet with a quilt folded neatly at the end. She twisted around. There were two small windows behind her that matched the two on either side of the door across the room. The walls were plastered, and whitewashed, and the ceiling was rough board above timbers.

"Theodore?" The sound of her voice startled her. She stood, became dizzy, and reached for the table. "Theodore!" Using the table and one of the chairs for support, she made her way to the door and, taking the handle in both hands, pulled. The door refused to yield. She tried again. It rattled but remained shut. It was locked.

The windows, Edith rationalized, even if they were locked, she could break the glass. She found a milking stool next to the door and decided it was sturdy enough to serve the purpose. She dropped it in disgust when she saw the bars on the window.

"Help! Can anyone hear me? I've been kidnapped." She looked through the window. She was deep in a forest. "I'm in a fairy tale," Edith said. "Theodore!" she screamed in frustration. She gave up shouting, found a water jug and a cup, and dipped herself a drink. The moment the cup was at her lips, she realized how thirsty she was. She drank deeply, filled the cup, and drank again. She set the cup next to the jug and cleared her thoughts. She remembered the church, the man with the white hair, and

Theodore's shouts. Nothing after that. Until she awoke.

Ether, she decided, or chloroform. A drug of some sort.

"What would Theodore do?" Edith asked herself. She became irritated with the question. "What will Edith do?" she said. A bath, she said, but realized the idea was absurd. She stank of sweat, and her hands were filthy. She could wash off easily enough if it weren't for the windows staring at her. Tonight. When it's dark.

A thought startled her. How long am I to remain here? Is there a ransom? No. There is no question of money. It's about the Prince of Wales and that poor girl. The cupboard caught her attention. She threw open the doors. There were a few chipped ceramic plates, a pitcher, a scattering of forks and spoon, and a miniature pyramid of can goods. Edith examined them. Pears, condensed milk, bully beef, and something called Stapleton's Fine Sardines in Fresh Oil. She shuddered at the thought of it. She pulled open the drawers below the shelves. There were worn rags in the top drawer. The bottom drawer was filled with newspapers. She found their presence odd, until she realized they had a very practical use.

Edith's search around the rest of the cottage revealed nothing of interest, and certainly nothing of use. There was no way out, except through the door or windows; and both were blocked to her. She guessed she was supposed to live on the cans of foodstuffs in the cupboard. But she had nothing to open the cans; and even if she did, it was doubtful she could eat the contents.

She returned to the bed, sat down, and considered her options. There was a tall, thin can to one side of the fireplace. Matches. She looked at the ceiling again. "This is probably the only quaint English cottage built like a fortress," she observed. If she tried to set fire to the ceiling or door as an escape, she would probably succumb to the flames or smoke.

Batter down the bars over the windows with a chair. She went to the window and examined the bars. They were iron, on the other side of the glass. She looked below the sill. Four carriage-head bolts ran the length of the window. The bolts extended through the wall, passed through the bars, and were secured on the other side.

"This is too much," Edith felt her anger rising. "I'm just one little woman," she shouted at the ceiling in anger. "Did you think I could batter down the walls? If I had Theodore's revolver, I'd shoot you dead." She laughed at her own absurdity. "If I didn't detest guns." She pulled out a chair and sat down. She was tired, a little woozy; and she hoped there was a tin of tea hidden in the cupboard. She would have preferred coffee, but she supposed she was not likely to find any.

Edith heard a soft jingle in the distance, and the muffled thud of horseshoes on the soft ground. She jumped to her feet, ran to the window, and peered out. The bars and filthy glass distorted the view; and she shifted, hoping to see something.

"Help! Anyone? Can you hear me?" She raced to the other window. Standing on her toes, she could see a two-wheeled cart pulled by a farm horse. A man drove, or rather held the reins. The horse appeared familiar with the lane. Next to the driver was a plumb woman with a basket on her lap. "Help," Edith screamed. "I'm here. Can you help me?" She returned to the other window. "Please. I've been abducted."

Edith ran to the door and beat its rough surface with her fists. She shouted, "Help me," until she grew hoarse. The muffled sounds of talking made their way through the cracks in the door. A key scraped into the lock, the latch jangled, and Edith jumped back from the door.

"Hurry, please," she cried. Her hands were clasped together in relief. She was free. Theodore? Was Theodore harmed?

The door was thrown open, and the middle-aged woman with bright red cheeks appeared. Edith did not have time to respond before the door was slammed shut and locked. She looked at the woman in disbelief. "Why did he do that? Is he insane?"

The woman, squat with stubby legs, waddled over to the table, and was just barely able to lift the basket. "Oh, no. Mr. Congreve is no more than I." Her voice twinkled in innocence, like a child's. "But he had a curious way about him." She turned to Edith, satisfied with the basket's place on the table. "Now, my dear, I'm Mrs. Sheraton."

Edith's voice was sharp with frustration. "I want to go home. Now."

Mrs. Sheraton didn't abandon her pleasant attitude. "I know you do, dear; and I'm sure everything will be worked out as soon as heavenly possible. All I was told to do, you understand, is see to your food and necessities; and since I can't manage one of those devilish conveniences, Mr. Congreve will see that I get to and fro." She dug through the basket. "I brought a spot of tea for you dear."

Edith felt hope drifting away. "Why am I being held? Who is holding me?"

Mrs. Sheraton continued to sort through the items. "I haven't the slightest idea what you're talking about." She looked at the goods in disappointment. "Oh. No butter. I forgot butter. How is a soul expected to have biscuits and tea without butter?" Her concern flew away like a sparrow. "Well, that's that, I suppose."

Edith said, "I've got to get out. I must return to London and see my husband. My husband is Theodore Roosevelt. He's a very important man." Mrs. Sheraton didn't hear her. Arranging the jars and tins in the cupboard required her full attention. "I can pay you. If you help me, there will be a reward." Edith watched as Mrs. Sheraton checked the night soil pan, made the bed, and stood with her hands on her hips, examining the interior of the house.

Mrs. Sheraton started for the door. "Mr. Sheraton was a lovely man but too fond of the drink by half. A footman he was. He drowned in Collier's Creek. No more than a foot of water. And I left with a child. Still, me and Margaret Jane got along splendidly."

"You can't leave me here," Edith said. "Please don't go. Help me. At least, send someone for me." She realized she had another option. "A note. I will write you a note, and you can send it to my husband."

Mrs. Sheraton knocked on the door. "Oh, no, I couldn't do that. Mr. Congreve and I have strict instructions. Now, you'd best step back away from the door before you're injured. Mr. Congreve can be difficult. Oh, and please take care with the cottage. It's Mr. Congreve's. He's the warder, you see; and he's very particular with his things."

Edith grabbed for Mrs. Sheraton, but she twisted out of her grip and was through the doorway. The door closed with a bang, followed by the key being inserted in the lock, and a click.

"Let me out!" Edith screamed. She beat on the door. "Let me out of here. I'm an American. Do you know that? My government will make you pay. You can't do this to an American." She continued shouting until her voice became weak. She slid down the door, slumping onto the cold stones of the floor. She was alone again, and all she had to show for it was some food and the acquaintance of an insane woman. She laid her arms across her knees and dropped her forehead. Shadows were lengthening across the floor. The sun's light was dying. The back of the cottage faced west, the fireplace south, the cupboard north, and the door she rested against, east.

She lifted her head and let it drop back against the door. She thought, fittingly, fragments of ideas and images swirling around in the darkness. They had no form.

Edith closed her eyes. She startled awake. She had fallen asleep. She climbed to her feet. The shadows had spread into the cottage, easing up the walls and filling the corners. She was not refreshed, but her mind had calmed; and her thoughts floated gently, rather than spinning wildly. She spoke to hear the sound of her own voice. It was comforting. "Mrs. Sheraton and Mr. Congreve. They couldn't have come far," she reasoned. "That poor animal was too fat and too old." She posed that idea to herself and accepted it as logical. "Perhaps, Mr. Congreve is mad. Or a criminal. Mrs. Sheraton is *certainly* mad." She thought it over. "Or feeble minded." Congreve appeared more than capable of defending himself. He guarded the door like Horatio at the bridge. She smiled to herself. Theodore would certainly appreciate that analogy.

Edith felt sadness slipping over her. Poor Theodore. Alice is gone, and now I am gone; and he could do nothing to help either one of us. He must feel abandoned, frustrated, and frightened.

She surveyed the interior of the cottage and laid out her plan for the evening. A bite to eat, a nice hot cup of tea, bath, and go to bed. It became apparent to her without any thought. She had to have plenty of rest and adequate sustenance to prepare for defense of escape. Bathing was just as important as rest. She was accustomed to a daily bath, and she meant to maintain that schedule. "I will take control from those scoundrel's piece by piece until my life is mine." It may start with a cold bath out of a wooden tub, but it was a beginning. Then what?

Fright was still with Edith. The emotion had subsided and been replaced with anger and outright rage. But it had never fully left her side. It remained, if only in a whisper. Now it leaned over her shoulder and in the coldest of voices reminded her: You could die here.

CHAPTER 17
WINDSOR CASTLE, LONDON, ENGLAND

Victoria R. I., Empress of India, Queen of the United Kingdom, Ruler of Scotland and Ireland, received Lord James Crittenton in Her Majesty's Private Sitting Room. She was dressed in mourning, the black garment contrasting starkly with her gray hair and pearl-white skin. She filled her chair with rotund corpulence, despite her small stature, and was so motionless she could have been one of the marble statues that lined the wall.

The gallery of family photographs in a variety of silver frames peered obediently at Her Majesty. The sight amused Crittenton. Except for the luxurious setting, Her Majesty could be a shopkeeper's wife in her waning years.

But she was not. She was the Queen of a great empire with children and grandchildren scattered around the royal houses of Europe. Royalty in their own right, they might yet receive a sharply worded letter if the Queen was informed of conduct unbecoming a member of the royal family. She was the moral compass of the empire and her family. There were dynastic principles at work in the heart of the old woman, and despite her grandmotherly appearance, she could be obstinate.

It was late in the day for an audience with Her Majesty, but Crittenton had been notified of the Queen's desire to see him as he left Parliament.

Crittenton bowed midway to the monarch and waited for her to grant permission to approach.

"My dear Lord Crittenton," Victoria said. Her voice was high and strained at times, like an old woman's who was likely to fall asleep in mid-sentence. Her age and intractability frustrated her ministers. She made no attempt to hide her dislike of some who served her. Crittenton was not among those. "Approach, please. We are happy to see you. Be so kind as to be seated." She motioned to a chair pulled close to hers with her tiny hand. It might have been a dove.

"Thank you, Your Majesty," Crittenton said. He made certain to sit erectly as a sign of respect for Victoria. Disraeli had a habit of slouching, but he had been one of her favorites. "How are you this evening?"

"We are dreadful," she said. "Just dreadful. Our spine is hardly better than the other day, and our temperament reflects it. We trust the news you carry will leave us much improved."

"I must admit that I have failed you, Your Majesty," Crittenton said. She should have expected his report would contain unfortunate news. While she secluded herself at Windsor Castle with an occasional breakfast under the trees at Frogmore to be near her late husband, she was well versed on the undercurrents of Parliament.

"So, Lord Crittenton?" Victoria said. "We are to be displeased at the news. We should have imagined that even under a common cause, those misguided souls in both houses could not secure Home Rule."

The Queen had to be led to the reality of the situation, Crittenton knew. She demanded what she thought best for the realm without admitting what was apparent to the members of Parliament. They controlled the British Empire, and she was reduced to wielding influence only. But influence, skillfully wielded, was as powerful as an army. Monarchs were an anachronistic species, some thought, their demise hastened by the approach of a new century. Still, Crittenton accepted; they had their place. "Lord Parnell leads sixty Irish Nationalists. Warren controls the Radicals, and the Liberals wander about as Moses through the desert. And, of course, Your Majesty, there is the Prime Minister."

Victoria's hand flew up. "We are heartily aware of Minister Gladstone's role in this disaster. Our Prime Minister," she said in a fit of betrayal, "would rather see the Irish free of our control than an end to this sectarian violence. You should know, Lord Crittenton, that we have been insulted only by the Irish and Socialists." She pushed herself back into the chair. A shock looked crossed her face. "We have failed to offer you tea, Lord Crittenton." She reached for a tiny silver bell on a table next to her chair.

"No, thank you, Your Majesty."

"We have never been so rude," Victoria said, aghast at her failing. "We must only suppose these recent events have been more troubling than we suspected."

"It is quite understandable, Your Majesty," Crittenton said. She was the Queen of the greatest empire on earth, but she was an old woman. She had held the throne for fifty years; and while she had aged, the world had gotten more complex, more dangerous. She thought she could simply turn her mind to any problem and solve it by force of will. Those days were gone.

"If I may suggest, Your Majesty," he said, certain that he could manage some good news for her, "Lords Churchill and Chamberlain are quite certain they can turn a goodly number of votes from the Radicals to Your Majesty's position."

She found a glimmer of hope. "Are they? We would be most appreciative of their efforts."

"I shall inform them," Crittenton said. "If I may ask Your Majesty's indulgence, I must return to Parliament for consultation with my peers." It was a mild lie. He was scheduled to discuss politics over cards.

"Yes," Victoria said, holding out her hand. The black sleeve of her mourning dress inched up a plumb, white wrist. "We are heartily pleased that you were able to spare the time to inform us of events in Parliament."

Crittenton took Victoria's fleshy hand in his and bowed deeply. "As always, Your Majesty, it is my pleasure to serve you."

Victoria's hand trapped his as a thought came to her. "Lord Crittenton, we would be very much pleased if you could join us for the Jubilee events of the twenty-first. We are so looking forward to it with much anticipation. Many of our children will be there."

Crittenton glanced at the photographs that swept over every available space in the sitting room. He smiled at Queen Victoria. "I will be most pleased.

Crittenton began backing away when Queen Victoria's voice called to him.

"That other matter, Lord Crittenton," Victoria said, barely hiding the distress in her voice. "Will you soon be able to inform us of its conclusion?"

She looked like a tiny doll. Eyes that nearly always pierced her visitors with unwavering perception, now glinted with tears. Crittenton was relieved he was several feet from Queen Victoria, less she be aware of the pity in his eyes. The Prince of Wales' indiscretions hung heavily in the room. The Queen counted on Crittenton to mitigate their impact. She had heard something about a drunken party. Nothing else. She was willing to accept the account, because she did not have the strength to deal with another of her son's scandalous episodes.

"You Majesty," he said, "the issue will be favorably resolved. You need not concern yourself with it in the least."

The Times of London
The Times has recently been informed that the American entertainer and frontier scout, Mr. Buffalo Bill Cody, will arrive shortly with his Wild West Show. Mr. Cody is well-known for his duel to the death with a famous Indian chief, after the defeat of General George Armstrong and his men.

CHAPTER 18
BEDFORD LANE, TOTTENHAM COURT ROAD, LONDON, ENGLAND

Benjamin Dugan, pulled his pipe from his pocket, watching Schiess assemble the batteries. The acid's stink was barely noticeable above the thick stench from Meux's Brewery next door. After a few days, Benjamin had become so accustomed to the smell of hops and yeast fermenting in the brewery's huge tubs that he no longer noticed it. The odor from the brewery's stables, even though they were on the other side of the four-acre brewery, was too powerful to ignore. Horseshit was horseshit, and you can't make perfume out of it.

"You can light your pipe," Schiess said as he examined the glass jars.

Benjamin pulled the pipe from his mouth and looked at the bowl. "There's no tobacco in it."

"Put some tobacco in it. That constant wheezing is irritating."

Benjamin dug a waxed tobacco pouch out of his pocket. "Aye, well, we can't have you irritated, can we?"

They were alone in the brick pump house. It had been part of the brewery; but so many residents of Bedford Lane had taken to stealing parts of the pumps, the proprietors of Meux's Brewery had removed the machinery and abandoned the house. Benjamin claimed it as his, after running off a pimp and two of his whores.

"How much dynamite?" Schiess asked. He took a drink of gin from a chipped ceramic cup. It calmed him.

"One hundred forty-two sticks."

Schiess chuckled and looked at his friend. "How did you arrive at that curious number?"

"Is it your job to know?"

Schiess turned back to the batteries. "It's my job to make them explode." He had lanterns surrounding the table in a bizarre devotional. Schiess was the monk, the unfinished batteries, precious relics. He worshiped in solitude, despite the presence of

Benjamin's bulk in the room.

Benjamin slipped his hand in his pocket and held out an abacus. "Do you know how to work it?"

Schiess glanced at it. "I do not. How did you come by such a devilish instrument?"

"A Chinaman holding a birdcage sold it to me."

"If you don't know how to use it," Schiess asked, "why did you buy it?"

"He wouldn't sell me the bird, so I bought this. One day, I suppose, I'll learn its secret."

Schiess grunted and continued working. "Where are the brothers?" he asked.

Benjamin lit his pipe, drew in the smoke, and stepped away from Schiess. He didn't want to send the old man into a coughing spasm. "Out."

"Considering they aren't in; one would assume they're out."

"Why the interest, old man?"

Schiess sat back, staring at the batteries as if they were his children. "I've been wondering. You came back to this hostile land. If you're caught, they'll hang you. Whatever enticed you to return had to be considerable."

"I'm a patriot."

"Oh, I've never doubted that. But for a government that doesn't exist?" Schiess had another idea. "A country under the heel of the despot. Why, Benjamin, you're a romantic. I've always believed the only cause you upheld was for the glorious Benjamin Dugan."

Schiess's efforts with the batteries fascinated Benjamin. His delicate fingers danced over the devices like tiny insects. The man was a genius, but he was a greedy bastard as well. "There is no more money to be had, if that's what this is about."

Schiess laughed. "Money? Look at me, man. I'm dying."

"Then what is it?"

"I'm a scholar. My intellect requires me to acquire knowledge. Allow me to learn, and that's payment enough."

"Curiosity killed the cat," Benjamin said.

Schiess gave him a look of mild disappointment. "I expected so much more from you. Very well, let's exchange information."

Benjamin shook his head. "You've got nothing I want."

"Pride goeth before the fall," Schiess said. "In fact, I do have a sliver of information. About you as it happens."

"Oh?"

"Yes," Schiess said. "You're about to be betrayed."

The Times of London
Reports have circulated that the Royal Navy Sloop Suspect was grounded off the coast of France near Pas de Calais. Three men have been lost, and no officers. It is doubtful the vessel can be saved.

CHAPTER 19
THE THREE SISTERS LONDON, ENGLAND

It was a building that years before had been filled with reputable residents. Now, it was a whorehouse. The passing years wore the neighborhood down until the buildings had degenerated, and a wave of the poor flooded the area. Three buildings, exactly alike, delicate structures that offered promise: They were now ragged reminders of a better life.

A black man, wide and menacing, let them in and then, without a word, stood aside as Abberline led them down a narrow hallway to a door next to the stairs. Theodore heard laughter and loud voices, muffled by the walls, followed by a high-pitched squeal. He heard a noise behind him. He turned to see a slight woman, her face worn and suspicious.

"You've got the nerve coming here, Abberline," the woman said. Her voice was unnatural, husky.

"Don't trouble yourself, Bert," Abberline said, opening the door. "We won't be here long."

"Bert?" Theodore was confused.

"You'll run off, my gentlemen friends, won't you?" Bert snapped. He glanced at Theodore's drooping mustache. "Traveling with walruses now?"

Abberline grabbed Bert's arm and thrust him down the stairs into the basement. Theodore followed. "Now, see here, Bert." The policeman lit a lamp just over Theodore's head. "You and I get along all right. I don't bother you and your kind, so let's come to an understanding before I lose my temper. My friend and I are staying in the cellar for a bit. Keep it to yourself, or I'll have so many constables here, that it'll look like a stationhouse. Get out." He grabbed the lamp, closed the door behind Bert, and pointed Theodore deeper into the cellar.

"Never fancied you one of us, Abberline," Bert called through the door. "Hope the walrus keeps you satisfied."

They found two more lamps, lit them, and looked around. The ceiling was low, but they had room to walk upright. Boxes, a few steamer trunks, and pieces of furniture hidden under muslin sheets were stacked against one wall.

Abberline gestured to a door close by. "That leads to Thomas Lane."

Theodore noticed a door in the far wall. "What about that one?"

"Coal chute."

"How is it you're so familiar with this establishment?"

Abberline gave Theodore an annoyed look. "I'm partial to women, Mr. Roosevelt, so don't worry. Every good cop knows where to get out of the cold."

"Very well," Theodore said. "We're out of the cold. What are your plans?"

"Give me your pistol."

"Absolutely not."

"I need it."

"That may be so, Mr. Abberline, but I have it; and I intend to keep it on my person."

Abberline set the lantern on a crate. "I'm going out, and I may have use of it. When I return, you will have it. So please, give me the bloody thing, before I fetch another stick."

"Sarcasm is not the way to gain another's confidence, Mr. Abberline. How do I know you will not abandon me in this evil place?"

"For God's sake, Roosevelt, I'm the man who saved you."

"From what, exactly? Edith is kidnapped, I'm led through some endless labyrinth to a house of ill repute, and now you find it convenient to run off. With my pistol. You catch my meaning, Abberline?"

"Only a solicitor can add two plus two and come up with eighteen," Abberline said in disgust. "I need your pistol because I'm going to confront the man who took your wife."

"What?"

"Bob Chamblis."

"You're going to arrest him, aren't you?"

Abberline looked at Theodore in disbelief. "He's the Black Squad, man. I could have seven witnesses swear he shot the Queen, and he'd still get away with it." He calmed, approaching Theodore. "Look. I'm an outcast, just like you. I don't have the department behind me."

"He has Edith, Mr. Abberline. We can't let that go."

Abberline was sympathetic. "Yes. He *has* her. He's smart enough not to have her anywhere around him. I know Chamblis. We were on the force together. I might be able to talk him into revealing something."

"I'm going with you," Theodore said. There was no other way.

"It's too dangerous. Give me the revolver."

"Too dangerous? You think I care about that now?"

"I do," Abberline said. "This is a delicate business, Mr. Roosevelt. I'm not all that sure I'm going to walk away from it."

Theodore didn't budge. "I'm going."

Abberline nodded. "Very well. Chamblis has a little café on the Strand. Very popular. When we get there, you wait outside. I'll go inside and talk to him."

"Find out where Edith is."

"I'll be lucky I don't find myself in the gutter with my throat cut." He remembered the pitch barrel on the banks of the Thames. "Chamblis is the sort that's hired to do whatever is necessary. For the right amount, he'd kill his own mother. He was a good cop at one time, and he knows London like a parson knows the Bible."

"He's a coward and a rogue. When I have an opportunity, I'll put a bullet between his eyes."

Abberline wasn't impressed. "Bob Chamblis is no coward. It's best you keep that in mind. This is not America, Mr. Roosevelt. This is London. If we're not careful, we'll end up floating in the Thames. That's not the sort of end I prefer."

The Times of London
The Queen's Jubilee
Constantinople. The arrangements for sending a representative of the Sultan to the Queen's Jubilee were more than once altered, and finally Ali Nizami Pasha was named.

CHAPTER 20
BEDFORD LANE, TOTTENHAM COURT ROAD, LONDON, ENGLAND

Benjamin laid his hand on Schiess's shoulder, stopping the little man's work. "That's a dangerous subject to broach. You know I have a Homeric hatred for traitors, don't you?"

"Please remove your hand, Benjamin. The pressure is likely to snap the few good bones I have left to me."

Benjamin did as he was asked, found a bottle of Scotch on a shelf near the door, selected two of the cleanest cups on another shelf, and poured a healthy dose of liquor into each. He nodded toward the unfinished batteries. "Come away from those devices so we can talk."

Schiess covered the table with cheesecloth, scooped up his cigarette makings, and joined Benjamin.

Benjamin slid a stool over to Schiess with his foot, and, when the old man sat down, handed him a cup. He toasted Schiess and watched his trembling hand bring the cup to his lips. "What is the illness that ails you?"

Schiess shrugged. "Something to do with my muscles and nerves. Some days are worse than others. That's Hell enough, but my mind fails me on occasion." He held out his hand, turning it back and forth as he examined it. "Somedays, my hands feel almost electrified. Tingling. Other times," he dropped his hand, "I have no strength."

"There's no cure?"

Schiess looked up at Benjamin and continued to drink. Answer enough.

"Let's trade confidences," Benjamin said. "I'll go first, so you know I'm honorable. I wasn't in America all these years. I was in Ireland. Sometimes I worked for the Rebels and sometimes the English. Fruitful employment is hard to come by. Whoever my employer, I never betrayed them."

"You mean when you decided whom you were actually working for?"

Benjamin raised his cup. "Ah, there's a fine line, don't you know. There were those who'd sooner betray their comrades than breathe. There were a number who tried to betray me."

Schiess handed Benjamin his cup. "Be so kind as to give me a bit more and tell me their fate."

Benjamin returned Schiess's cup, half filled. "Let's talk about the other."

Schiess handed Benjamin his tobacco pouch and papers. "Favor me with a cigarette, will you?"

Benjamin slapped the pouch and papers from Schiess's hand and jerked him to his feet. His cup crashed to the floor. "You think this is a game, you ugly little cripple? You play me for a fool, and I'll break you over my knee like a twig."

Schiess, hanging between Benjamin's hands, swallowed heavily. "And who will make the electricity to fire your bombs," he gasped. "Kill me, and you'll have to run your fuses eight hundred feet or more."

Benjamin relaxed his grip, trying not to show his surprise. "How do you know the length of the fuses?"

Schiess tapped the hands, trapping him in a vice. Benjamin released him. "I'm a voracious reader, my friend. It's no great thing to determine why you're here, or what you intend to do."

"I ought to kill you."

"We've already discussed the folly of such an action. Besides, I'm not the enemy."

Benjamin picked up his cup, wiped out the interior, and poured Schiess another drink. "What else do you know?"

Schiess took a long drink. "Let me catch my breath." He held two fingers up in the universal plea for a cigarette. Benjamin retrieved the pouch and papers. As he fashioned one, Schiess continued, "From the newspaper accounts, I suppose you could use one of a dozen sites. Of course, there must be several hundred stands being constructed along the procession route. I haven't told a soul, because I value what remains of my miserable existence and because I don't care." Benjamin handed him a cigarette, struck a match, and held it until Schiess managed a few feeble pulls. "Now," he said. "I'm satisfied with a drink, a few cigarettes, and a few more hours of life." He exhaled with a raking cough. "Does that constitute my confidence?"

"Who will betray me?" Benjamin asked.

"It's that damnable temper of yours that troubles me," Schiess said. "I'd feel better if you stepped to just the other side of the table. And remember now, everything we need is under that covering."

Benjamin took Schiess's cup, filled it, and went to the opposite side of the table. He took a drink, and then another, and waited.

"Another name for Judas is Michael," Schiess said. He waited for Benjamin's reaction.

Benjamin's voice was stripped of emotion when he spoke. "Little man, if you weren't already dying, I'd kill you myself."

CHAPTER 21
THE STRAND, LONDON, ENGLAND

They took an omnibus, Abberline paying the eight pence to the conductor who stood sentry at the rear, and climbed the iron steps to the top deck.

Roosevelt saw an endless stream of streetlights glowing in the darkness, banners and flags celebrating the jubilee, swaying in the night air, and weary street vendors making their way home. "Is it like this every night?"

Abberline shrugged. "It's the Queen's Jubilee. Everyone is trying to squeeze the last shilling out of the visitors. When the celebration's over, and the bunting comes down, the streets will be empty by ten. That's when London really burns."

"How do you mean?" asked Roosevelt.

"The good citizens of the night. The panel thieves, buggerers, sweet dollies, and Nancy boys come out. The gin houses and black-and-tans unlock their doors; and respectable clerks, merchants, and reverends go about looking to have their pickles tickled one way or another." Abberline was amused by Theodore's innocence. "The opium dens do such a striving business at night; it's difficult to get a pallet. Take any lane to Hell; but take care the demons don't swarm out of the darkness to cut your pocket for your purse or your throat, because it's less trouble. Sin piled on top of depravity, with only the dead left to greet the dawn. The sights I've seen are beyond description. The worst is the children. They die of neglect or disease, if they're lucky. Sometimes, they fall prey to the perversion of adults. Perhaps, a good Christian will happen upon their bodies; and they'll get a good, decent burial."

"You use the word Christian as if it's an expletive. You're not one of those free thinkers, are you?"

Abberline's tone hardened, "I've seen good, Christian men pay money to rape children, boys and girls. And I've seen mothers so destitute they had to sell their children."

The thought sickened Theodore. "I am truly sorry that such practices exist. If I happened upon a scoundrel taking advantage of a child, I'd shoot him without giving it another thought."

Abberline smiled before answering. "Well, you've got the gun, haven't you?"

They swung off the bus near a shop with a sign that read *Romford & Burton Ales*, under a festive red arch that ran from one side of the street to the other. The air over the street was filled with decorations, flags, bunting, portraits of the Queen, an explosion of patriotism. The largest arch bore the legend *God Save the Queen* in gold lettering, and below that, in case anyone forgot, was a stern Victoria, glaring down at the passers-by.

Abberline motioned Theodore toward a storefront. "Listen very closely to my instructions, Roosevelt. I am convinced you're the sort of fellow that will go off on his own if the impulse arises."

The comment stung Theodore. "Not at all."

Abberline said, "That little white building down there is Chamblis' restaurant."

Theodore saw a storefront with red half-curtains on the front windows and a row of flower pots underneath the windows. "Charming," he said. "Let's go."

Abberline stopped him. "It's your wife, and if it were my wife, no power on heaven or earth could stop me from going in there and ripping the man's head off. But it's not revenge we want or retribution. It's information. If he sees you, the jig is up."

"I will not abandon, Edith," Theodore said.

"You've got to stay here. Keep your pistol handy and keep out of sight."

Theodore said. "What of you? What if you need assistance? How will I know?"

"Mr. Roosevelt, if I need assistance, all of London will know." Abberline found the ideal location for Theodore. "In this doorway, if you please. If anyone approaches, just speak American."

Theodore watched as Abberline walked down the sidewalk, stopped to study a store window, and disappeared into the front door of the café. He stepped back into the doorway and slipped his hand into his pocket, feeling the reassuring bulk of the revolver. He felt himself tremble. I'm behaving like a fool. It was anger, and fear, and frustration. Abberline was right. He was burning to race into the café and pistol-whip a confession out of Chamblis. Abberline was right as well about the danger of taking matters into his own hands. This was no time for thoughtless action. But for the first time in his life, Theodore knew hatred.

Abberline entered the café, and his first thought wasn't of danger but how wonderful the food smelled. The last time he had eaten was breakfast.

There are a dozen tables in the dining room, half of them occupied. White tablecloths shimmered under candlelight. The three modest chandeliers hung from a low ceiling, and paintings in gold gilt frames hung on the walls. Chamblis had done well for himself.

A waiter approached him. The man wore a starched white shirt with black bowtie, and a clean white apron that extended from his waist to the tops of his shoes. A napkin, neatly folded, hung over his left arm. His attitude told Abberline that the place was for the better class only, not an inspector on the run.

"I've sorry, sir," the waiter said. "But we've stopped seating customers."

"I didn't come to eat," Abberline said. "I've come to see Bob Chamblis."

"Mr. Chamblis is otherwise occupied in the kitchen."

The man was so earnest Abberline almost laughed. "I'm sure he's not too occupied to see an old friend." He pushed the waiter aside and walked back to the kitchen. He pushed open the swinging door to find Chamblis, standing over a stove, cooking. His apron was splattered with stains.

Chamblis smiled a greeting. "Just frying a few eggs, Fred. Fancy something to eat?"

"Not just now, Bob." Abberline backed away from the door and leaned against the wall. It wouldn't do to expose his back around men like Bob Chamblis. There were two other men in the kitchen. One was washing dishes, and one was consulting a list of some kind.

"Take a bit of butter, salt, and pepper," Chamblis flipped the eggs. "Add some cheese, onions, and some bacon if you're a mind. Serve it with freshly baked bread." He looked at Abberline. "Slice it nice and thick now and butter it. Simple pleasures."

Abberline listened, waiting for Chamblis to finish talking.

"Some tea topped off with milk. Now, some folks want kippers with their eggs, but that spoils the taste." Chamblis flipped his eggs onto a plate, picked up a fork, and began to eat. "What's on your mind, Fred?"

"What do you hear about the Black Squad?"

Chamblis took a bite of bread and wiped a spot of butter from the corner of his mouth with the back of his hand. "Nothing to it." He pointed to the dining room with his fork. "What do you think of my place?"

"Lovely," Abberline said. "About the Black Squad?"

"Long gone," Chamblis said. "If there ever was such a thing. Thinking about writing a story? The Doyle fellow sparked your interest? He writes fiction, doesn't he?"

"What about it, Bob?"

Chamblis set the plate on the stove. "Fred, I've few things I can call my own. One is cooking, and the other is eating, and now you've gone and spoiled things with all this talk." He turned and whistled, catching the other men's attention. He jerked his head, sending them out through a back door. When they were gone, Chamblis turned to Abberline. His playful manner was gone.

Abberline said, "This murder at the St. Denis Hotel…"

"Was there?"

"And the whole deed was neatly tied up by someone used to that sort of thing."

"Everybody has a talent, Fred," Chamblis said, brushing his hair back off his forehead with the edge of his hand.

Abberline glanced at the white streak. "Was it to protect the Prince of Wales? Did he kill the girl?"

Chamblis picked up his teacup and blew across it. "That's a lurid question, isn't it, Fred? That sort of reasoning could get a chap in trouble. You know the royals wouldn't let a thing like that out. You are on the force acting like you just came to town. I'm heartily disappointed in you, Fred."

"Who killed Harvey?"

"Is he dead?" Chamblis said.

Abberline eased himself off the wall.

Chamblis offered an opinion. "He was a filthy sot. He's been dead ten years but never had the common sense to admit it."

"He was my friend," Abberline said.

Chamblis answered with a cruel smile. "He would have sold his soul for a thimble full of gin. Worse, he would have sold yours."

"Well," Abberline said. "He heard something or saw something; that's what I think. There's more to it than that dead girl, isn't it?"

"Ask Hasselbach. He's your governor."

"Why kidnap the American? I know all about it, Bob. Hasselbach wouldn't get his hands dirty with any of this. That's why he came to you. He wouldn't have, unless it was bigger than one tart's death."

"Fred, you've got a sharp mind. Smart in some ways, perhaps, but dense as a brick in others. I don't know anything about Americans, but if I were a betting man, and I am, much to my saintly mother's regret, I would say that American lady is unharmed and will remain unharmed, if everyone just keeps their bloody mouths shut."

"Excellent advice."

"I'd feel so much better, Fred," Chamblis said, "if I knew you were going to take it."

"Hand Mrs. Roosevelt over to me, and I will."

Chamblis shook his head. "Fred, you've been a disappointment to me since I've known you. Go home, wait a bit, and the Roosevelts will be reunited by-and-by."

"This isn't like you, Bob, getting citizens involved. Something went wrong, didn't it?"

"You know, Fred. Even powerful men get in the shit. Now go home. Get a good night's sleep. Tomorrow, the sun will shine. I'll have a lot of fine folks in for breakfast, and you'll see there's nothing to worry about."

Abberline always thought that Bob Chamblis was probably the most dangerous man he'd ever encountered. Now, he was certain of it.

"All right, Bob."

"Come by for breakfast," Chamblis tossed after him. "And try the crepes."

Abberline walked through the dining room. A big man with a red beard, a laborer from his dress and manner, held a cup of tea in his hand, watching Abberline pass. They exchanged glances. Abberline had seen that look before. The man was just as dangerous as Chamblis.

When he was outside, he looked up and down the street. He turned left, and, when he was clear of the café windows, hurried to Roosevelt's doorway. "Give me the pistol. There's a man I need to club."

The request startled Theodore. "What are you…?"

"Chamblis had a man on me the moment I left the place."

"Just let the miscreant follow you, and I'll take care of it. I'm not a babe in the woods, Mr. Abberline."

Abberline warned, "Don't bungle the job, then. I'm off."

Theodore stepped back into the doorway and watched the reflection of the café in the shop windows across the street. If the big man with the bushy beard he saw going in was his target, Theodore judged it would have to be a solid blow. No hesitation. He'd always judged the English to be small people, pale skinned, lacking muscle. This fellow with the red beard shattered his hypothesis. He pulled the pistol out of his coat.

Theodore saw a movement in the window, a shadowy reflection, distorted in the glass. A man stepped into the street and turned to his left. He walked rapidly. A light man with a trim mustache. He was the man sent to follow Abberline.

Theodore tightened his grip on the pistol barrel, raised the weapon above his head, and watched the man's progress in the window. With a start, he realized that he might be visible by the same method as well. He pushed himself into the doorway. His target's reflection floated over store windows, breaking into pieces on glass panes, reassembling again.

Before he knew it, the man was in front of him. Theodore caught the flash of a knife blade as the man's arm came up.

The world slowed.

Theodore swung the pistol and knocked the knife out of the man's hand. There was a cry of pain, and the man threw his fist at Theodore but missed. As he did, Theodore brought the butt of his pistol down. There was a dull thud, and the man collapsed in the street.

Abberline appeared. "Not badly done."

"He's out, isn't he?"

"Too right. Now rob him."

"What?"

Abberline pushed Theodore aside, knelt next to the unconscious man, and searched through his pockets until he found a purse. He held it up in triumph. "I have no money. Do you have any money? I thought not; most gentlemen trade on their good names. Now, we have money." He stood. "Come on."

When they were a safe distance from the café, Abberline said, "There was a big chap in there. Red beard. Could have been a boxer. He didn't belong. He's trouble all right."

"I saw him go in. What did you learn from Chamblis?"

"Mrs. Roosevelt is safe and will remain safe as long as we are silent."

Theodore wasn't satisfied, "Where is she?"

"I don't know."

"You had time to memorize the Guttenberg Bible while you were in there. Tell me you learned more than that?"

"I did," Abberline said. "And I will tell you. Let us return to the whorehouse, get a good night's sleep, and in the morning," he tossed the purse in the air and caught it, "our unconscious friend will treat us to ginger cakes."

Theodore threw Abberline against a doorsill. "Mr. Abberline, where is my wife?"

"Step back from me, Roosevelt," Abberline warned. "The one thing we can do to ensure your wife does not return is make a mistake. You know these people are murderers. We appear to say nothing and do nothing, and she remains safe from harm. Chamblis is in it up to that white hair. We'll take it as slow as molasses."

"Edith is everything to me. I could do nothing to save her. I failed, Mr. Abberline. I let them take her."

"Had you tried to interfere, you'd both be dead. Of that, I am certain. I shall do everything in my power to see her safely returned," Abberline said. "I may look like a day clerk at a counting house, Mr. Roosevelt, but I'm a bloody good detective. We'll get them and hold them to account." He saw the poor sot Harvey, stuffed in the pitch barrel. "For everything."

CHAPTER 22
THE CHAMBLIS CAFÉ

Benjamin knew the man was a copper. He watched him go out the café door and set the empty teacup on its saucer. The man was gone, but the look that passed between him and Benjamin was one of recognition. Yes, you're a cop and I'm a criminal, but we'll let that be for now.

Chamblis had done something stupid, something to attract the attention of the Metropolitan Police Department. This was not the time for such nonsense; but there was the cop passing by, and there was Benjamin, enjoying a cup of tea.

Chamblis came out of the kitchen, saw Benjamin, and ordered a waiter to close the front window curtains and leave them alone. He sat down, his back to the wall, at Benjamin's table. "More tea, then?"

Benjamin said, "What the bloody hell are you doing having me come here, when you're playing at cops and robbers?"

"Why are the Irish always so emotional?" Chamblis said, unfazed. "I didn't know Abberline was coming for a visit. So? He saw you, and you saw him, and there's no harm done. You don't know each other, do you?"

"No," Benjamin said, but he wasn't satisfied with Chamblis' reasoning. The man was far too convinced he could outthink or outtalk anyone. "But he knows what I'm about, all the same."

"No, he doesn't. Not *that* in any case."

Benjamin wasn't reassured. "I've come for my five hundred pounds."

"Tell me, Benjamin, and it's only a matter of curiosity, nothing more. What have you done to deserve that princely sum?"

Benjamin hated bantering words. "You came to me."

"I came to Daniel," Chamblis corrected him.

"Yes, and you know that neither brother could piss in a pot if they were standing over it. You know what I do. If I make a bargain, I keep it. We made a bargain. A thousand pounds, five hundred in advance. I'll take my money now, and I'll contact you about the dynamite tomorrow. This is a tricky business, royalty and all, and it won't be done easily. The streets are swarming with citizens and soldiers every hour of the day. It'll be a closely run thing." Benjamin stood. He was ready to leave. "Do we have a bargain or not?"

Chamblis rose. "We do. You know me to be a fair bloke. As good as my word."

Benjamin didn't move.

"Very well, then," Chamblis said. "I'll get your money. Just be a minute." He returned, tossed a bundle of five hundred quid at Benjamin, and then stood back watching Benjamin count it. He pulled an envelope from his pocket and handed it to Benjamin.

"What's this?" Benjamin asked.

"A ticket to paradise."

"I've been to paradise."

"Open it," Chamblis said.

Benjamin pulled out a heavy stock card. The Queen's crest, flanked by a lion and unicorn, was printed across the top. Below it in restrained font was *Royal Jubilee Procession,* and below that *Tuesday, 21st June 1887.* "By Order of The Queen," Benjamin read. "J. H. Leon has been appointed Master of Fireworks for the Royal Jubilee Procession."

"What's a celebration without a few explosions, I ask you?" Chamblis said. "Show that, and you can go where you want to, when you want to."

Benjamin examined the card, "Where did you get it?"

"Send for the dynamite when you're ready," Chamblis said, ignoring the question. "From now on, stay away."

"You used to be so sociable. I'll need caps as well. Dynamite is useless without them. And cord." He wanted cord in case Schiess's batteries failed. The old way was infailable.

Chamblis said, "When you're ready, send word."

"Who else is in this?" Benjamin asked.

"That's not important," Chamblis said. "You'll do the thing right, won't you, Benjamin? I need to know all that you know when the time is right. There's more to this than you realize."

"There always is, isn't there?" Benjamin returned. "If I need you, I'll let you know. Otherwise, you won't hear from me. Oh, and your tea tastes like shit."

Chamblis, hurt, picked up the cup, and examined the contents. "Everybody's a bloody critic."

Benjamin walked to the street, hounded by the idea that he was being a fool. He'd put his faith in Chamblis, and he knew the man was a liar. If I'm to do this thing, he thought and realized how stupid the thought was because he knew he would, I've got only myself. Everything that had come about thus far, Chamblis, Schiess, the planning and direction, had come from Benjamin. You're the strongest of my sons, his mother had said to Benjamin. She had meant his will and conviction, not the fists as thick as wheel hubs he'd used to beat others into submission.

A whore slid next to him. "Fancy a bit of fun, dearie?" she said, reaching for his crotch.

His hand wrapped around her wrist. "Go away from me."

She winced in pain. "Here. You're hurting me. Let go. Please." He did, and she ran off.

Benjamin had rented two rooms above a tiny tobacco store near Shaftesbury Park that offered more privacy and more comfort than the dank pump house. He'd ordered the others to move everything to the new rooms. Leave nothing behind, he'd told them, not a sliver of wood or scrap of food. Nothing to tell anyone they'd been there. Not the police, nor Chamblis.

"Be careful in all endeavors," his mother had said. "Don't let a soul get near to you."

"Not Michael or Daniel?" he asked himself. "My brothers?"

It wasn't the plan that worried him. The thing was simplicity itself. They would hide in the bedlam of Jubilee construction and lay the dynamite at will. They'd lose themselves among the thousands of men swarming over the streets, driving wagons, throwing up seating stands along every inch of sidewalk. The Jubilee had flooded London, and a handful of men wouldn't be noticed. Just more Irish trudging from site to site, invisible, worthless.

It was a jubilee of profit for London, the Queen's celebration. Merchants added additional stories to buildings, or on tops of their roofs to accommodate the two hundred thousand or more who would line the parade route to see Her Majesty and nobility from fifty countries.

The streets stank of green wood and paint, and the sound of hammering echoed throughout London from sunrise to sunset. Every seat filled meant money. Benjamin had seen a leaflet pasted on a brick wall, *T. Foster & Company*, announcing its Cheapside stand. Ground-level seats were ten pounds, ten shillings, but the top row was a modest two pounds, two shillings. Under the pageantry and wealth of a monarch's golden jubilee lurked the basest of motives: greed.

Benjamin would sink into the ocean of humanity and do as he pleased. He was satisfied that he would be safe.

A sense of grief overwhelmed him as he arrived at the Pump House. Michael was gathering up the last of their belongings.

"Michael," Benjamin greeted his brother.

"Nearly done," Michael said with a smile.

Michael. Even the sound of the name burned itself into his heart. He had wanted to kill Schiess, even though he knew what the old man had told him was true.

"You've seen him yourself, Benjamin," Schiess had said. "He goes about, especially at night, when we've got things to tend to. He's secretive about it. You've asked him, and Daniel has asked him, but Michael's walking here or going there. I just want to see, the boy's face when he answers your questions, his head dropping in shame."

Benjamin had listened without speaking, because it took all his will to keep his rage in check. You've got one brother then who can't be trusted. What of the other?

Michael, boyish, innocent Michael, with his corn silk hair and slender frame, hid his intelligence behind a quiet demeanor. The city had stolen the boy's heart; but, in return, what did it offer?

Why are you here, boy? Benjamin wondered. You and your brothers come all this way from Liverpool? What have you come to see, child?

Michael, the innocent, stripped of guile, was more than willing to talk, because he didn't see the danger of a few words. And the other thing, his love of little children. A sickening love, burning to be close to them, to possess them. There was a deep chill in Michael, a dark place that cried out to be filled. It was an unnatural calling, but to Michael, as natural and necessary as the rising of the sun.

Michael loves his children, and maybe someone notices and passes on to the Metropolitan Police that a boy is after children. The filthy bastard.

Early some morning, constables would crash through the door and sweep them up because Michael could not keep away from children.

"There's the last of it," Michael said.

"That's good, Michael," Benjamin, lost in the darkness of the night, said. "Let us go on."

CHAPTER 23
THE WARDER'S COTTAGE

Edith was up before dawn, she had made her bed, run her fingers through her hair in place of a comb, and, lighting a lamp, examined the interior of the cottage again, as methodically as she could. The only hope of escaping other than the door and windows was a mouse hole next to the fireplace. Some enterprising rodents had managed to nibble away a segment of mortar between two stones.

There were no tools, no objects that could be turned into weapons, and nothing to indicate where she was. Stranded, far from Theodore. Edith clasped her hands, closed her eyes, and prayed. "My Dear Heavenly Father, please give me the strength to survive this travail."

Theodore would have approved. It was short, to the point, and it took very little of the Almighty's time.

"God is a busy divinity," Theodore had assured her. "He doesn't have time for long-winded communications."

She finished her prayer with, "And if you would be so kind as to provide a weapon, I would be most grateful."

Edith heard a wagon approach. It was the mad woman and her driver, Mr. Congreve. Perhaps, he did not pose an immediate threat, but a threat, nevertheless, she decided. He would have to be dealt with, but not now.

Reconnoiter, she told herself. Learn all you can. Find a weakness.

The woman.

Get close to her. Lull her into complacency. Edith decided she would become Mrs. Sheraton's best friend.

She heard the familiar jangling of the lock, and the door swung open. Edith caught a glimpse of Mr. Congreve's arm. He let the old woman in. Of course, her arms were filled with goods, and she couldn't manage the door. The door was the only thing that separated Edith from Mr. Congreve. Edith grew excited about possibilities. Congreve and Mrs. Sheraton. She could slip by them and disappear into the woods.

The plan evaporated as quickly as it appeared. I haven't run since I was a child, Edith admitted to herself. Three steps, and Congreve would have me.

Mrs. Sheraton, a basket looped over each arm, walked to the table, smiling with good cheer. "Good morning, good morning, my dear, how are you? The sun is just popping up, and Mrs. Sheraton comes bearing gifts." She set the baskets on the table with a thump and began sorting through them. Edith stood next to her.

"Here are some lovely cheeses, two cans of pears." She drew out a bundle wrapped in cheesecloth. "Bread." She held it close to her nose and smiled in satisfaction. "I could eat a loaf myself in one sitting. Here's a crock of butter, and a bit of ham. A tin of sardines."

"Mrs. Sheraton, do you know why I was brought here?"

"Oh, bless me, no. Such things are above me. I was told to meet your needs and that Mr. Congreve would bring me out each day. I don't drive, you know. The more I don't know, the less to explain. That's from the Bible, you know. One of the Psalms."

Edith tried a different tact. "Then you live nearby?"

Mrs. Sheraton emptied the last basket. "At the manor house, of course. But no names, His Lordship was very specific about that. I was to be polite and helpful at all times." She leaned toward Edith and said in confidence, "He can be very short-tempered, you know. His type always is."

"The manor house?" Edith said, trying to keep Mrs. Sheraton's mind from wandering. "Are we far from London?"

"London? Goodness gracious, I wouldn't know. I haven't been there, have I? No good Christian has any business in that wicked town," she lectured Edith. She quickly forgot her own advice. "Now, Mr. Congreve goes to London at the Lord's bidding, but that's business between men. But if I were you, being the lady you are, I'd stay far away from that horrible place." She folded her hands together in satisfaction. "Now, can I fix you a spot for breakfast? It'll have to be cold, I'm afraid."

"Yes, please," Edith said, sitting down. She thought for a moment. "Do you know who my husband is?"

"No," Mrs. Sheraton said happily. "Now, Mr. Sheraton was a fine man before he drowned." She sliced the cheese, wiped off the knife on her apron, and did the same to the ham. She looked up in alarm. "Oh, my goodness, you're not Hebrew, are you?"

"No."

"Mr. Disraeli came to dinner once. He's a Hebrew, you know. Was, poor soul, he's dead now. I heard he and Mrs. Brown were quite close." She continued with breakfast. "He was very fond of Margaret Jane. My daughter, you know. He said that she was lovely. She is. She never liked her Christian name; it was too common, she said. But she's a child. Gentlemen prefer good, strong Christian names. What is your name, dear?"

"Edith."

"Oh," Mrs. Sheraton said, with a trace of pity. "Well, I suppose that suits you perfectly well." Mrs. Sheraton waved her knife. "But a good name and a shapely figure will capture a gentleman's eye every time."

Edith was tempted to snatch the knife out of her hand, but she couldn't do it. There must be another way. "Mrs. Sheraton, will you please join me for breakfast. I've been horribly lonely all night, and your presence would mean so much to me."

Mrs. Sheraton hesitated, looked in the direction of Mr. Congreve, and sat down. "Just for a bit, dear."

Edith ate slowly. "Is there a railroad track nearby? I swear a train woke me last night."

"His Lordship detests the filthy thing. Now, there's a lovely, well-treated road just through the forest. Mr. Congreve constantly complains about it. It's too rough, he says. Bad for the spokes, he says."

"I see. Would you like some cheese or ham?"

"Oh, no, no. I have oatmeal every morning. Tea as well."

"Mrs. Brown," Edith said. "Does she live nearby?"

"London," Mrs. Sheraton said. She tore off a tiny sliver of ham. "Just a bite, I suppose. His Lordship has some very unkind things to say about Mrs. Brown, and her a widow and all, with those many children. Did I tell you about my daughter, Margaret Jane?"

"Yes." She didn't want to hear about this lunatic's daughter. She was near a road, or might be, and within earshot of a train track.

There was a muffled shout through the door. Mrs. Sheraton stood and wiped her hands on her apron. "The man has no patience. And even fewer manners."

Edith was sorry to see her drop the knife in one of the baskets and carry both off. She walked the woman to the door and stood back, while Mr. Congreve unlatched the door.

Mrs. Sheraton smiled at Edith. "Now, don't worry about a thing, dear. Everything will work out perfectly."

She disappeared, and the door closed with a thud. The familiar jangle of the lock followed. Edith had seen Mr. Congreve through the window. The man was calm but alert; the horse's reins draped over his fingers. He had sullen features, not a person who revealed much of anything. A dangerous man, she concluded. A violent man.

Edith began to pace. "A woman who is clearly touched and a silent man to watch her and me." She nestled her hands in the small of her back, fingers interlocked. Her steps were deliberate. She was focused on what she knew. She stopped, surprised by the obvious. "I can drive a buggy. What's the difference between an English buggy and an American buggy? That horse looks capable of no more than a walk." She resumed walking. "How do I separate Mr. Congreve from the vehicle? He's much larger than I."

She paced the cottage floor. She sat down at the table. "I have to distract Mrs. Sheraton." She bit into a piece of cheese, looked at the remnant in her hand, and exclaimed, "That's it! She's afraid of mice. Every self-respecting woman hates the little vermin. I'll scream there's one at her feet, and Mr. Congreve will rush in to save the day." She finished on the cheese, laid a slice of ham on a piece of bread, and considered the next step. "I must dispatch Mr. Congreve." She dropped the ham and bread and propped her chin on her fists in thought. She stared at the cupboard. The stoneware water pitcher stared back. No weapons, eh? Make your own.

"Oh, Theodore," she said. "You'd be so proud of me."

The Times of London
The House of Lords undertook a debate on the Childers Reforms of 1881, over the appropriate colours of labels, cuffs, and collars of regimental uniforms. As enacted, Welsh and English regiments where to have white facings, Scottish yellow, Irish green, and Royal regiments dark blue. Some members of the House support the reintroduction of historic facing colours.

CHAPTER 24
THE STRAND, LONDON, ENGLAND

Abberline counted out two pence to the vendor. The old man slipped two ginger cakes from the tray hung around his neck and handed them to Abberline. "You don't know where I can get a quart of milk, do you?"

"I do," the vendor said. "Mr. Dymond will be pushing his cart down this very street in half an hour. Four pence a quart he charges, and the milk's so sweet you'd swear it was made from sugar."

Theodore was famished. He had nearly consumed his cake when Abberline began eating his. He and Abberline had spent the night on thin mattresses thrown over crates. He had not slept well. All he saw was Edith. She was in a mirror, pushing against the glass, calling for him, her face pleading for him to save her. He beat on the glass with his fists, but he could not break through. He shouted her name, but they were both trapped in a world of silence. He had awakened so many times he wasn't sure he had slept at all.

"Let's toast the generous chap that bought us breakfast," Abberline said.

"I recommend," Theodore said, tired and short-tempered, "we go back to speak to Mr. Chamblis."

"That won't do any good," Abberline said. "In fact, it may do more harm than good."

"Then I take it you have a plan?" Theodore said. Abberline was irritating him. He was too plodding, far too methodical. Action was needed to save Edith, not thoughtful consideration.

"Ah," Abberline said, "here comes our milk."

A bearded man pushing a three-wheeled cart appeared on the street. Empty pails hung from the axle; and a variety of cans swung back and forth, banging loudly against one another. "You can get anything on the streets, Mr. Roosevelt. Iced cream, fish. Mind the cats, of course. Clothes, matches, crockery, a lady's companionship." He looked down the street. "A gentleman's companionship."

"Mr. Abberline," Theodore snapped, "are we going to set out after Edith or elaborate on street life?"

Abberline waved to the milkman. "Mr. Roosevelt, sustenance is fuel for the body, as contemplation is fuel for the soul. Besides, I sent for reinforcements this morning, while you slept."

"I thought you said we couldn't trust your colleagues?"

The cart stopped in front of both men, and the driver tipped his hat. "Good day, gents. What can I help you with?"

Abberline looked at Theodore. "Two quarts?"

"Yes."

"Two quarts, it will be then." The man tipped a large pewter can, pouring milk into an earthenware jug. He handed it to Abberline, who paid him for both.

Theodore said, "Thank you," when he received his jug.

"I know a chap called Christy. How's your milk?"

"Fine," Theodore said.

"He's a conniving little bastard, but he fears me enough not to lie to me."

"What can he do for us?"

"I haven't decided." The sound of hammering erupted down the street, echoing from building to building. "God, I'll be happy when all this foolishness is over. It'll be nothing but a pickpocket's heaven, when all those citizens are crammed together, hoping for a glimpse of Her Majesty."

The two men finished their milk and returned the mugs to the vendor. He pushed his cart down the street, whistling happily.

"I am beginning to detest London," Theodore said.

Abberline said, "Be charitable, Mr. Roosevelt. Let's go back to our room."

"Can we stay out a while longer?" Theodore asked. The basement stank, and everything surface was damp to the touch.

"No," Abberline said.

"Have you been to New York?" Theodore followed Abberline to a stoop and sat on one of the steps.

"No," the detective was watchful, his eyes sweeping the street.

"It is a remarkable city," Theodore said. "America is the greatest country on earth."

"Yes," Abberline said wryly, "aren't we all?"

"When my first wife, Alice, died, I was crushed. My mother followed days later. I went west, intent on losing myself. It was a difficult time, you understand. I relied on my faith in the Almighty and my own character. I became a cowboy, Mr. Abberline. Drew my strength from the clean air and vast plains of the West. Hard work, sir. Tax the body, and the spirit will heal. In time, I resurrected myself, and became the man I am today. Then I fell in love with Edith. She saved me, sir.”

“Why don’t you two buggerers hold hands?” Christy said. He was crouched in a doorway, below the stoop, leading to the basement. “Don’t look down here,” he warned the two men. “Just keep looking straight ahead.”

Abberline said, “Good morning, Christy.”

“You call this hiding out? I don’t know about the Yank, Abberline, but you should know better. You’re a wanted man, aren’t you?”

“Am I?”

Christy chuckled. “Your own boys are looking for you, Hasselbach’s leading the way. And then you’ve got three or four lying in wait outside Bert’s.”

Abberline spat. “That bloody bastard turned us in.”

“Bert doesn’t have the balls,” Christy said. “You were followed.”

“Bloody hell,” Abberline sat against the step. He turned to Theodore.

“That first chap was a decoy. There was another who followed us after him, and I fell for it. Well, that’s what arrogance gets you.” He stood. “Mr. Roosevelt, you saved us both. Had we not lingered on the street, we would have run into an ambush.”

“You’re both quite welcome, I’m sure,” Christy said. “So Hasselbach’s running the show?”

“Hasselbach?” Theodore queried.

“A cop,” Abberline said. “Police Superintendent Hasselbach. Running it? I don’t know. But he’s the sort of chap that would gladly look the other way if the money’s right. Let’s go. That way.” He waved Christy from his position. “We’ll need a place to hide out.”

Christy joined them on the crowded sidewalk. “You’ve done well on your own. Why involve me?”

Abberline gestured toward Theodore. “This is Mr. Roosevelt. His wife’s been snatched. Chamblis is involved.”

“Chamblis?” Christy turned to run, but Abberline grabbed his arm. “Don’t leave the party yet, Christy,” Abberline said. “The fun’s just begun.”

“Are you trying to get me killed, Abberline?” Christy said. “I want nothing to do with this mess. Chamblis, indeed. I’m begging you. Spare me involvement in this unholy affair.”

“Shut up,” Abberline said.

“No Christian would do this to another,” Christy said. “Can’t you help me, Mr. Roosevelt?”

“I’m not a Christian,” Theodore said, feeling cantankerous. “I’m a Republican.”

Christy, confused, looked to Abberline for clarification. “What’s that?”

“It means he eats raw seals and frozen butter.”

“God blind me.”

They resumed walking, with Abberline’s arm thrown over Christy’s shoulder.

Theodore searched his pockets frantically. "Damn!"

"What is it?" Abberline asked.

"I left the pistol behind."

"A gun?" Christy said. "You have a gun?"

Abberline looked at both men in disgust. "You left it at the Three Sisters?"

Theodore said, "I kept rolling on it in my sleep. I took it out of my pocket and set it aside."

"And you left it?"

"I had other things on my mind."

"Apparently, staying alive wasn't one of them."

"If you weren't so consumed in finding money for ginger cakes last night, we wouldn't have been found out," Theodore said.

"You do have a fondness for ginger cakes," Christy said. "I might have known."

Abberline ignored him. "It's your job to find us a lair for the time being." He turned to Theodore. "And your task is to pay more attention to what we're about."

"Don't lecture me, Mr. Abberline."

"Then keep your wits about you, Mr. Roosevelt. Let's have no more talk about cowboys and wild, red Indians."

Christy looked at Abberline. "Are all Republicans like this?"

"Just the worst of them."

"Mr. Abberline, sir," Christy said. "If you would kindly unburden my shoulder with your arm, I can avoid those coppers."

Theodore saw two policemen pushing their way through the crowd. They were headed their way. "Gentlemen?" he said in warning. "We have company."

Abberline saw them and looked up the street. "Three more this way. Blast. We've got to scatter."

"I can't outrun them," Christy cried.

Theodore began moving away. "Let us reassemble at Cleopatra's Needle tonight."

Christy looked at Theodore. "I'm a cripple. I can't run."

"You'd better learn to fly," Abberline bolted for an alley across the street.

"Good luck," Theodore shouted, running after Abberline.

Christy stood in disgust. "Isn't it always the way? Leave the crippled boy to fend for himself."

The Times of London
*The Royal College of Organists has chosen a selection of works to be performed
each Saturday afternoon for the month proceeding Her Majesty's Jubilee. Works
include familiar pieces as well as those commissioned by the RCO to commemorate
the Jubilee.*

CHAPTER 25
FROGMORE GARDENS, LONDON, ENGLAND

It was the tranquility of Frogmore that drew Queen Victoria there for a secluded breakfast. Its thirty-three acres of heavily wooded grounds were a royal refuge sprinkled with mausoleums. There was no opportunity at Windsor Castle for solitude, far too many people buzzing around, always anxious to see to her wellbeing. For their own benefit, of course.

There was such a thing as an overabundance of attention. She found the journey to Osborne House on the Isle of Wight too taxing, and she would only travel to Balmoral Castle in Scotland if she were free of the memories of that solemn place.

When she had come to Frogmore, she entered the grounds as the young girl, slim, and a bit awkward, who found it hard to suppress a smile, until she was reminded that she was the Queen. She came to Frogmore for solace, a solitary figure walking gracefully across the grounds. She was trailed, at a distance, by a few members of the household staff who set her table and then discretely disappeared, leaving her alone. Save for Papa, of course.

She poured hot water into two cups, stirred in his tea first, and then hers. They both took milk, and she preferred sugar. He did not. He kept trim, he told her, by disavowing himself of all unhealthy foods. Prince Albert, formerly of the House of Saxe-Coburg and Gotha, took the cup of tea and sat back in his chair.

"You have more will power than I," Victoria said. She meant refusing sugar, of course. She thought he looked splendid. His black suit complimented his black beard and hair, and the stark whiteness of his color and shirtfront gave him a ministerial confidence. He could have been more than a prince; had he been allowed.

The cup floated gracefully to his lips. After a sip and a polite smile to indicate it was to his liking, he asked, "How are the children?" His German accent was rich, and his words were leavened with authority.

"Quite well."

He was a demanding father, but fair. The children looked to him for direction, as did Queen Victoria. He reminded them that they were all members of the royal family and that they should conduct themselves as such. "Albert Edward?"

She did not like to hear him speak of their eldest son. It was his misadventures at Cambridge that brought Prince Albert from his sickbed. It was that journey that killed him. "He taxes me, my dear," Queen Victoria said. "Nothing compared to the trials of his poor wife, but the weight is difficult to bear."

"But you must." Albert was calm and majestic, if only in her mind.

Despair swept over Victoria. "You are my father, my protector, my guide and advisor, in all, in everything, my mother, as well as my husband."

"Let us return to Albert Edward," Prince Albert reminded her.

She did not want to speak of her son. She wanted them to be lovers again, to have him entirely to herself. "There is some incident. I'm not sure. I prefer not to know. Lord Crittenton is devoting his utmost attention to the matter."

"Albert Edward should know better than to visit such difficulties on you during this period."

"If you're speaking of the Jubilee," Queen Victoria replied, long sick of the event and its demands on her, "it gives me scant satisfaction to celebrate the occasion without you at my side."

"But I am always at your side," Prince Albert pointed out.

Victoria poured herself another cup of tea, and said, "Do you know what I wrote just after you and I met? I wrote 'Albert is extremely handsome; his hair is about the same color as mine; his eyes are large and blue; and he has a beautiful nose and a very sweet mouth with fine teeth; but the charm of his countenance is his expression, which is most beautiful.'" She imagined Albert flushed at the compliment.

"And what of Alexander?" Albert teased. Victoria's father favored Prince Alexander of the Netherlands of all the eligible young men who sought her hand.

"I wrote that Alexander was very plain."

"You were a very naughty young lady."

She felt the longing for his company again. "Yes," she said without enthusiasm. "I suppose." She knew the staff would return shortly, and she must leave through the delicate cast iron gate in Albert's Mausoleum. She could not return for many weeks. There was too much that required her attention. Her life would be taken over by ceremony. "So much has changed," she blurted out. She felt tears sliding down her cheeks.

"Life is change," he said. "My departure from you was ordained, even before we met. Almighty God directs all." Albert did not often deal in spiritual observations.

She returned to her tea.

"You should take care," Prince Albert said, standing. "There are men who would see you harm." He stood and continued the warning. "Every monarch is never far from the anarchist's bomb or the assassin's knife."

She wanted him to remain. "Oh, no, my love. Don't go."

"There have been attempts on your life. There will be more. The Irish, for certain. Perhaps, the Indians, but I believe the Irish." He circled the table, leaned down, and kissed her gently on the forehead. It felt like a breeze across her skin. "But don't forget your own."

The words filled her with sickness. "What?" She was at his side, trying to grasp his arm, but it melted away. He was gone. Her beloved had disappeared. What did he mean? Don't forget your own?

"Your Majesty?" It was Duchess Humbert. She saw to the Queen's needs at Frogmore Gardens. Mr. Westbrook and Mr. Bruner were at her side, waiting for orders. Duchess Humbert prompted Victoria. "Your Majesty?"

Queen Victoria stood in the shadow of the cold, forbidding massive stones of Prince Albert's Mausoleum. It was a modest monument, a reflection of Albert's simple taste. It wasn't as grand as her mother's. It reminded Victoria of a little Italian church. Something one expected to find in the countryside. Albert would not be happy with a tomb that smacked of ostentation. Here, he would rest for eternity; and one day, she would join him. "Yes," she replied sharply. "Let us return."

Westbrook and Bruner stood in one corner of the mausoleum, waiting for the servants to clear the table. The work was done without speaking.

Bruner slid closer to Westbrook and whispered, "Did you hear the old girl? Talking to him, who ain't there?"

"I'm not deaf, am I? God, I could use a fag."

"Too right. She'll never make it through this Jubilee, you know. Heart's too frail. One day, she'll up and collapse."

"Ain't you the cheery one? That means his Randy Royal gets the crown. Picture that now. Eddie the king, and the castle filled with tarts."

Bruner followed the servants to the carriage. "Who do you suppose will be at the old boy's shoulder, giving him kingly advice?"

Westbrook joined him. "It won't be me now, will it?"

"Too right," Bruner agreed, "unless your name's Crittenton."

The Times of London
Metropolitan Police Inspector Prescott reported the most unusual results of an argument between thieves, occurred on Chest Street last night. The two unknown criminals, overcome by avarice as they divided the night's booty, fell into a knife fight that ended in the death of both.

CHAPTER 26
HAYMAKER'S ALLEY, LONDON, ENGLAND

"Why are you following me?" Abberline said to Theodore as they ran. "I don't know where I'm going." He looked over his shoulder. Three bobbies were racing across the Strand toward the mouth of the alley.

"Up here," Abberline said, "the alley splits. You go left. That's take you in the clear. Mind the hole. See you tonight." He sped off, and Theodore turned left.

The alley fell off to the right and then back to the left. Theodore decided there wasn't a straight line in this city. He heard a noise ahead, sounds of construction echoing off the alley walls. More stands, more seating for the Jubilee.

He was out of the alley. He stopped to get his bearing. The noise was tremendous, steam whistles, incessant hammering, almost a solid wall of sound. In front of him was a train, stopped on its tracks, the engine chugging lazily. Beyond it, several hundred yards, a row of buildings. He turned back into the alley, listening for his pursuers. He could hear nothing, and the alley bent sharply to the right. If the bobbies were close, he wouldn't see them until they were almost on him.

He ran across the street. Get on the other side of the train, he thought. What in God's name was that noise? The air thundered around him; but there were no stands, no construction, just a train idling on the tracks.

He made it to the train, stopping near a flatbed loaded with huge stone blocks. He looked back at the alley for an instant, rolled under the train, and ran.

The earth disappeared. He slid to a stop, rolling to his knees on the edge of a chasm nearly a hundred feet deep.

Abberline's hole. Inside, steam shovels, pile drivers, block and tackle were suspended on huge frames carrying buckets of dirt out of the hole: two hundred feet long, a hundred feet wide filled with men swinging pickaxes and shovels, pushing carts filled with dirt to collection points, and in the middle, timber frameworks nearly fifty feet high. At either end, ramps were cut into the sides of the hole, with men streaming in and out. It was monstrous. The Pyramids in reverse.

Theodore realized what he was looking at and bresthed, "The Underground. It's a station." He had to move. He forced himself to run along the edge of the chasm. He heard shouting behind him. The bobbies. Could he make it around the hole, get to the other side, and lose himself in those buildings? No, that wouldn't do. They'd be on him, before he knew it.

Hide. Run down the ramp and hide about the hundreds of men in the hole. A bundle of thick timbers, drifted over him, suspended on cables that ran to a derrick against the wall of the hole.

He ran to the ramp but had to slow, stepping carefully. The surface was too steep and uneven, covered in a corduroy of cut timbers. Workers, tools slung over their shoulders, trudged up the ramp. He stepped to the left, picking his way over the ragged surface.

He was at the bottom of the hole. Looking up, he saw three bobbies in the distance, perched on the edge of the massive dig, looking for him.

Theodore searched for a place to hide. A gigantic steam engine was in front of him, smoke billowing from its stack, gears rolling and screeching, the bucket digging into the earth like the teeth of a hungry monster. He looked up. The bobbies were making their way to the ramp.

He ran deeper into the hole and saw a group of men with picks, digging at a mound of earth. Theodore circled around a surveyor and his assistant and stopped near one of the diggers.

There was a shovel stuck in the ground at his feet. Theodore scooped up a handful of dirt, rubbed it on his face, and picked up the shovel. He began digging, head down.

A short, wiry man next to him stopped. "What the bloody hell are you doing, mate?"

"Digging," Theodore said.

"So, you are, but in the wrong bloody place. We've got our grade here." He pointed to the other side of the mound. "Go over there, you stupid bastard."

"Don't talk to me," Theodore said.

The man threw his pick on the ground and pushed his shirt sleeves up. "By God, put that shovel down, and I'll show you talk."

Theodore heard a shout behind him.

"Williams! Get back to work, you daffy Welshman." A big man wearing a straw hat, leading three bobbies, picked their way across the uneven ground.

Theodore continued to dig. He couldn't run. They were too close. Williams glanced at the bobbies and then back to Theodore. "Peelers, eh? So, that's it," he said in disgust.

"This looks like out man," one of the bobbies said.

Theodore tightened his grip on the shovel. He had a weapon; use it. Throw it at them. Your gun! No. He had lost it. He threw the shovel on the ground. He was trapped.

"What's this?" Williams said. "Why James wouldn't hurt a fly?"

The bobbies surrounded Theodore. "Stand back," one of them ordered. "This is police business."

A worker next to Williams stopped digging. "What is it, Williams? Have you got the Peelers called on you?"

"They've come for poor James, here," Williams said. "And him practically a saint. Mr. Howard, you know James, don't you?"

Howard, the man in the straw hat, caught on and nodded. "As well as I know my own son." He turned to the bobby. "James hasn't left the pit in a day and a half."

The bobby tapped Howard on the chest with his day stick. "Don't be playing games with me. He's our man, and I've got orders."

Three more workers joined the crowd. One began nudging Theodore to one side.

"I can vouch for James," a man said. "Seven years I've worked with him and never a harsh word between us."

The bobbies looked at one another.

"This is our man," one of the bobbies said, "and I'll advise you to stand back. We're on the Queen's business."

Two more workers came up. Theodore was pushed back a little more. A shriveled man puffing on a dirty clay pipe said, "Mr. Howard? Begging your pardon, but why would Peelers come down in our lovely pit, except to ferment rebellion and discontent?"

The others agreed with him.

Howard nodded. "The very question I asked myself, Andy. And them on the Queen's business, or so they say." Howard turned to a bobby. "We're on the Queen's business as well, and well, you know it. These tubes ain't going to be finished, if we have to stop every hour and discuss matters that don't pertain to this project."

"This man is coming with us," the bobby said, but a veil of uncertainty slipped over his words.

Theodore eased back into the crowd, and more workers showed up. The argument became general and confusing, with the bobbies demanding their suspect and the workers resisting. Soon, there were nearly a hundred men surrounding the bobbies, who began to fall back toward the ramp.

Theodore ducked below the crowd, ran to a pile of timbers, made his way through a row of wagons, and, grabbing a pile of empty burlap sacks, threw them on his shoulder to hide his face. He fell into a line of men filing up the opposite ramp.

He didn't dare look back or break his stride. He hoped his new friends would detain the bobbies long enough for him to get away.

"Well, look what we have here?"

Theodore lowered the burlap sacks. Two bobbies stood at the top of the ramp; day sticks in hand.

"It's that Roosevelt bloke, isn't it, Carly?" one of the bobbies said.

"'Detain at all hazards.' Isn't that what Hasselbach ordered?" Carly said.

"Gentlemen," Theodore said.

"'Gentlemen,' he calls us," Carly said. They were both short but with thick bodies. Men not easily dislodged. Carly motioned with his stick. "Just drop those at your feet, Mr. Roosevelt, if you please, and we'll go easy on you."

There was nothing else to do. Theodore knew the other three bobbies would be coming up the ramp at any moment, and five on one would certainly be no contest. But two on one? Well, that bettered the odds.

He threw the pile of sacks at Carly, rushing him at the same time. Theodore drove his shoulder into the bobby's chest, knocking him off balance. The policeman rolled into the dirt.

The other bobby shouted an oath and swung his day stick at Theodore, striking him on his shoulder. Theodore cried out in pain but twisted enough to land a fist into the bobby's face.

Carly was up and rushing at Theodore.

Theodore jerked the day stick out of the other bobby's hand and turned on Carly. Their sticks collided in midair. He swung at Carly and dropped back to meet an attack by the other bobby. As he rushed forward, Theodore brought the day stick down on the man's shoulders, sending him careening into a pile of timbers. He brought the day stick up in time to parry a blow by Carly.

"Hold still, you bloody bastard," Carly said. "I'll beat the life out of you."

The other bobby, stunned, tried to rise; but he couldn't find his feet.

Theodore charged Carly. The two men swung their sticks, the solid crack of the wood against wood piercing the air.

Carly jabbed at Theodore to throw him off and then tried to jam the end of the stick into Theodore's chin. Theodore bent back, so that the blow missed; but the movement threw him off balance. Carly closed in, drawing the stick back, aiming for Theodore's skull.

Theodore dropped to his knee, and the stick burred through the air, inches from his head. Theodore swung his day stick, catching Carly fully on both shins with a horrific crack.

The bobby screamed and dropped to his knees. Theodore's stick connected with Carly's forehead, and the policeman crumpled into the dirt.

Theodore jumped to his feet and saw the other bobby, back against the timbers, cradling his arm.

"If I could get up, I'd show you a thing or two," he growled at Theodore.

Theodore, his chest heaving, dropped the day stick at his feet. "I'm certain you could." He turned and trotted off as quickly as he could. Mr. Abberline was right. Carry a big stick.

He was safely away from the pit, when he realized that all the bobbies had followed him, and none Abberline.

Why?

What was the man's name? Abberline's superintendent? Hasselbach? Hasselbach, Crittenton, Chamblis.

There was something more, Theodore sensed. A thing he could not see or understand. More, something more, was apparent. Sweat trickled down his forehead. He wiped it off with the back of his sleeve.

"An itch you cannot scratch," his grandfather had said. "A thought that has no place, yet exists."

Theodore grew angry at himself. The entire Metropolitan Police Department on your trail, and all you can do is rely on old proverbs; but the thing would not leave him alone. What was it that would not go away?

He answered his own question. Nothing is of any importance except finding Edith. The Queen, Abberline, Crittenton. The Prince of Wales. They mean nothing to me.

I must find Edith.

The Times of London
American newspapers have reported the collision and subsequent fires aboard two ferries on the Hudson River, New York, New York. It is a common practice for American ferries to race one another to their destinations. English ferry captains never undertake such a deadly practice.

CHAPTER 27
THE VICTORIA EMBANKMENT, LONDON, ENGLAND

Christy studied the stars in blackness. "You know, seeing them shine down on us almost makes me think there is a God in Heaven."

He lay on his back, arms under his head, on a stone platform built to house a cast iron sundial.

Abberline, pacing back and forth behind him, said, "I'm sure the Almighty is pleased to operate with your approval." They'd been waiting for nearly six hours. "If that American has gone and gotten himself in trouble, I'll kill him."

Christy propped himself up on one elbow. "How many stars are there, I wonder?"

"I'll kill him," Abberline said. "We're already in the soup, and he makes it worse." Cleopatra's Needle blotted out the city's lights. They'd moved from the obelisk to the sundial. They were less exposed, and it would be easy to slip over the edge of the Embankment and down to the river's edge, if they were discovered.

"You don't see any coppers out there, do you?" Christy asked. They had a clear view up and down the Embankment, past the park, through the tree line to a gleaming row of buildings. They couldn't be taken by surprise, but they couldn't stay there forever.

"All I see is a dozen lovebirds on the walkway," Abberline said, resting his arm on the sundial, "holding hands and stealing kisses."

"Aren't you the romantic?"

"Christy?"

Christy sat up. "What is it?"

Abberline nodded across the well-kept lawn. "There's a man in that stand of trees. Bloody hell, I wish I could see in the dark."

Christy joined Abberline. "What's he doing just standing there? He sees us, doesn't he? He's got to see us? He's not a copper, is he?"

"I'm not playing at twenty questions with you," Abberline cut him off. "Come on. If it's Roosevelt, he'll wait for us. If it isn't, we'll soon find out."

"That isn't me," Theodore said, climbing up to the crest of the Embankment. "I'm down here."

Christy gasped. "I nearly shit my pants, Mr. Roosevelt. Don't sneak up on a fellow like that. My God, have you been rolling in a pig sty?"

"Let's have it," Abberline demanded. "What happened to you?"

"We can talk later, Mr. Abberline," Theodore said. "If you two would be so kind as to drop over the edge, we can find refuge for the night."

"Christy," Abberline asked, "has that bloke moved?"

Christy gazed at the tree line. "Not an inch. He may be a tree stump."

"Right," Abberline said. He slipped over the waist-high stonewall and dropped down next to Theodore. "Well?"

"You failed to mention the hole was the size of the Grand Canyon."

"Does it matter? You're here, aren't you?"

Theodore slumped to the ground. "I don't think I could go another step."

Abberline said. "Well, you have to, Mr. Roosevelt."

Theodore said, "Why, suddenly, do they want me?"

"I don't know," Abberline said, "Chamblis told you to remain silent, and everything would be all right." He gave a disgusted growl. "Ah, I can't fathom this bunch."

"No more so than I," Theodore said.

"Hasselbach sent the bobbies after you. Not us. You."

"Say what you mean," Roosevelt said, falling back on the grass. "I'm too tired for riddles."

"I'm not sure what I mean," Abberline said. "I'm not sure what any of this means."

"We must find Edith," Theodore said. "That is what I intend to do."

Christy's head appeared over the top of the wall. "Pardon me, gentlemen, but while you two catch up old times, do you mind getting out of the bloody way so I can join you." He nodded toward the tree line. "I'm certain the man over there is no friend of mine."

Abberline helped Theodore to his feet. "There is a point to this, isn't there?"

"Oh, by Jupiter, there is," Theodore said. "But what exactly? I'm not certain. Something dreadful, more than involves the Prince. Mr. Abberline, they're biding their time."

"Let us go find a refuge for the night," Abberline suggested.

"I know just the place," Christy said.

Abberline said, "In the morning, Mr. Roosevelt. We'll make our plans in the morning."

They made their way along the base of the Embankment. Theodore spoke, more to himself than to his companions. "My sense is they are working against time. In regard to what, I have no idea."

"A schedule?" Abberline mused. "Perhaps. A timetable? Trains? Ships?"

"What has either to do with the Prince of Wales and Mrs. Roosevelt?" Christy asked.

"I have no idea. Except she is in danger." Theodore realized the futility of his answer. "And there is nothing I can do."

***

Police Superintendent Hasselbach joined Bob Chamblis in the line of trees. "We nearly had him," he said.

"Yes, and I am nearly the King. You should have taken my advice, Superintendent," Chamblis said. "Grab them both up at the same time. Man, and wife."

"Those were not your orders."

"Yes," Chamblis said. "That sort of thing just isn't done? Is it?"

"What are you complaining about? I came around to your thinking."

"Oh, of course, you did." Chamblis said. "But you sent the wrong chaps to do it. You think your Peelers have it in them for this sort of game?"

"All right," Hasselbach said. "Send your boys and have at it. I don't want to hear anything more from you about it. We have his wife. Get Roosevelt. When this is over, I'll see that the American is taken care of."

Chamblis peered across the meadow to the rise of the Embankment. "You get used to that sort of thing. When you're in my line of business. This whole thing has turned to shit, you know. A simple little effort mucked up beyond belief."

"Quit complaining," Hasselbach said. "We'll do what we need to."

"It's not a complaint," Chamblis said. "It's a criticism. A simple murder. The Prince firmly in hand, and then this American and his wife. God likes his tricks, wouldn't you say?"

Hasselbach wasn't pleased with Chamblis' comments. "If I were you, I would remember what's at stake." He turned away from Chamblis and headed for his carriage.

Chamblis followed him. "Don't send more of your bobbies, will you? They turned this into a bloody circus."

Hasselbach said, "I told you I wouldn't, didn't I?"

"I'll have my chaps follow them, and in the morning, when the sun is up, take them," Chamblis said.

"Splendid," Hasselbach said.

"Lovely night, isn't it? Look at the stars? Just for the Queen, I suppose," Chamblis said. He signaled to two men to follow Theodore and the others. At Hasselbach's carriage, Chamblis lit a cigar and handed one to Hasselbach. "What happens if the wheels fall off this particular cart? It won't be Dugan, because we've set him at it; and he won't stop until the thing is done. He'll make a pretty penny and be gone. But your kind, I mean. Do they have the backbone to follow through?" He moved closer to Hasselbach. "You see, I ask because I've been at this sort of thing awhile, with never a misstep. If it all goes to Hell, will men like me end up on the gallows, while men like you stand by, untouched?"

"I wouldn't know," Hasselbach said. "Life is capricious after all, isn't it? I shouldn't worry, if I were you. The lower class is seldom noticed and never guilty of original thinking."

"Yes, you could say that," Chamblis agreed, "but the thing about the lower class is there are so many more of them than your sort. Once you start a revolution," he drew heavily on his cigar, "it may not be an easy thing to stop."

Schiess finished the glass of gin and made a face. "I don't like this swill."
Benjamin, rolling a cigarette for the old man, ran the paper over his tongue, pressed it into place, and handed it to Schiess. "Then don't drink that swill."

Daniel laughed. Michael smiled. They were in a room on the second floor of the tobacconists. The next room held bedrolls, blankets, and the few belongings the group carried with them. They had planned to go back to the pump house to see if anything remained.

Benjamin watched Michael over the table filled with Schiess's batteries. There could be nothing as innocent as that boy's face, he thought. If that's so, he questioned, why do I find it so troubling? Michael? There wasn't a cross bone in his body.

Schiess rapped Benjamin's knuckles with a pencil. "Pay attention. You must have vexed the sisters."

"He didn't last a week," Daniel said. "They tossed him out without even praying for him."

"Go on with it," Benjamin told Schiess. "I'm listening."

"Good," Schiess said. He stood, leaning over the six, gallon-sized glass jars. "These are called Daniell Cells. They aren't very sophisticated devices. They are also known as the Exchange Telegraph Cell, because they were used by the Exchange Telegraph Company. Other people call it the crowfoot cell, but that seems so indelicate."

"Fascinating, I'm sure," Daniel said. "But what does it mean to us?" All it took was a look from Benjamin to shut Daniel up.

"Bear with me, Daniel," Schiess said. "It's an obsolete device but effective enough for our needs. It's also rather simple to construct." He pointed to a metal hook that hung over the side of the jar. "This is the negative terminal. This is attached to a zinc electrode, which is suspended in a zinc solution. The shape of the zinc electrode, which is distorted by the solution, gives the device the name crowfoot."

"It stinks," Michael said.

"I'll add a layer of oil to cover the solution. That should reduce the smell. Now," Schiess continued, "at the very bottom of the jar, if you look here, despite the refraction, you can see a copper electrode. It's suspended in a copper solution." He pointed to a copper wire hanging over the jar lip. "The positive terminal connected to the wire that passes through a circuit break leads to the explosive. At the appropriate time, the circuit is activated, the Brighton Fuses catches it, and detonation follows."

"Why not just use a powder fuse?" Michael asked.

"Time and distance," Benjamin said. "We want to be as far as possible from the dynamite when it goes off." He wanted his brothers to understand. "We'll run the electric wire from the charge to the terminal, a safe distance away, set the switch, and ignite the charge."

"At the appropriate moment," Schiess continued with a smile, "whenever that might be." He took a drink. "And wherever."

Daniel shot Benjamin a cold glance. "Don't you think it's time we know?"

Benjamin didn't bother returning the look. "Time and tide, brother. Isn't that what Shakespeare said?"

"Chaucer, actually," Schiess corrected him.

This time Benjamin's eyes were on his brother. "The meaning's the same, Daniel. You'll know when I think it best to know."

*Construction of the towers on the new Thames River
Bridge is progressing. Selection of the steam engines to power the roadway
structures is expected to take place within a month. Completion of the bridge is
highly anticipated, and it is acknowledged as yet another triumph of British
engineering.*

CHAPTER 29
THE WARDER'S COTTAGE

The teacup shattered against the rock fireplace, sending bits of China flying in a dozen directions. Edith swept up another cup and threw it with all her might. It burst against the fireplace.

Edith stepped back from the table, her breath coming in angry spurts, her arm aching. It felt good to feel pain, to destroy something, no matter how inconsequential it was. Gradually her rage subsided. She felt a little foolish but, somehow, energized.

Dawn was nearly done, and its end had reminded her that she'd spent another day in this wretched place, away from her husband.

Edith stared at the fireplace and decided today was the day she would escape. She had lain awake last night, stacking reality atop potential, until she had reached the conclusion that escape was feasible and a matter of life and death. She had grown irritated at herself, feeling that the phrase was too melodramatic. In the beginning, she had convinced herself that she was in no real danger. She was a lady after all, from the best class; and Theodore was a gentleman. As she repeated the rationale she was certain would keep her alive and unharmed, a tiny voice whispered it was a lie. She knew it was true. Abduction and murder were separated by intention only. The thought had sickened her. She had slid in and out of sleep, putting some distance between herself and that horrible thought.

Edith tore off a bit of bread to nibble on. Mr. Congreve was not my abductor. Mr. Congreve, as much as I've seen of him, was lithe and middle-aged; the man who carried me away from Theodore was a large man, young. Mr. Congreve is a game warder, she concluded, a man comfortable with nature. Like Theodore.

Mrs. Sheraton? Edith's thought stopped. It was too much of a coincidence to suppose the poor child lying in a pool of blood had anything to do with that poor, demented woman. Edith found the idea disturbing, though. Margaret could be Maggie. The Prince's Maggie.

Edith slid into the chair, brushing particles of China from the table. Maggie was a token offered to the Prince of Wales. For what purpose? To entice him? Entrap him?

"Poor Mrs. Sheraton," Edith whispered. "First your drunken husband drowns, and now your darling daughter is murdered." But Maggie is a common name for Margaret. It could have been any one of a thousand unfortunate girls.

But the thought nagged Edith until she grew weary of it.

"Perhaps, I can enlist Mrs. Sheraton's help?" Edith said. She felt her courage rising. "If I can convince her." She knew she could not reveal Maggie's murder to her mother. "If I can convince Mrs. Sheraton that Maggie needs help, perhaps, she would throw in with me." Edith worried. It may be too complicated for Mrs. Sheraton to comprehend. She rose and looked in disgust at the mess she had made. She must control her emotions. She laughed at herself. You think too much.

She heard the grind of the cart's thin wheels on the dirt road. They were coming. "Now or never," she told herself. She smoothed her dress, stood by the table, forced her breathing to slow, and waited. Mrs. Sheraton's voice drifted through the wooden door. She chattered aimlessly, a continuous stream of unrelated thoughts, strung together by nonsensical observation. The chain rattled, the lock fell against the door with a hollow thud, and Mrs. Sheraton laughed. The door swung open.

"Mrs. Roosevelt?" Mrs. Sheraton called. "I trust you're up." She entered carrying a basket covered with a checkered cloth. She saw Edith. "There you are. My, how pretty you look." She saw the particles of teacups strewn over the floor. "Oh, my!" She glanced at Edith in surprise. "Oh, my! Look what you've done to that lovely China. Why, I'd expect that from a child rather than a lady? You ought to be ashamed of yourself. Yes, indeed. Waste not, want not, I always say. You don't think I'd let my Margaret get away with this sort of behavior, do you?" She set the basket on the table and retrieved a broom from one corner.

"Mrs. Sheraton, I think we ought to talk about Maggie. Margaret."

She began sweeping with a vengeance. "Now, she's gone off to London, with her gentleman. She hasn't time to write; and even if she did, I never learned to read. She's very happy, I'm sure. She has a fine gentleman who takes good care of her."

"Yes," Edith agreed. She didn't have time to be gentle. "My husband and I…We found a young lady under most unfortunate circumstances."

Mrs. Sheraton continued sweeping, gathering the pieces together in a modest mound. "Well, I don't doubt that. London is a horrible place for those young ladies that don't have a gentleman to care for them."

This was not working. "I think I'm owed an answer, Mrs. Sheraton. Who is your employer?"

Mrs. Sheraton leaned on the end of the broom and gave Edith an impatient look. "I've been told to mind my own business and mind my own business I will. I suggest you do the very same thing. I've worked for his lordship all my life, and I follow his orders without hesitation." The basket on the table caught her attention. "My stars, I forgot to fix your breakfast. What a silly, addled, woman I am." She dropped the broom and hurried to the table. "Now you sit down, and I'll fix you right up. My, you must be nearly starved."

Despite her situation, Edith pitied Mrs. Sheraton.

Mrs. Sheraton unwrapped a slice of apple pie, fetched a plate from the cupboard, and set it before Edith. "Mrs. Brown was in the papers. Again. Goodness, she has a way about her."

Edith was suddenly tired. "Yes, I'm sure."

"She was very lovely and lived in a beautiful house with a dozen children, like the old woman in the shoe. The nursery rhyme." She began singing a nonsensical tune. "But then she turned evil, and the good prince came to cut off her head and restore the throne to the rightful heir."

A fairy tale. The poor woman.

Mrs. Sheraton gave her a motherly look. "You appear a bit under the weather, dear. Are you ill, my dear? Perhaps, a douse of Castor's Oil. That always brings me around."

"I'm in tip-top shape," Edith said. She knew she had to act. She stepped away from the table, closer to the door. The jug was on the floor near the wall. It was heavy and unwieldy, but she had practiced knocking it against the head of an imaginary Mr. Congreve.

He had to be brought into the cottage. Now, Edith. Now.

The old woman was bent over the table, carefully arranging breakfast, humming tunelessly.

The door was hanging open a crack. Mrs. Sheraton hadn't closed it. Edith glanced at the jug. Now, Edith. As you've planned.

"A mouse!" Edith screamed.

Mrs. Sheraton turned with a chuckle. "No, don't pay the least bit of attention to that little beast."

Edith froze. She isn't afraid of mice. Think of something. Do something.

Edith slapped Mrs. Sheraton as hard as she could. Mrs. Sheraton's mouth dropped open in horror. Then she screamed.

"Help! It's murder!" She raced around the table and became so confused; she nearly ran into the wall. "Help, Mr. Congreve. Murder."

Edith stumbled around a chair, picked up the stone jug, and held it ready. Her heart beat wildly. She measured the distance to the door and calculated the height of Mr. Congreve's head. She realized how heavy the pitcher was and was frightened the silly old woman was right: There would be murder done in the cottage.

Mrs. Sheraton ran around the length of the single room, arms flapping, spouting a combination of shrieks and wailing.

Edith heard Mr. Congreve's rough voice. The door was thrown open and bounced against the wall.

Mr. Congreve was taller than Edith suspected, older as well, but heavier.

"What's all this, then?" he shouted.

Edith swung the heavy jug, her body spinning. She saw Mr. Congreve's dark eyes widen in surprise and heard the single exclamation, "Damn," before the jug landed with a solid thud against the man's temple.

His legs folded, and he collapsed like a sock doll.

It was quiet in the cottage. Even Mrs. Sheraton stood rooted in place. The pitcher slipped out of Edith's hand; she stepped over the unconscious Mr. Congreve.

"But you're not allowed to leave," Mrs. Sheraton said helplessly.

Edith, angry and afraid, turned long enough to say, "Oh, shut up." She ran through the doorway to the cart, gathered the fabric of her dress around her legs, and climbed into the vehicle. She fumbled for the reins, took a deep breath, said a quick prayer, and clicked her tongue against the roof of her mouth. The horse began to walk, a rolling motion.

"Oh, my God," Edith cried, snapping the reins. "For Heaven's Sake, can't you run?"

The horse broke into a trot. Everything passed in slow motion, the distance from the cottage barely increasing, the horse's heavy body swaying back and forth, the wheels of the cart squeaking in protest.

She slapped the reins again, and the horse managed a canter.

She looked over her shoulder, expecting to see Mr. Congreve racing after her. The lane ahead, cutting a gentle curve through the forest, was empty.

Edith laughed and saw the horse's ears perk up. "I shall call you Mercury. You don't know where London is, do you?" The ears twitched. "Well, neither do I." She remembered Mrs. Sheraton's words. A railroad and a road.

Mercury seemed pleased at his sudden burst of speed. "This is an adventure, is it?" Edith said. She felt light, free.

Now she had to find London. Then she must find Theodore. One man in a city of millions. How do I find my husband?

Her plan had been successful, and now she was free; but there was no plan for finding Theodore except to drive in the general direction of where she believed London to be. She knew she was being foolish. Millions of people, she thought, probably many more. As big as New York, maybe more so. "How will I find Theodore?"

Mercury snorted and tossed his head in response.

"Let us find London first," Edith said, "and then we'll see to the other."

The Times of London
The West Kensington Literary Guild will discuss the merits of the popular French novelist Mr. Jules Verne. Mr. Verne is a recognized authority on various scientific theories.

CHAPTER 30
GREAT SMITH STREET, LONDON, ENGLAND

Benjamin thought the street looked like a village fair: drapes, flags, banners, and in every crude format available, hand-painted broadside salutes to Queen Victoria. No matter your feelings, it was best to display your patriotism prominently. A wagon filled with freshly sawed boards, still stinking of sap, rolled by.

He walked back to the doorway that held Schiess. The old man alternated between his cigarette, and a pint. When he saw Benjamin, he slipped the pint into his coat pocket, pulled out a pencil and pad of paper, and waited.

"Three hundred, twenty-one paces," Benjamin said. "Too far, is it?"

"Too far for comfort, yes. It's to be Tothill Street, then?" Schiess thumbed through the pages, consulting his notes. "Tufton Street puts us right behind, but the wires will be exposed for some length. There's the weather, as well. You know it looks to rain."

Benjamin gazed at the hazy sky. "Not likely."

"Or some club-footed Englishman takes just that moment to stumble over the wires."

Benjamin tapped the pint in Schiess' pocket. "Keep it there until we've finished." They began walking, side-stepping a man on a ladder painting God Bless Queen Victoria on a shop window.

"Where are we going?" Schiess asked.

"There's a lane off Tothill Street."

Schiess wasn't impressed. "So? There's a lane off Tothill Street? We just passed a perfectly good lane off Great Smith Street."

Benjamin kept walking.

Schiess struggled to keep up with him. "Be kind, will you? Your legs are twice the length of mine."

Benjamin ignored him.

"The least you can do is offer to carry me." Schiess was breathing heavily. "If only this much care were given to the welfare of the poor and needy," he observed.

"Since when do you care about the underprivileged?" Benjamin asked. He pointed to a structure taking shape over the entrance of Westminster Abbey. "You see that?"

Schiess studied the skeleton taking shape. "The Queen's grandstand, is it?"

Benjamin said, "It offers possibilities."

Schiess searched his pockets. "My bottle? Do you have it?"

"Now is not the time to play at games."

"Are you threatening me, Benjamin?"

"I am indeed," Benjamin said and began walking toward the construction site.

Schiess followed him. "You've lost your humor." Benjamin stopped and Schiess nearly ran into him. "Be kind enough to roll a cigarette for an old man, won't you?"

Benjamin took the makings from Schiess without looking. "You see how they have the portico built out, don't you? And wings to either side? I'll wager the carriages go there to unload." His finger traced the route for Schiess. "And come out again there."

"Or the reverse," Schiess said, waiting hungrily for the cigarette. "Well, one or the other, it has to be. Either will work."

Benjamin waited for two beer wagons to rumble by their high sides blocking his view. He stepped off the sidewalk, moved to the north a few feet, and studied the scene before him. The canopy would be properly done; he thought, temporary as it was meant to be. Well braced, anchored, and finished off by carefully planed boards. Thirty feet up the east side of the Abbey and plain as a butcher's daughter. Built to shade heads and receive royalty, it would come down as fast as it went up. Benjamin smiled. Trust the English to desecrate their own. And why not? They had done the same to half the world's treasures. He began to see it would be more of a problem than he anticipated. "There's no room under the portico or to be had on either side. They've used the Abbey's stairs, so they wouldn't have to build any anew. If I could crawl under it, I would." He picked apart the framed addition; his eyes traveling over the beams, uprights, and the timbers of the floor joists. He knew he could plant his dynamite anyplace, if he only had a way to get to it. But the explosives had to be positioned where they would have the best impact. If the blast bounced off the stone sides of the Abbey, then all was well and good. No timbers or planks made in England, or any land could stand up to that blast.

The answer was there, Benjamin thought, trying to see into the half-completed platform; but it was hiding from him.

"Step out of the street, Benjamin," Schiess said. "You're drawing attention to yourself."

"Inside the Abbey, then. That's how I'll do it."

"Here? You two." Two bobbies approached them, the brims of their helmets hovering just above their eyes. "The sidewalks for walking. Not gawking."

Schiess said, "We were just discussing that, sir."

The older bobby looked at them suspiciously. "French, is it? Or Belgium." He turned to his companion. "You see that, Earl. The city's up to its neck in foreigners. And not a one with enough sense to get out of the street when he should."

"Swiss," Schiess corrected him.

"Shut up!" the bobby said. He looked at Benjamin with a smile of recognition. "But you're not Swiss, are you, Paddy?" He tapped Benjamin on the chest with a day stick. "You see here, Earl. It's plain as the nose on your face. He's a Mick all right. Bred for size and nothing else." The bobby enjoyed the game. "See that broad face. That thick chin. How about it, Paddy?" The bobby leaned closer. "Will you sing us a song? Dance us a little gig?"

Earl said, "We ought to be moving along, Phil."

Phil smiled at Benjamin. "You're a mongrel race, aren't you? Are you one of those who murder innocent women and children? Come up out of hell to rob and kill. You're Papist scum and God, as is His right, ought to wipe the lot of you from the face of the Earth. Better you under the church instead of in it."

"Phil?"

Phil stepped back, measuring Benjamin in disgust. "Let's be off then. Jews, Micks, and Wogs, Earl. They'll be the downfall of this empire yet."

Benjamin stepped onto the sidewalk and headed toward Tothill Street. He rolled the cigarette as he walked; but as Schiess reached for it with a shaking hand, Benjamin slipped it between his lips.

"I could have used that," Schiess complained as Benjamin lit the cigarette.

"Roll your own."

"I was certain you would break that copper's neck," Schiess said. "For the love of God, will you roll me one as well?"

Benjamin handed Schiess the cigarette, struck a match, and watched as Schiess puffed on it gratefully.

"My compliments to you, Benjamin," Schiess exhaled with a burst of smoke. "You took council of your patience."

"Did I?" Benjamin said.

"Touching on this other matter," Schiess was careful in his approach, "have you given any thought to young Michael?"

Benjamin covered the length of the Abbey, crossing a churchyard blossoming with half completed stalls. When the great day came, you could find a bite to eat, some drink, and souvenirs in this little village in the shadow of Westminster Abbey.

Schiess followed in a clumsy half trot. He drew alongside Benjamin. "You know, I bring it up," Schiess said, "only because I have your best interests at heart."

They stopped at the entrance of a narrow lane. A dozen yards across, the Abbey towered on one side, and in its shadow, a long run of small shops, broken by a livery and carriage rental. The buildings were shoulder to shoulder; and the livery, its biggest doors thrown back, was one of the largest of them.

"Come on," Benjamin ordered Schiess. They hurried across the street, stopping to let wagons pass.

"You know, for all the order the British Empire brings to the world," Schiess observed, "they could spare a bit of that to organize traffic."

It was cool in the lane, the heat kept at bay by the deep shadows of the Abbey; and the noise of the streets was now distant and muffled. They stopped near a China shop. Tiny flags raced around the shop window. On a ledge inside the window was a steel engraving of Queen Victoria. Schiess leaned against the door jam.

"Are you having trouble?" Benjamin said. There was no emotion in his voice.

"Thank you for asking," Schiess said. "I would feel honored if the inquiry was sincere."

Benjamin looked up, tracking the Abbey's copper gutters, now a rich green from exposure to the elements. He studied the features with the intensity of a craftsman.

Schiess followed his gaze, perplexed. "Remember Icarus." The comment didn't break Benjamin's concentration. Schiess tried again. "He flew too close to the sun."

"I'm not that ambitious," Benjamin said. He pointed to a strand of telegraph lines. They were attached to a single arm jutting from a pole, rising and falling like the swells of a calm sea. "Will your wires look like that?"

Schiess straightened, interested in Benjamin's question. He calculated the gauge of the wires and then mentally compared them to his. "They would. Very nearly. You have a plan?"

Benjamin remained silent, his eyes tracing the lines before looking at Schiess. "Even idiots can make plans. The intelligent man knows when to change a plan, and the successful man knows how to change it."

Schiess considered the lesson. "Intriguing. The detonation wire runs overhead to hide among the telegraph wires, down the side of the Abbey, and onto the explosives located near the entrance. But as I see it," Schiess reminded Benjamin, "we still have a problem to overcome. Getting the explosives under the platform."

"The story should rightly be about Daedalus," Benjamin said, "not the boy who ignored his warnings."

Schiess followed Benjamin down the block, slowed with him in front of the livery, and then continued.

"Mr. Schiess," Benjamin said, his voice strangely vacant, "if you have misled me in any fashion about the device, I will kill you."

A coughing spasm overtook Schiess before he answered. "Mr. Dugan, do you really think that death frightens me at this juncture of my life. You're a man of actual accomplishments; yet here you are reluctant to believe in me or my instruments."

"It's my neck if you're wrong."

"Oh, but I am right. Eminently correct. As right as I am about Michael. The wrong word, the nature of his complaint gets out. Suppose he had been the one approached by the bobbies? He would stink of nerves, and then they would snap him up and take him to a nice quiet spot to beat the truth out of him." Schiess threw the spent cigarette away. "He couldn't help himself."

"You're the sort who isn't happy unless he can tear someone down," Benjamin said.

"A prophet in his own land," Schiess shrugged.

Benjamin slammed Schiess against a wall, glancing up and down the street for the two bobbies. "This is Michael, you despotic little man. My brother."

"But you know I'm right," Schiess said.

"Michael could have been a priest if God had but laid a hand on his shoulder. A kind man. A good man. He can't be held responsible if his mind isn't what it should be. He has a terrible hunger. His mind is corrupted. He graves the company of children. You, with your education and big words. You're well-read and knowledgeable, but your soul is rotten with drink. You can't be happy; and you can't stand to see others happy, so you foul every nest you make for yourself."

Schiess gently pushed Benjamin's hand away. "Mr. Dugan," the old man said, "are you trying to convince me or yourself?"

Benjamin stepped back, watching Schiess straighten his clothing.

"The livery," Schiess said, as if nothing had happened. "That would serve us perfectly. Yes?"

Benjamin felt a shiver. Someone walking across our grave, his mother would have said. My grave? Or Michael's? The livery? Schiess said something about the livery. He measured the distance between the livery and the Abbey with his eyes. "Yes."

Schiess nodded. "I thought as much. You see, Benjamin. We are likeminded."

Benjamin didn't hear the little man. He was thinking of something altogether different. "When I was a boy, I read a poem by a man named Knox," he said. "It was the language of angels. I thought 'how wonderful it must be to make words sing.' Now, I've come right back around, standing in a courtyard of poets. You see the irony of that, don't you, Mr. Schiess? God has led me to this place, and me thinking He and I were at odds. We're close to solving the problem now, I feel it."

"Benjamin," Schiess said reluctantly, "our problems are just beginning."

The Times of London
Familiarities of Westminster Abbey
The Times is pleased to feature interesting features of this magnificent building to commemorate its role in the Queen's Jubilee. An important monument in the Abbey is Joseph Wilton's work of Major-General James Wolfe, mortally wounded at the Battle of Quebec in 1759.

CHAPTER 31
INDIA DOCKS NEAR BUGSBY'S REACH

Theodore was tired of running. They were hiding in a dilapidated warehouse near the river because they did not have the energy to continue.

"This won't find Edith."

Abberline kicked a pile of straw into a mound, sat down, and crossed his arms over his knees. "And running from the police will, I suppose?"

Christy found a discarded crate, searched the interior for anything of value, and then flipped it over. He sat down and looked from Theodore to Abberline.

"What do you suggest, Mr. Roosevelt?" Abberline said. "We seem to be at a disadvantage, being just three against the whole of the Empire."

"Four," Christy corrected him. "Don't forget my little brother. He'll throw in with us. He's a good sort."

Theodore's frustration erupted. "There must be someone we can go to someone who can assist us. By Jupiter, you're an agent of the government. Surely you know an official we can trust."

"The instant," Abberline pointed out, "the very instant we make ourselves and the situation known, Mrs. Roosevelt will be in the greatest of danger."

Theodore knew Abberline was right. Still, he argued because there was nothing else he could do. "Don't you," he searched for an answer, any answer, "know this city?" He fell into helplessness. Finally, he gave into reality. "Blast this situation."

"Our situation is bloody awful," Christy said. He caught Abberline's harsh look. "I mean, if I were to sit down and talk things over."

"We've talked this to death, and nothing has changed," Abberline said. "If you look closely, Mr. Roosevelt, you will see that you and I are sharing the same dirty warehouse."

Theodore dismissed his comment. "Yes, I know. Can't you go back to that other fellow? The one with a streak of white. Maybe learn something more from him."

"Chamblis?" Abberline said. "What he knows, he won't tell us."

"I have never felt so lost in my life," Theodore said. No, that wasn't true. Alice's death. Every bit of him was stolen away the moment she and his mother died.

Christy felt compelled to speak. "Oh, what a tangled web we weave when first we practice to deceive." He was pleased with himself. "I snuck backstage at a play once. Didn't see much before they tossed me out. You blokes may have the advantage on me, schooling and all, but all I see is a tangled web."

Somehow, Christy made sense. Theodore spoke first. "He's right. We've got to unravel this a bit before we understand it."

Christy savored the word. "Unravel."

"Don't speak," Abberline ordered.

Theodore paced the filthy board floor, stopping on the edge of a sunbeam that pierced the battered roof and pooled on the floor. He removed his coat, pulled his tie free, and rolled up his sleeves. "I number the natural sciences among my many interests."

Abberline glanced at him.

"Years ago, the Earth was considered the center of the universe. Galileo proved otherwise, but not without some difficulties from the authorities."

Christy turned to Abberline and whispered, "What's a universe?"

Theodore swept his hand through the sunbeam, scattering a galaxy of shimmering particles. "The nine planets, captured by the Sun's gravity, revolve around it, in effect, paying it homage. Every celestial event …"

Abberline was interested.

Theodore turned, stunned at his own thoughts. "What a fool, I am. Right there in front of me. In the note. An event. I didn't see it. How could I have not seen it?"

"Seen what?" Abberline asked.

"Everything we've become embroiled in," Theodore continued. "A schedule, Abberline. What is to happen will do so in a timely fashion."

"I have no idea what you mean," Abberline said.

"We are involved in something greater than the sum of its parts."

"In English," Abberline said.

"The Queen," Theodore exclaimed. "Can't you see it, man? We are only a threat to those villains if we come forward. We'll do no such thing, because they have Edith."

"The Prince," Abberline reminded him. "This is about His Majesty…" He slowed, looking at Theodore. "The man who becomes King when the Queen passes."

"Nothing to worry you on that point," Christy said. "She's in the shadow of a hundred and twenty. She'll cross over Jordan any day now."

"That's the conspiracy," Theodore said, pieces beginning to fall into place. "Every conspiracy has a purpose. I saw Lincoln's casket pass by my grandfather's front door when I was a child. I never forgot the sorrow of the thing. For some reason, these men we face are not content to wait for a natural death. They plan to assassinate the Queen and advance the Prince of Wales to the throne.”

Abberline said. “You’re talking about murder on a grand scale.”

“I am,” Theodore said. “Because no other single event ties these supposed unrelated actions together. The nation is embroiled in a continuous battle with Fenians, is it not?”

“That’s common knowledge,” Abberline said,” at least to them, the Boers and the Indians. We didn’t become an empire by dispensing good will.”

Theodore turned to Christy. “You mentioned Irish terrorists?” He looked at Abberline, linking the two thoughts. “You saw one of them at Chamblis’ place?”

“A big man with a beard,” Abberline countered. “Fenian or not, I can’t be certain.”

“But you’ve investigated the Irish?” Theodore said.

“I was on the Fenian Squad,” Abberline agreed.

“Too right, he was, and the best man at it,” Christy said. “It was a sad day for the Empire, when they gave Detective Abberline the sack.”

“Was the man Irish?” Theodore said.

“I’m not certain,” Abberline said.

“Don’t quibble, Abberline,” Theodore pushed. “Was he Irish? You’ve seen enough of the race.”

Abberline thought. “He was.”

Theodore relaxed. “I think we should proceed as if I’m correct.”

“It’s a theory,” Abberline said to Theodore. “You’ve no proof that what you say is true.”

“Detective Abberline,” Theodore said, “logic takes us down no other path.”

Abberline said, “Conspiracy. Just once, I’d like to hear about sturdy thieves and righteous scoundrels.”

Theodore said, “You did. They are the very men who should protect the government; yet they are the enemy.” He saw a shadow move in the doorway; and two men, one holding a pistol, appeared.

“Let’s all be civil,” the man with the pistol said. “We’ve been all over Kingdom Come looking for you, and I’m too tired to chase you anymore.”

Abberline recognized them. The two men from the Hotel, the Black Squad.

“Did you bring your bona fides with you?” he asked.

“Right here,” the man holding the pistol said. “It trumps anything you have.”

The Times of London
Members of the West End Merchants Association have completed movement of three shops from the Strand to new locations on Regent Street. Members of the Association have declared they will entice all the merchants from the Strand to Regent Street before the Queen's Jubilee.

CHAPTER 32
ALONG THE LONDON POST ROAD

Edith was terribly disappointed in Mercury. He began the journey as excited as a colt, keeping a steady walk and occasionally breaking into a cantor. The horse appeared to enjoy this unexpected adventure, tossing his head and letting the warm sun run its fingers over his coat. But he was an old horse used to a steady routine. The experience lost its novelty, and his energy deserted him. He slowed, falling into a walk that was hardly more than a drift, dropping his head so that it was nearly to the ground.

Edith stopped him at a shallow stream, concerned she couldn't convince him to continue. Holding the reins, she hoped off the cart and felt the cool water wash her feet and calves. She knelt, cupping water in her palm, and drank gratefully. Mercury joined her. She knew she shouldn't let him drink too much, but she couldn't break herself away from the water. She splashed it over her face and neck and drank more. Edith had a tight grip on Mercury's reins. She stood, leading him farther down the stream, into a valley of overlapping trees and flimsy, russet reeds. Mercury followed without interest.

They had passed a road sign some distance back. London was just nine miles away. Edith began to wonder if Mercury would last.

"We must try to do better," she said. Emily, her own horse, had always responded to her gentle urging, but Emily was a filly with spirit. "You've done wonderfully." She stumbled over a patch of gravel and guided Mercury onto a low bank. "You must meet, Theodore," she continued. She couldn't decide if the monologue was for Mercury's benefit or hers. It wasn't important; it comforted her. They stopped, and Edith looked back to the road. They were well concealed. She would not feel safe until she was in Theodore's arms. She wasn't used to the pitch of the two-wheeled cart, and her buttocks ached.

"I'm on my honeymoon, you see." Mercury began drinking again. Evidently, he was not a romantic. "Then the most dreadful incidents befell us. First, a young woman was murdered; and then we were attacked; and I was carried off and held in that cottage where you first beheld me.”

Mercury splashed a hoof.

“Yes, I know. Very melodramatic. But very frightening, I can tell you.” Edith stroked his flank, thinking. “And now,” she confirmed, “I have to locate my dear husband.” She was convinced of one thing. “I will not go to the police. That dreadful Mr. Abberline set this tragedy in motion. I must be circumspect.” She heard riders approaching. Two, she thought, on the road. Her hand froze on Mercury. It could be nothing, someone out for a ride, a galloper on official business; but she knew better. These men, she was convinced were men who rode with urgency and purpose.

Mercury lifted his head in interest, and water cascaded from his muzzle. Edith stepped close to him and began caressing his wet cheek. “You must remain calm,” she whispered. The horse’s ears twisted toward the road. “Those men might plan to do me harm, you see.”

She saw the riders through a break in the branches. They stopped on the road near the steam. Edith froze. They would see the broken reeds and cart tracks. She knew she could escape on foot, up the bank, or into the trees. She looked around, searching for a route. There was nothing. Edith dropped her head against Mercury’s shoulder. Only a blind man could miss the trail she left behind.

Mercury shifted on his right forefoot.

She watched the men. They were talking to one another, arguing it seemed. Edith could tell even at that distance they weren’t comfortable on horseback. They were sent out to look for her, but they were tired. She saw the bottle appear and pass from man to man. With the least bit of luck, they were blinded by alcohol. Tired, hungry, and caked in road dust, Edith realized. So was she.

Edith looked up. The road was clear, the men had gone. Mercury dropped his head and pulled at a fern growing near the bank. Edith hooked her hands in his bridle and lifted his head. “We were lucky; so now, we are going to hasten. If we can find London, we can certainly find the Russell House; and that is where we are going.” She began leading him back to the road. “I think Theodore is going to be amazed that his bookish wife has now turned into a regular adventuress.” She climbed into the cart, looked up and down the road, and ordered Mercury on. “Adventuress or not, I am going to be very happy when I can take a nice, long bath.”

The Times of London
Colour lithographs of the painting of Prince Albert Edward in a sailor suit by Winterhalter are being sold at a reasonable price to benefit the widows and orphans of those men gallantly lost in Egypt. The painting was commissioned in 1846 and resided in the Royal Collection, St. James Palace.

CHAPTER 33
THE ALBERT DOCKS

The man holding the pistol was Rupert. His partner was Wilson. They advanced on Abberline and Theodore.

"Mr. Roosevelt?" Abberline said. "You asked after the Black Squad. Here are two of them in person."

Rupert, scanning the warehouse, held a Webley. Eight shots, but it was a very awkward piece with no balance.

Abberline turned on Christy. "You treacherous little bastard!"

Christy looked at him in shock. "No, Mr. Abberline, I swear."

"You led them here," the detective said, "you bloody piece of filth."

"You're not a man for trust, are you, Abberline?" Rupert said, making his way to the right. Wilson glanced behind a stack of bales and walked around a pile of rotting lumber.

"No one else here," Wilson said to his partner. He posted himself with his back to a beam scoured with rope burns. "Well, let's all relax and enjoy each other's company."

"Edith?" Theodore said. "Please? I need to know."

"Why ask us?" Wilson said.

"We've come after you two, Mr. Roosevelt," Rupert said. "You and Abberline." He pulled his coat off, keeping his pistol aimed at Theodore. "I never could stand heat. How about you, Wilson?"

"Not I," Wilson replied.

"You had better get used to it," Theodore said. "You're both on the short line to Hell."

Wilson laughed. Rupert smiled. "Clever chap, isn't he?"

"You little bastard," Abberline said to Christy, "by God, I'm going to kill you for betraying us." He grabbed Christy around the throat, choking him. Christy tried to break away, and Abberline drove his fist into Christy's stomach. The little man cried out and fell to the floor. A cloud of dust erupted around him, as Abberline pulled him up by his lapels and slapped him. Christy screamed.

"I swear! It wasn't me," he said, collapsing on the floor.

"Get up, you little shit," Abberline ordered. "If I get out of this, I'll hunt you down and kill you."

"Abberline?" Theodore said. "For God's sake, let the little fellow alone." He noticed a pile of broken boards at his feet.

Abberline shot a hateful look at Theodore. Christy crawled to Rupert and threw his arms around the man's leg. "Please save me. Tell him, please. I didn't betray him."

Rupert kicked Christy away. "Get your hands off me, you little gutter snipe."

Christy lay in the dirt, sobbing.

"Get out, you bastard!" Abberline said. "But run and hide well. You're a dead man. You and all your kind. Dead!"

"Should we keep the little one?" Wilson asked Rupert. "Or what's left of him?"

He gestured to Abberline and Theodore with the Webley. "These two, we was told."

"Please," Christy cried. "Let me go with you."

"Maybe he can lead us to the woman?" Wilson said.

"What?" Theodore said. "Edith? Where is Edith?"

"You didn't hear?" Rupert said. "The lady rescued herself. Ran off. We'll find her. More money for us, eh, Wilson?"

"More, indeed."

"Edith?" Theodore said. "She's free?" For the first time in days, he felt joy.

Wilson tossed Abberline a flyer that landed at his feet. "You ought to keep informed of current affairs."

Abberline picked up the flier and opened it. He read it and handed it to Theodore. "It seems I'm posted a murderer, Mr. Roosevelt. I'm the one who stuck poor Harvey in pitch."

"What about Edith?" Theodore demanded.

"Worry about yourself," Wilson said

"It's not us, Mr. Roosevelt," Rupert said. "It's orders."

"If this is about me, then," Abberline said, "you've got no reason to hold Mr. Roosevelt."

Rupert smiled in mock regret. "Do you have so little regard for us, Abberline? Bring the two we were ordered. And two it will be."

Christy began wailing. "Murder! For God's sake, leave me out of it. Let me go." He grabbed Rupert's legs again.

Rupert stumbled as Wilson rushed at Christy. "Get off him, you little piece of shit!"

Christy threw himself on the ground, locking his arms around Rupert's ankle.

Wilson began kicking Christy, who screamed for help.

Abberline rushed the three men. Rupert saw what was happening and raised his pistol.

Theodore snatched a board and threw it with all his might. It struck Rupert just about the elbow with a sickening thud. His shrill scream filled the warehouse.

Abberline drove his elbow into Wilson's throat. The man collapsed, gagging. Christy rolled clear of the fight, as Theodore picked up Rupert's pistol and held the two men at bay.

Rupert cradled his arm, hate-filled eyes on Abberline. "You bastard!"

"Shut up!" Abberline kicked him in the shin. He picked up the other pistol and looked at Theodore. "Speak softly, eh?"

"And carry a big stick."

"Well played," Abberline said, "I'll give you leave to keep it."

Theodore walked over to Wilson. "Your friend doesn't tell me, so I suggest you do. One of you will or suffer the circumstances. Where is Edith?"

Wilson took a breath and coughed out the reply. "I swear I don't know. They said find her, that's all I know."

"Who said?" Theodore asked.

Abberline supplied the answer. "Hasselbach."

Wilson nodded.

"Where was she being held?" Theodore asked.

"I don't know," Wilson said. "I swear I don't.

Christy joined them. "Splendid work, if I do say so myself."

"Find some rope," Abberline said. "Tie them up."

"What do you know about this?" Theodore said.

Wilson shook his head. "Nobody says nothing to us, except what they want done. They give us money, and me and Rupert do as we're told."

Abberline gestured for Theodore to step to one side, as Christy began tying the men's arms. When that was done, he kicked their legs out from under them and tied them securely back-to-back.

"This confirms it. It's more than the Prince's good name," he whispered to Theodore.

"Mr. Abberline," Christy said as he wrapped a rope around Wilson's wrists, "kindly pull your punches the next time you pretend to hit me. I think you ruptured something inside."

Abberline ignored him, waiting for Theodore to respond.

"Why else risk so much?" Theodore said. "What is worth the risk? Prince and scandal and such? To have power over the Prince of Wales?"

"No," Abberline said. "The Queen is the power to the people. Parliament to her government." He searched for an answer. "Albert Edward would never enjoy the popularity his mother does. What is expected of this?”

“Abberline,” Theodore said, “we have been looking at Albert Edward as the center of this conspiracy. Suppose it is not the Prince of Wales, but is instead, Parliament?”

Abberline shook his head. “Then why kill the girl and implicate the Prince? And even if the truth of the incident is known? Let me see the letter again, if you please?”

Theodore handed it to him.

Christy finished and brushed the dirt from his hand. “What’s that?” he asked.

“A real mystery,” Abberline said, handing the letter to Christy.

Christy looked up from the letter. “Who is ‘C’?” he asked.

“‘G,’” Theodore and Abberline corrected him.

“I don’t know much about letters, but this is a C,” Christy held the letter out for them to see. “There’s a blemish in the paper. It looks like a G, but it’s a C.”

Theodore was not convinced. “Are you certain?”

“Mr. Abberline,” Christy said, “you know that I know paper. I’ve passed enough in my time. This is a C, not a G.”

“C?” Theodore queried. “It can’t be.”

“Crittenton,” Abberline supplied.

“The girl knew,” Theodore said. “There was something going on, and she found out about it. That’s why she was murdered. She knew Crittenton was planning something. The girl’s death gave him a way to control the Prince.”

Abberline took the letter from Christy and looked at Theodore. “This is a damnable business.”

“Albert Edward becomes King,” Theodore said, “with the swords of Damocles over his head, the murder of that young woman.”

“Well, chaps? Shouldn’t we be off?” Christy suggested.

“Right you are,” Abberline said. “

“We have to find Edith,” Theodore said.

“We have to find a place to hide,” Abberline pointed out.

“Edith comes first,” Theodore said. “Nothing else matters.”

Abberline saw the futility in arguing with Theodore. “Oh, all right, but let’s talk as we walk.”

They left the warehouse and the two men tied up in the dirt. Two blocks away, in a narrow, serpentine alley, Abberline stopped Christy. “We need reinforcements.”

“What do I look like?” Christy asked, “The Duke of Wellington?”

“Abberline?” Theodore began.

“Yes, I know. Find Edith. We can’t go about searching for her all over the city. We need men who can.”

“Yes,” Theodore reluctantly said. “We need help.”

Christy reminded them, “I told you. There’s my little brother.”

Abberline said, "Someone. We can trust."

Christy was mildly offended. "Are you deaf. Me little brother, I said. Trust him as you do me. He's the one man who knows the streets better than yours truly."

"Do you trust him, Mr. Abberline?" Theodore asked.

"Have a bit of faith, why don't you?" Christy said.

Theodore looked over his shoulder. Christy was gone.

"Don't worry about him," Abberline said. "Nothing will catch that little mouse."

"He didn't betray us?"

"He didn't. And he knew I didn't suspect him. But we had to put on a show to get him outside." Abberline waved Theodore forward, cautiously. "I'd give my right arm for a simple stabbing. The good old days. When bad blokes killed other bad blokes. Not this mess of royals and rebellions."

The Times of London
Wallis and Sons, Florist to Her Majesty Queen Victoria has created an arrangement of flowers in honor of the Queen's Jubilee.

CHAPTER 34
NEAR WESTMINSTER ABBEY

Benjamin was convinced the world regained its innocence at dusk. The day's heat, thick as clotted blood, began to dissipate. Winds stirred by the falling sun swept the filth from the sky, and golden clouds floated overhead.

It was better for a man to die at dusk, Benjamin concluded, easier for a man to be killed than in the heat of the day. He did not always have the luxury of killing a man at the proper time. Circumstances usually dictated when and where, without regard to the hour. But if he had his druthers, he would pick dusk.

Most killings came with a pinch of regret; he wasn't a soulless man, but regret was short-lived. Eventually, the emotion and incident became vague memories.

He walked with Michael, listening to the boy, but thinking about the Abbey, the livery stable, and the way he would go about things. Benjamin had given up having a dozen or so eager men at his elbows. He'd learned that lesson in America, with the Mollys. The more mouths, the more likely one talks. He never understood why a man had to talk. Silence was an underrated commodity.

They crossed the street and stopped to watch workmen swarm over viewing stands; traffic had lightened considerably. Work never stopped because of darkness. Oil lamps, bonfires, streetlights, and if need be, candles glowed so the men could see to cut boards, hoist lumber, and drive nails. The Jubilee was days away, and its proximity called for urgency.

A burly man in a tattered suit, carrying a sheaf of papers, stopped them at the front steps of the Abbey. "Here now! We don't allow sightseers to wander about. Stay on that side of the street and enjoy the view."

Benjamin fished out the pass that Chamblis had given him and held it up for the man to see.

The man wasn't impressed. "You can buy those on any street corner for a quid. You blokes don't impress me; and if you're not on your way, I'll send for a constable."

Benjamin understood. "Any man running about with a bundle of papers like that should be able to read."

"Who said?"

"This is a Queen's Warrant, and I've got the one and only concession for fireworks at the Abbey. Summon your constable if you must, but I'm willing to wager he can read, and when he sees this and learns of your reluctance, you may be the one on your way."

The man held his ground for a moment, but it was only to save face. "Well, then, go about your business," he said grudgingly. "But don't get in the way of the chaps doing the real work."

Benjamin stuffed the pass in his pocket, glanced at Michael to join him, and made his way up the stairs. When he got to the top, he pushed open the huge doors and walked into the Abbey. The darkness swallowed up the light thrown off by clusters of candles on iron pedestals arranged along the nave. Thick columns rose and disappeared into the darkness. Benjamin did not like this place. His belief in God had eroded over the years, but his appreciation of the supernatural had grown stronger. Sometimes, he felt the spirits of the men he had killed, and in the Abbey, in the thick threatening shadows, they walked alongside him.

He turned and closed the doors, cutting off any contact with the outside.

"You can't hear nothing," Michael said in awe. His head rolled back, and he stared overhead. "That must be a hundred feet."

Benjamin waited, listening.

"What is it?" Michael whispered.

"Nothing," Benjamin said. "I wanted to make sure no one was here." He moved off, Michael trailing, searching for a doorway that led to the cellar. He had seen it walking with Schiess. He had seen the telegraph wires that would disguise the charge wires, and he had seen the crescent windows that ran along the base of the Abbey. A man could not get into the Abbey through them; they were too small, and four iron bars blocked the entrance. But a man could slip bundles of dynamite through them, clearing the Abbey wall. Then the same man could use a broomstick to push them under the wooden platform on the front of the Abbey. The charge wires could be wrapped around the bundle, tied off, and then inserted into the blasting caps. "Over there," Benjamin motioned. The doorway led to a narrow stairway that would take them to the cellar.

Before Michael entered the passageway, he said, "How can so few have so much?" He was in awe of the wealth that surrounded them.

"They get it," Benjamin said, "by taking it from others."

Schiess had been wrong about Michael. He was not a danger; he would not betray them. But the children? That was a different matter.

Benjamin had followed his younger brother, not immediately after Schiess accused Michael, although he should have. It was bloodguilt that traveled with Benjamin following Michael at a distance long after the sun had set.. Through the crowded streets and into the dark alleys until Michael happened upon a girl of the streets. Small, rail-thin, dressed in soiled rags. He watched as Michael gave her a penny and spoke soothingly to her, and then led her into the recess of a locked door. And there. And there as Benjamin watched he harmed the child. And then strangled the child. He readjusted his clothes, the pitiful bundle at his feet, and walked away.

Benjamin stood frozen in the alley, tired of the whole rotten mess. Of death and deceiving, and the realization that Michael, poor, weak Michael, was doomed.

Michael was his brother and one to be looked after, their mother had said. "You must care for him after I'm gone," she had told Benjamin. "Give me your word that you will, Benjamin. See that no harm comes to Michael."

But he now knew there was something terribly wrong about Michael's journeys into the darkness. The children he sought. What he did to them. What Schiess said bordered on the truth, but even a man who betrays can be excused. What Michael did, sickened the soul.

"Wait," Benjamin placed his hand on Michael's thin shoulder. He pulled a lantern off a peg jutting from a huge timber, lit it, and adjusted the wick. He kept the flame low, providing just enough light to burn away the gloom. "Now, go straight ahead."

Michael turned on his brother in surprise. "You've been here before."

"Straight ahead." Benjamin held the lantern to cast some light ahead of Michael. They were underneath the center of the nave; the light was too faint to be seen through the basement windows. The Abbey was surrounded by bonfires and lanterns and men rushing to finish their work. Here, the sounds were muffled to the point of extinction. You could set off a cannon in the Abbey, and no one would notice. Yes, I've been here before, Benjamin thought. Here, and London Bridge, and the Houses of Parliament, and three other places with Chamblis, looking for the ideal location. The best of the best, Chamblis was fond of saying; but Benjamin thought Chamblis was being foolish. "I'll just find the one that will do," Benjamin had told him, and Chamblis was silent after that.

"Why didn't Daniel come with us?" Michael said.

All Benjamin could see was a ring of soft light being cast over Michael's shoulders. Michael's halo. He was relieved not to see his brother's face. The thought came to him before he could stop it. He tasted disgust, as the old religion came back to him. There was nothing angelic about Michael.

"Benjamin?" Michael sought his answer.

"He and Schiess are minding the batteries."

"Does it have to be complicated?" Michael's voice was so soft in the darkness it could have been a child speaking.

"Watch where you're walking," Benjamin ordered. "You'll fall on your face." They were almost at the windows in the west end of the Abbey. They were covered by the platform, so light didn't reach them. But they could not be seen either, and a thousand coppers or Queens Guards could stand within two feet of the windows and not see him slipping bundles of dynamite between the bars.

He and Michael walked through the darkness, until Benjamin stopped.

"Here?" Michael asked. "You're going to put the dynamite here?"

Benjamin set the lantern on a stone pier and faced Michael. Now he would say what he had to say. "Why do you treat the little ones so? It's a sickness. I thought…I thought, maybe, you'd come to your senses. The children? Why do you do it, Michael? You know, if you're found out, you'll betray us. Schiess came to me and said that very thing."

Michael's eyes widened in the light. "Betray? No, Benjamin. No. Never would I do such a thing. You're my brother. You've taken care of me my entire life and never asked for one thing in return."

Benjamin's huge hand came up, the thumb and trigger finger nearly touching. "It's that close to wringing his neck that I came for that accusation."

"I never," Michael began but the look on Benjamin's face silenced him.

"Don't you think what I see of you sickens me?" Benjamin felt cold, but it was flushed away by disgust. "The children, Michael?"

Michael was confused. "What a horrible thing to say."

"Horrible," Benjamin said grimly. "You can't keep your hands off the children. God made you do this terrible thing. But you? You enjoy it."

"Benjamin …?"

"It has to be said, Michael." Benjamin's voice was tight and hollow, and he forced himself to continue. "I see the worst of the city in you, Michael. The whole of mankind."

Michael started to speak, but Benjamin's fist shot out and knocked him to the ground.

"Benjamin? For God's sake, why?"

"You think I like this?" Benjamin cried; his words strangled by pain and rage. Michael looked up at him in shock.

"I failed you, Michael. I failed mother, and myself." He extended his hand and pulled Michael to his feet. Benjamin smoothed Michael's hair and brushed the dirt from his coat. His big hands gripped Michael's arms, and his voice was soft with finality. "I could have forgiven you anything, boy. Murder, robbery, and betraying me, and in the end, I would still have loved you as my brother." Tears rolled down both men's faces. "But I followed you, Michael." He had pulled Michael up so that he was just inches from his chest. "How many is it, boy? How many children did you kill?"

Michael struggled to break free, but his brother was too strong.

"I saw you with the child. Her little legs, thin as reeds, kicking in the air. I should have stopped too you, Michael. I've learned that once some men get the taste of killing in their mouths, they can never stop. Not your kind, Michael. Not with the sickness you have." Benjamin let Michael step back.

"I'm sorry, Benjamin," he gasped between sobs. "It just comes over me. Like I'm a different man. But I won't do it again. I swear to God. It was just the one time."

Benjamin's eyes grew soft with understanding. "Just once? The girl was the only one?"

Michael nodded. He had condemned himself with a lie.

"Good," Benjamin said. "Let's be done with this place, then." He handed Michael the lantern and, as Michael turned to lead the way, picked up a stone from the pier, and slammed it into the back of Michael's head. Benjamin grabbed the lantern, as Michael collapsed into the dirt. He did not move.

Chamblis and two men appeared from behind a set of piers. "You could have picked a more convenient location."

"That wasn't my concern, was it?"

"It'll be a task to get him out of here."

"You've got the money," Benjamin said. "You agreed to the bargain."

Chamblis said, "So it's justice for the buggering of a few children?"

"I didn't do it for the dead children," Benjamin said. "I did it for him."

CHAPTER 35
THE TOBACCONIST'S SHOP

It was done.

Michael was dead, and the body carried off with a canvas sack of stones tied to his waist and dropped into the darkness of the Thames.

Benjamin slipped his hand into his pocket, as he strolled back to the rooms and felt the familiar shape of the abacus. Maybe that's what the Devil used to calculate human suffering. Yes. It all made sense.

Benjamin reached the tobacconist's shop, opened the narrow door that led to the stairway to their rooms, and saw Daniel sitting on the steps. He stood when Benjamin appeared.

"He's gone," Daniel said.

"What?" Benjamin said, puzzled. Then he understood. Benjamin raced past Daniel, slamming him against the wall, clearing three steps at a time. He burst into their rooms, with Daniel just behind him.

Benjamin dropped to his knees next to the body of Schiess, the little man shrunken more as his spirit, vacating his body, left so little behind that it was worth almost nothing.

Schiess's eyes were open, fixed toward Heaven.

Benjamin's fists game up in a rage, ready to beat the dead man. "You bloody, inglorious bastard. You couldn't have waited a week before you died, could you? You filthy, little man." He rolled off his knees and slumped to the floor, his arms covering his head. "What happened?"

Daniel, in the corner, far from Benjamin's rage, said, "We were talking. Just talking. He was drinking a little, not much at all. I rolled him a cigarette, like you do. He was smoking. He said something he thought was funny. I didn't understand it." He glanced at the body on the floor. "He started coughing. Like he always does. Then he was choking. I said, 'Take a drink.' I thought that would help. Then. He fell off the chair. He didn't move."

Benjamin offered the benediction. "I'd kill him, if only that would bring him back to life."

"I didn't know what to do. As God is my witness, Benjamin. He just died."

Neither man spoke for several minutes, each trying to sort out their place in the death of Professor Schiess. His famous batteries were now useless.

Benjamin climbed to his feet. "It's up to us now. I'm going to Chamblis and get some of his blokes to help us."

Daniel was confused. "Where is, Michael? He won't be with us?"

"We've got to move the batteries. Hide Schiess's body."

"Benjamin? Where is, Michael?"

Benjamin laughed softly. It was the Devil's humor, give and take away, lift up and then hurl to the earth. "Go to Chamblis tonight. Tell him what's happened. Tell him we need a wagon and two men. Do you understand me?"

"Yes." It was a reluctant answer. Daniel did not understand. "Can you use the batteries?"

"I don't know," Benjamin roared. "Do I look like a genius? Can I use the batteries? Can I lift the Earth?" He calmed. "Go to Chamblis." He thought he could. The old man had told him enough about the batteries, had shown him what to do. How to hook up the wires and throw the switch to send the charge to the blasting caps.

"I will," Daniel said.

"Don't tell him about Schiess," Benjamin said. "Don't ask. Tell him if he wants it done, the job he hired us to do, he had better come through. I'll need a few things."

"Yes," Daniel said. "Benjamin? Where is, Michael?"

"He's gone home," Benjamin said. "Do as I say." Daniel left, and Benjamin knelt next to Schiess's body, delivering the eulogy. "What have you done to me, you worthless piece of shit. I don't know a thing about batteries and electrics, and now it's been locked up in your head forever. I think you've doomed me, old man." He rolled a cigarette and stuck it between Schiess's lips. "You know how much I hate to be disappointed."

The Times of London
Paris—Engineers continue to assemble the iron framework of Mr. Eiffel's tower despite a slight delay due to this past winter's inclement weather, which impeded the installation of the foundations. The tower, which sits on the Champs de Mars, will be 1,100 feet tall.

CHAPTER 36
THE VILLAGE OF DEBTS ON THE LONDON POST ROAD

Edith knew she could not coax a few more miles from Mercury. She felt guilty. Her body ached, she could smell her own odor, and she dozed off constantly. It was not fair to ask more of the poor animal when she had no more to give.

They were on the outskirts of London. The progression had been almost mathematical. There were farms parceled by low stone walls, clusters of separate villages, chains of houses strung along the road, until they became unbroken links to the city. And London, a low, brown mound in the distance, spread across the horizon, church spires jutting into the sky.

The sky above London shone; lights gleaming in the city, a string of diamonds to match the stars overhead. Horsemen, wagons, carriages, carts, and pedestrians passed her. Some with a curious glance, most ignoring her. She was too tired to care. She had a single thought, find Theodore. The harsh reality of hours in a two-wheeled cart reminded her there were some things love couldn't overcome. Her back ached so badly she wanted to cry, her legs were locked in cramps, and her buttocks were on fire. Tears rolled down her cheeks.

She saw the inn on the left, brightly lit, with a stable next to it. A sign hung above the door, and she could just make out the word 'Spanish'. A groom stood outside, brushing a horse by the light of a lamp. He was a child, probably not much more than ten. He stood on a stool to reach the animal's back.

Edith guided Mercury toward the boy, wiping tears from her face with the hem of her dress. "Excuse me?" she called.

The groom hoped off his stool and hurried to the fence. Edith could tell her appearance stunned the boy. "Yes, mum. What can I do for you, mum?"

"I'm afraid I'm in a bit of a predicament," Edith said.

"A what?"

"Trouble," Edith tried. "You see, I need some help. A place to stay." Her stomach growled a reminder. "Perhaps, something to eat. I need to contact my husband."

"I'm sorry, mum," the boy said. "We ain't got no rooms. Full up we are, 'cause of the Queen's birthday."

"Oh," Edith said. She was so tired. She couldn't go on. She told herself that somehow, she would find her way to London and then contact Theodore. She knew she could do it. She was certain. But it was such a long way, and Mercury was so slow.

A rich voice burst through the darkness. "Preston! Those animals won't tend to themselves." A large woman, her black skin nearly hidden in the night, approached Edith. "What have we here?" Her voice was English but was accented with a pleasing sing-song manner. She had to be nearly six feet tall, with broad shoulders and thick arms, a woman used to hard work. But she was graceful and assured. "Why child, you've been crying?" She turned on Preston. "Young man? Did you …?"

"No," Edith protested. "Please. I've come such a long way, and I'm very tired."

"I told her we ain't got no rooms," Preston said.

"And this is your establishment, boy?"

Preston gave her an irritated look. "Everybody uses big words I don't understand."

"I'm Mrs. Norton," the black woman said. "This is my inn. You come down off that carriage, and we'll get you everything you need. Preston? See to the lady's horse and carriage."

Mrs. Norton threw her arm around Edith, helping her down the short stone walk to the door. "You're an American."

Edith said, "Yes. But you aren't English, are you?"

Mrs. Norton slapped her chest in pride. "I'm Jamaican. I met that scoundrel Boswain's Mate Norton when his ship stopped for victuals. Twenty years in the Royal Navy, and here we are. Except that lovely man has gone on, these past ten years. And what of you? You're a lady with no business driving yourself."

"It's a long story," Edith said and then realized how ridiculous she sounded. "Please, I need your help."

The Times of London
News has reached the Times from the Foreign Office that Zululand has become a
British Colony. The British army was victorious in 1879 in securing the territory for
the Empire. Not least of those triumphs was the engagement of Roarke's Drift,
resulting in the award of five Victoria Crosses by Her Majesty.

CHAPTER 37
ST. JAMES PARK LONDON, ENGLAND

Theodore couldn't sleep. He had wanted to build a fire, not for warmth but for comfort; but Abberline pointed out that fires in London's parks generally brought the night wardens, who were always followed by the police.

"Like the races at Ascot and big hats," Abberline, on the edge of sleep, had said.

They were in a thick stand of trees, hiding from the authorities once again, the city's lights barely visible to them. For the fourth time, he calculated. They had accomplished nothing. Edith. Theodore smiled. She had gotten away. It was a victory. Edith had escaped.

"There was always the chance she would be found," Abberline said. "If they find her …?"

"I know," Theodore had cut him off abruptly. She would not survive. Theodore lay on his back and built his argument to Abberline's dreadful theory. She was intelligent. She was creative. She was in good health. When last you saw her, she was in good health, Theodore's common sense reminded him.

He locked his hands behind his head as a pillow and propped himself against the base of a tree. Abberline, awake, lay next to him. Christy had gone off to find food and his brother.

Theodore vowed to remain awake to find a solution to their predicament. "No sleeping, old chap," he ordered himself.

"There's no reason for both of us to remain awake," Abberline said. "Go to sleep."

Theodore dismissed the suggestion. "I was deliberating our situation."

"Our situation is bloody awful," Abberline said. "There's no debate about that."

"How will they do it?" Theodore asked.

Abberline raised himself up on his elbow, peering passed the bridal paths and over the cricket fields, looking for intruders. "A bomb," he said. "Dynamite. It's not the most certain way of doing things, but it will cause the most damage. A gun's the thing, but that would have to be close-up; and the Queen will be surrounded by a hundred soldiers. The chap I saw with Chamblis, a big bloke, sounds like one of the brothers Christy told me about."

"Brothers?" Theodore said.

"Irish. Dynamite Patriots. Set off a bomb big enough, and you can kill a hundred. But you've got to get close enough to the Queen. If you want to kill her, you have to make sure the bomb is right under the carriage." He sat up. "Or you can chuck a load of dynamite right in her lap."

"What a twisted, filthy business this is," Theodore said.

"It is," Abberline confirmed. "Us right in the middle of it, and nothing we can do."

"We can do something," Theodore said. "There is always something to be done. I won't stand idly by and watch murder committed. Edith and I are going home, Mr. Abberline. We're getting out of this mess and going home."

"Very good, Mr. Roosevelt. How do we suggest we prevent the assassination? The entire Metropolitan Police Force is looking for us. The Black Squad has been enlisted to see that we leave this Earth with all dispatch. We would die in the effort like poor, Mr. Brown."

"Mr. Brown?"

"A servant of the Queen, Mr. Brown was," Abberline said. "A madman meant to assassinate the Queen; you see. 'Gallant Mr. Brown,' the newspapers reported, threw himself in the path of the bullet."

"I do remember something. A scandal?"

"The press," Abberline said, "condemned the poor man when he was alive. Victoria's lover, they taunted. Well, after the death of the Prince Consort, naturally. Queen Victoria survived the attempt, Brown died, and England prevailed. Until now."

"Edith is safe," Theodore pointed out.

Abberline chuckled. "You have me there. She has true grit, Mrs. Roosevelt. I'll grant you that."

"She is remarkable," Theodore said.

"When she makes her way to London, of which I have no doubt," Abberline asked. "How will she try to contact you? You must have thought of that."

"I have," Theodore said. "I shall leave it in the hands of Cupid."

"Cupid?" Abberline said. "The little chap with the bow and arrow?"

"Love, Mr. Abberline," Theodore explained, "conquers all."

"Excellent, Mr. Roosevelt," Abberline said. "But how do we prevent an assassination?"

Theodore shook his head. "Mr. Abberline, I'm afraid that is well beyond Cupid's purview."

The Times of London
Finch and Lester's, outfitters of gentlemen's sportswear, have just received the wondrous telescopic fishing rod, invented by American Everett Horton of Connecticut. The fishing rod consists of steel tubes that slide into one another for ease of transport.

CHAPTER 38
ABINGTON STREET, NEAR POETS CORNER LONDON, ENGLAND

Chamblis arrived just before midnight driving a delivery lorry, its cargo concealed by a faded green canvas tarp. Two men sat on the tailgate, their legs swinging back and forth, like children on an outing. Daniel was sandwiched between them. A large lamp swung from a wrought iron hook to the left of the dashboard.

The street swelled with wagons filled with lumber, workmen stretching red and white striped canvas across the frame obscuring the west front of the Abbey, and street sweepers shoveling horse dung, removing errant pieces of wood, or resetting stones that had been dislodged. It was a scene of desperate activity, and Benjamin watched it all.

There were a few cops strolling up and down the street, but they looked bored. Foremen, painters, builders, tentmakers, and those who wore red sashes strutted about like music hall kings. They could, with the wave of a hand bring order from chaos. That was the English way, Benjamin thought. Bellow and bully until unity is imposed and mark on a sheaf of papers all that has been accomplished. It was the country of the official officer.

God had been replaced by the Counting Clerk.

Benjamin didn't signal Chamblis; it would be too obvious. It wasn't likely that anyone would take notice and even if they did, there was no reason to believe they'd care. But necks had been snapped on slim threads before, and Benjamin never wagered against fate. He began walking across the Old Palace Yard. There was no thought of Michael to accompany him. He had taught himself that when a thing was done, not to linger on it. Others might have dwelt on Michael's head exploding when the stone crushed his skull, and the crimson spray of blood and tissues that fanned into the air, if they'd been the ones to do it. But they weren't, and he was, and the image was already beginning to fade. It was the same with Schiess. Regret was a useless commodity.

Benjamin glanced over his shoulder and saw Chamblis on the lorry. He wanted to be away from this, Benjamin knew. Chamblis, the chef, had kneaded the dough and smeared a thick layer of lard on the pan, until he was content with the loaf. Then he slid it into the oven and waited for it to bake. It was a very tidy arrangement. It was a way of doing things that Benjamin found dangerous. It was that English method again, where the reward was not what was accomplished but maintaining the ritual.

Benjamin turned onto the street facing the south side of the Abbey and stopped. When the lorry got close enough, he saw the words *Epic Fireworks*, painted on the sideboard. Epic. Someone appreciated irony.

Chamblis jumped off the lorry. "Don't touch a thing," he ordered his men.

Benjamin saw Daniel appear around the rear of the wagon. Benjamin motioned for him to stay back, and turned, leading Chamblis toward the abandoned livery. He suspected treachery, but it was a familiar ingredient in any event.

Chamblis approached, keeping close to the building's wall. Nothing about him said beware. But it would not. Chamblis was too cautious to reveal how he felt. He slipped his hand in his pocket, smiling at the same time. It was a tired man reaching for a cigarette, a thirsty man after a bottle, a disarming man.

Benjamin said, "You know I can snap your neck before the pistol clears your trousers."

Chamblis was about to protest but reconsidered. His smile disappeared, but his hand remained buried in his pocket. He stepped within inches of Benjamin. When he spoke, his voice was sharp. "What the fuck have you done, you stupid Mick? Your wizard is dead, and he was the man." He turned sarcastic, "You said would make it all right."

Benjamin saw Daniel look away in guilt. He had told Chambliss about Schiess.

"Take Daniel and go get the batteries and wire."

"You didn't answer me."

"I haven't time for recriminations and insults. You've paid me well, but I'm willing to wager you'll get much more if it goes as planned. If I fail? Well, I'll answer for it. One way or another."

"Oh, not just you, my friend. Things have gone just about as badly as they can, and through no fault of mine. Hasselbach is running about looking for that Jew whore, and Abberline, and the Yank."

"I'm not acquainted with those names."

Chamblis anger swelled. "They can turn this thing up-side-down, and it means the gallows for all involved."

"Does it? Does it so? And what if you were to do as I ask, and I were to do what I promised? All would be right then, wouldn't it?"

Chamblis calmed, but barely. "You can still do it? Everything? Just as you say?"

Benjamin's silence was answer enough.

"I'll get the batteries and wires." Chamblis told Benjamin.

"Yes, you do that," Benjamin said. He could make them work, Schiess's wonderful invention. Hope glimmered, not brightly and not without despair but it was there.

"It's two days," Chambliss pointed out. "Two days and every copper and soldier will be on his guard. If they see the least thing awry, it'll be over."

"Don't you know?" Benjamin said. "We Irish are invisible. We can stand in the street naked as a jaybird, and not an Englishman in the city would lower himself to raise the alarm."

CHAPTER 39
RUSSELL SQUARE, LONDON

Abberline removed his jacket. He and Theodore sat against a stone stoop that jutted out into the sidewalk, well clear of the street.

The city was just awakening. Fish sellers, milkmen, crockery sellers, and cobblers shared the broad street with wagons, carriages, and buses. Match boys, rabbit sellers, and cinnamon cake dealers kept one foot on the sidewalk and one in the gutter, suspended between the worlds of the well-to-do and the legitimate tradesmen. Chimney sweeps walked in the gutter, dressed in a thin veil of soot, shaken loose with each footstep.

A clerk walking by slowed as something in the newspaper he was browsing caught his attention.

"Finished with that paper, sport?" Abberline asked.

The clerk glanced at the pair in disgust. "Filthy beggars. Shouldn't be allowed on the street."

"Give him the newspaper, you contemptuous fop," Theodore said, "or I will beat the shit out of you."

The clerk's face sagged. He folded the newspaper, handed it to Abberline, careful to keep his distance, and raced to the other side of the street.

"What is that unpleasant odor?" Abberline asked, unfolding the newspaper.

"Us," Theodore said. "We reek of filth."

Abberline gave him a look of admiration. "You're not so nearly polite as you pretend to be, are you?"

"I am not," Theodore said. "I once had a ruffian insult me because I wore glasses. I knocked him out with one blow, thereby, establishing myself as a man not to be trifled with."

Abberline said, "The Queen's Jubilee is tomorrow, Mr. Roosevelt. Have you a plan?"

Theodore peered down the street toward the Russell House. "I could use a good pair of glasses.”

“You’re wearing glasses,” Abberline pointed out.

“Not spectacles,” Theodore explained. “Binoculars.”

Abberline returned to the newspaper. “How did that fellow insult you? The one you boxed.”

“He called me Four Eyes,” Theodore said. “He meant to belittle me. I wouldn’t have it.”

“I see,” Abberline said. He did not.

“If that villain had called me Old Four Eyes, it would have been a sign of respect instead of an insult.”

The statement caught Abberline’s attention. “That’s a rather fine point, don’t you think?”

“Not to an American.”

Abberline threw the paper down. “We must be inconsequential. We’re not even mentioned in the *Times*.”

“Patience, Mr. Abberline,” Theodore said as he picked up the newspaper. “We’ve come for Edith. Let us not lose sight of our mission.”

Abberline stood, resting his arms on the steps, looking down the street. He turned and said to Theodore, “My father was a saddle maker. My mother owned a small shop. Men from the peerage down listen to me because I’m a cop. That authority ends when I question them.”

“In America …”

“In America, it’s the same thing.” Abberline was troubled. “We could go to the palace right now to warn the Queen, and we’d be clapped in the madhouse.”

“Surely, there are others charged with the Queen’s protection?” Theodore said.

“It’s all ceremony, Mr. Roosevelt. Polished brass and red coats. As far from violence as the Earth from the Moon.”

Theodore scanned the paper. “Do you see anything?”

Abberline returned to his vigil. “No. Carriages coming and going. No sign of Edith. There must be a dozen bobbies scattered around the hotel.”

“They’re the least of our worries,” Theodore said, turning a page.

“Are they now?” Abberline said.

“You’re not wearing a uniform, do you, Mr. Abberline? Who’s to know you’re a policeman?”

“What of it?” Abberline said, and then realized what Theodore was getting at. “Mr. Roosevelt, you continually amaze me.”

Theodore joined him at the steps. “We must get closer.”

“Have you any money?” Abberline said. “We can rent a carriage, if you have money.”

“No,” Theodore said. “But you have a badge, haven’t you? The hackney drivers don't know we're fugitives. It's official police business."

Abberline was impressed. "A splendid idea."

Theodore took his arm. In their short, tumultuous time together, Theodore had not seen Abberline so overwhelmed by circumstances. He was right, of course. There was very little they could do about the Queen's safety. Theodore had comfort to offer. "I know you are troubled, and you want to act. I promise you, as soon as Edith is safe, I'll throw in and do all I can."

Abberline nodded. "What concerns me, Mr. Roosevelt, is I don't know when the crime is to be committed, by whom, and how. All I have is a possible victim. It's worse than a theory, sir. It might as well be a vision through a crystal ball."

"Here comes a cab," Theodore said. "Put your coat on. You don't want to be taken for a common thug."

The cab pulled to a stop in front of them, and the cabby touched his fingertips to his hat brim in greetings. "Good morning to you, gentlemen. My name is Fields. Off for a long ride, I trust?"

Abberline thrust his badge at the cabby. "Here it is, old chap. You're to take us down the street, turn around just past the Russell House, and park on the other side."

"Like hell, I will. I know my rights. I must take you to and from, but I don't have to waste my time. Go hail a cabby who doesn't know the law."

"Hang this nonsense," Theodore said. He took hold of the seat rail, planted his foot on the iron step, and pulled himself up. He jerked the Webley from his pocket he had taken from one of his assailants and stuck it in the surprised man's side. "Shut up. Get down. Get in the cab." As the man was obeying, Theodore tossed Abberline his pistol. "I'll drive. Keep him quiet with this."

Abberline opened the cab door and shoved the cabby inside. He grinned at Theodore. "Old Four Eyes, was it?"

CHAPTER 40
THE LIVERY, NEAR WESTMINSTER ABBEY

Benjamin tested the double doors of the deserted livery across the lane from Westminster Abbey, nodded to Daniel, and then threw his weight against them. The two wooden handles, bound by a padlock and chain, snapped off and the doors flew open. Daniel pulled the wagon forward, waited for traffic to clear, and backed the wagon to the edge of the building. Two men jumped from the wagon and began stripping the harness from the horses. The batteries were in the bed under a tarp.

Chamblis sat on another wagon two blocks from the livery, waiting. He carried the dynamite, buried in layers of sawdust. Benjamin watched him.

"Here, Daniel," Benjamin called. "Toss me the wire."

Daniel ran to the rear of the wagon, pulled himself up, teetering on the sideboard, and jumped back with a roll of wire in his hand. He held it up triumphantly.

Maybe, I've been wrong about Daniel all these years, Benjamin thought. Maybe, all he needed was a cause.

Daniel heaved the coil at Benjamin and returned to the horses.

Benjamin glanced down Abington Street and across Old Palace Yard. No one took the time to notice him; they were too concerned with their own business. He traced a path from the livery, over the telegraph lines, through the limbs of an elm tree, and to the base of the Abbey. He counted cellar windows until he found the one he wanted; the window that intersected the cellar stairs. He didn't want to waste time hunting for the wire in the darkness.

"Get out of the bloody road, you bloody idiot!"

A bobby stood just behind Benjamin, his helmet pulled down squarely on his head, the chin strap held in place by the man's lower lip.

"I'm working, here," Benjamin said, matching the bobby's irritation. "Can't you see the wire?"

"I can see an Irishman about to be run over by any number of vehicles. And me left with the report to file."

"Well then, I'll be about my business," Benjamin said. He doubted he could just walk away. This man looked like the sort that needed answers.

"Just a minute," the bobby said. "Step over to the sidewalk and explain yourself." Then the man recognized him. "The Mick. I've run into you before. Me and Earl. You was with that little squid of a man."

Benjamin knew before the bobby did. Phil, his mate Earl called him. Benjamin had met his kind before; in Ulster, Dublin, New York, and working for the Coal Police in Luzerne County. They were the kind who hated his type, bullies who taunted him into a fight and then brought the law down on him. First came the beatings when he was outnumbered ten to one, and then the magistrate, and then a cold cell. Phil could be a Pinkerton, or a Black and Tan, or a Roundsman swinging an ebony nightstick.

"Where is he?" Phil said. "The Swiss man?"

"Dead," Benjamin said. "He was in ill health when last you saw him. Then he died."

"Ah, it's a shame," Phil said without compassion. "Here you are back on my street." He pointed at the roll of wire in Benjamin's hand. "And carrying that device." He unbuttoned the button and fished his whistle out of his top pocket. He swung it back and forth taunting Benjamin. He was a cat torturing a mouse. "I could have a dozen of my brothers here in ten seconds with one call of my whistle. They'd take one look at you, and before a filthy Papist prayer passed between your lips, they'd have you beaten to the ground."

"I'm supposed to be here," Benjamin said.

"What's that?" Phil said. "I barely stop talking, and you've gone and started your lies."

Benjamin set the roll on the sidewalk, being careful to move slowly, and straightened, looking at Phil. "I have a pass in my pocket that says I'm to be here. I'm going to take it out and show you."

Phil brought his fist up, ready to act. "You may have the weight, but I've got two good fists. You had better not try anything foolish."

He was too close, Benjamin thought. He had the dynamite and the wire, and he knew where and how to set it, and all it would take to spoil it was one bloody cop with a tin whistle. This was his time. He had gone to America, and come back, and came to Ireland. Living between what was right and what he had to do, looking for the time he could sail to China and see a world that was paradise. Michael, dead now by his hands, and Daniel, who had come around and with time might become a man of considerable value. Where is my time, Benjamin demanded? When will it come to me?

Benjamin held the pass out and watched the cop slip the whistle between his lips. It hung from his mouth as he looked at the pass.

"Fireworks?" Phil said skeptically. "You don't look like the fireworks man to me, Mick. Anyone with a good hand and a slip of paper could make up a thing like that."

"He could," Benjamin agreed. "But no man I know could produce a seal like that. There's the seal, and there's the signer; and you can see I have the starter wire right there. I've got to set this up today, or there'll be a lot of people asking me why, when Her Majesty came out of the Abbey, the fireworks didn't go off. If they don't, I don't get paid. Then I've got to say, 'There was this constable who kept me from doing my job.'" The cop's face flushed bright red. Benjamin read the hate in his eyes and watched as Phil calculated his position. He chose to compromise.

"Listen to me, you bloody aberration. Don't you ever again threaten me with consequences. As far as I'm concerned, you can shove that bloody paper up your ass." He smiled to show he still controlled the situation. "You can place your fireworks or do whatever it is that paper gives you license to do. I'll be by once every four hours, and if I see something that doesn't suit me ..." Phil withheld the threat. There was no need to speak it.

Benjamin understood. He had always understood. Every Irishman knew about the power that Englishmen had. "I'm only doing my job," he said. "When the celebration is over, I'll be gone."

"Good," Phil said. "And I'll still be here making sure that vermin like you don't come back." He had said what he wanted to. He turned and walked toward a file of workmen carrying thick rolls of canvas awning to the front of the Abby.

Daniel was at his side. "Is there trouble?"

"Not now," Benjamin said. "I can't vouch for later." Daniel's presence broke the spell. "Do you have the horses in?" He looked at the front of the livery and asked before he realized he had no need to. "And the wagon?" The wagon and horses were gone, and the door closed. He nodded his approval at Daniel and handed his brother the roll of wire. "Pull off a hundred feet, while I find a weight." Benjamin walked the length of the low cast iron fence along the Abbey, looking for a stone. He found one under a rain barrel. He picked it up, testing the weight in his hand. He could wrap the electric wire around it and toss it over the telegraph lines.

He returned to Daniel, looked at the wire coiled neatly at his feet, and took the end from his brother. He wrapped the wire around the stone, tucked the exposed length under the coil, and gauged the distance to the cross arms on the pole supporting the telegraph lines. He looked at the coiled line to make sure it wouldn't foul as it played out. He would take three steps, a bowler on a cricket field. One, two, three, with an overhand toss, and the stone would sail up over the cross arm, pulling the length of wire with it.

"Yes," Benjamin told himself, and then stepped off. The stone flew into the air, arching over the cross arms, the wire trailing smoothly. It fell clear, bounced twice, and rolled. Benjamin raced to the edge of the Abbey. He pulled gingerly on the electric wire, keeping the wire close to the cross arm but not on it. He didn't want it to snag on the rough timber. He pulled about forty feet of slack and held it loosely in his left hand. He motioned for Daniel to join him. "Take that roll into the livery. You've got to stay close by, Daniel. You've got to make sure no one tampers with the electric wire."

"What if he comes back?" Daniel asked. "The policeman?"

"I'll take care of the Peeler." Benjamin saw his brother smile for the first time in years. "I've got big fists, haven't I, Daniel? I mind the uniform and see to the batteries. When it's dark, I'll come and get you and we'll finish up."

"I wish Michael could have seen this." Daniel didn't know about Michael. Benjamin would never tell him. "He'll feel it in Heaven," Benjamin said. "There'll be such an explosion to knock God off His throne." He left Daniel to carry the roll of electric wire to the livery. One of Chamblis' men stood outside, rolling a cigarette. He was a thick-headed sort, a boxer, or dockhand, with plugs of brown hair jutting from his skull. There wasn't a bit of life in the man's eyes, Benjamin decided. He would be useful in a set-to.

"You're getting well-paid for this, aren't you now?" the man said in a way that told Benjamin he expected an answer.

"Am I?" Benjamin said. The men took stock of one another. "If I am, you'll need to take that up with your boss." He waved Chamblis forward. He looked at the man's head. "How long has your barber been blind?"

The man's face flashed in embarrassment. "I had the scourge on my head. A fellow said, 'Put kerosene on it.'"

"Well," Benjamin said, "I wouldn't stand under any streetlamps."

The Times of London
The Thames Iron Works on Trinity Row and the Thames Plate Glass Works have announced plans to expand into Bow Creek, for the purpose of creating three new wharves. The Thames Iron Works has just recently completed the addition of Shipping Building Yards next to Orchard Stairs.

CHAPTER 41
RUSSELL SQUARE

Theodore had switched coats with the cabby. He felt it made him look more authentic, even if it was small and smelled of sweat. As Abberline wielded the pistol, he heard the cabby's frightened voice. "Here, now! There's no need for artillery."

Abberline climbed into the cab. "But can you be peaceful and quiet all at the same time is the question? All right, Mr. Roosevelt, let's proceed."

Theodore shivered despite the heat and remembered the familiar feeling. It was anticipation mixed with fear and spiked with excitement. He saw a break in the traffic, flicked the reins, and sped up to slide between two vehicles. He heard cursing behind him and felt the cab fishtail. If his vehicle brushed another, they were lost. He felt safe enough disguised as a driver, and he was sure that Abberline could handle their reluctant passenger, but if they were found out…. All he could think of was Edith.

They were nearing the hotel, and traffic was beginning to slow. Buses and cabs stopped, depositing people and luggage. Bellboys ran from the hotel, gathering up suitcases, handbags, and traveling cases. The steamer trunks and larger cases were taken to the rear of the hotel where tradesmen unloaded.

It was a wild scene of doormen, gentlemen and their ladies, and fashionably dressed children, gawking at the flags and bunting hanging over-head. The noise equaled that of the street, shouts, orders, and the frequent shrill whistle of a doorman calling for a cab. Joy and excitement swirling over the heads of people who had come for the Jubilee, and London had welcomed them.

Theodore glanced from side to side, picking out the stoic figures of plainclothes detectives peppering the building's front. Bobbies stood sentinel, arms thrown behind their backs, walking casually along the sidewalk. The sight of their uniform alone was enough to warn off criminals. Theodore saw a bobby glance in the window of a stopped cab.

He eased the cab toward the middle of the street. The horse resisted, accustomed to his place close to the curb. Theodore wanted to keep his distance between the bobbies and the cab. He gambled Abberline and the cabby would be hidden in the darkness of the vehicle, unless he was ordered to stop for inspection. Then what? There was no question about making a dash for it; the street was clogged with vehicles. No, keep as close to the middle of the street as possible, pass the hotel, turn around, and wait. He knew Edith's walk, the way she moved. There could be ten thousand souls on the sidewalk, but there was no way she'd escape his notice. What if she came in a cab? Or on a bus?

They were passing the hotel, and Theodore could feel the eyes of the bobbies and plainclothes men plucking at his disguise. He forced himself to relax, gripping the reins with the familiarity of a practiced hand.

Theodore leaned forward, elbows on his knees, a cabby worn out by hours and fares. He listened for a bobby's order to stop. He cleared the hotel, allowed himself a glance over his shoulder, and guided the cab to the gutter.

"See anything?" Abberline called from the cab.

"Nothing," Theodore was overtaken by disappointment. He'd expected to see Edith. He wanted to see her so desperately his body ached.

A man rushed up and took the cab's door handle. "Fosters on Sterling," he said, pulling open the door.

Before Theodore could say anything, he heard Abberline bark, "Don't you see the vehicle is occupied. Fuck off!"

The man slammed the door shut and looked at Theodore accusingly. "Well, you could have told me you had a fare. I'll get your number and give it to the Taxicab Commission."

Theodore glared at him. "Didn't you hear the man? Fuck off!" He saw a break in the traffic, snapped the reins, and made a wide U-turn to the other side of the street. "All right," he said. He watched vehicles stop in front of the Russell House, unload, and pull away. There was no sign of Edith. "Mr. Abberline?"

"I can see, Mr. Roosevelt. They must have half the division there. I never felt so wanted by anyone in my life."

"Edith will have a bad time of it," he said. He hoped he was wrong. "Perhaps, they have descriptions of us, but not her."

"Whatever the Metropolitan Police Department is, Mr. Roosevelt, it is efficient. They have everyone's description. But she's an intelligent lady, I'm sure she'll give them the slip," Abberline said. But his voice lacked hope. "Still, there's nothing to do but wait. And keep the fares at bay." He must have been talking to the cabby when he said, "I'm sorry about that, chum, but there's nothing to be done about it."

"Can you keep him quiet?" Theodore said.

"The poor chap is concerned about his horse," Abberline said. "They've been a couple for years."

Theodore was about to answer when he caught some movement out of the corner of his eye. Another fare. He turned to tell the man the cab was occupied, but his words failed to materialize.

A giant, nearly seven-feet tall, with shoulders the width of an ox, threw a big hand on the seat edge. His voice, deep and as rumbling as thunder, froze Theodore. "You're Mr. Roosevelt, ain't you?"

CHAPTER 42
BUCKINGHAM PALACE

Her Royal Highness received the thirty-eight trustees of the Jubilee Celebration Committee in the Palace's second floor State Room one day before the Jubilee was to begin.

The room's large table was capable of seating all the members of the committee. It was a matter of nostalgia as well. The Prince Consort had often sat next to her when important questions were discussed at this table, but he was gone, and she was alone.

Victoria was pierced by pangs of bitterness, made almost palatable by her sweet longing for Albert.

He was gone and she was alone, facing a murder of crows, chattering over one another for attention. Her only solace was Lord Crittenton; and she ordered him, with an imperceptible nod, to restore order. He rose to speak, as Queen Victoria had been kind enough to bid them be seated during the meeting. "My Lords, shall we bring this, our final assembly before Her Majesty's Jubilee, to order?"

Their lordships, old men mostly, somber in black suits, fell silent. Collectively, they were a polite body, particularly in the presence of the Queen. In small packs, they were vicious, even if politely so, gentlemen whose position had been assured them before birth, and whose manner was especially proscribed towards superiority.

"How enchanted we are at what you have accomplished," the Queen said. "Most appreciative of your hard work and dedication of honoring us during this jubilee. We are also aware that your sacrifice extends well beyond Tuesday's ceremonies. We have had the privilege to consult the schedule developed by you for this summer's activities. We are pleased beyond measure."

The old woman can still be flattered, Crittenton thought. "Your Majesty," he said, "On behalf of the committee, may I state that we are so honored to contribute to this monumental event, and that we, humbly, feel that the program will be the first of many such occasions to acknowledge your reign." The group thumped the table with their open palms in concurrence. "If Your Majesty pleases, Lord Austin will recount the Royal Processions."

Queen Victoria nodded her permission.

Lord Austin, a handsome man with a sculpted beard and a poorly hidden interest in boys, began. "With your permission, Your Majesty." Too vain to rely on reading glasses, he held a sheet of paper at arm's length. "'The Royal Processions,'" he read. "'The first procession will leave Buckingham Palace at 10:30 and proceed as follows.'"

Crittenton listened patiently, knowing that nothing had changed since he negotiated the route three months before. It was a circuitous passage through London, Constitution Hill to Piccadilly, to Regent Street and Waterloo Place, Pall Mall East to Cockspur Street and Northumberland Avenue. Then to the Embankment, and Bridge Street, and finally, the Abbey. Every street would be packed with thousands paying homage to the Queen and trying for a quick glimpse of royalty. Give the London mob bread and circus, and they'll stand cheering in the presence of the Devil. Perhaps, they will be.

It didn't matter the color of their majesties' skin or if the mob had ever heard of their distant nation, royalty from faraway lands would be dressed in silks and gold splendor, riding in carriages that cost what the average man made in a lifetime of hard labor.

Crittenton began to appreciate the result of his own handiwork. There had never been such a regal procession in modern times. Even the old girl's coronation was overshadowed by the Jubilee celebration.

Soldiers, red coats brilliant in the sun, would stand at attention in continuous ranks on either side of the street along the parade route. A human line of demarcation that warned the Queen's subjects they had no right to approach Her Majesty. A thousand ranks of the Royal Navy, white straw hats gleaming in the stands, would stand guard in front of the Abbey. Two full squadrons of the Life Guards were detailed to protect either flank of the Queen's royal carriage, and those admirals and generals not too fat to mount a horse would ride in sets of four, close to Her Majesty. She was, Crittenton concluded, protected by the might of her empire.

Lord Austin drank from a tumbler, preparing himself to continue. Ceremony could parch the best of men. "There will be three processions, Your Majesty. One quarter of an hour between each departure. The first is composed of carriages drawn by bay horses."

"We are concerned over so fine a timetable," the Queen said.

Crittenton was about to respond when Lord Austin replied, "With respect, Your Majesty, we have conducted numerous rehearsals and have determined that one quarter of an hour is ample time."

The Queen gave a noncommittal royal shrug whose meaning was clear; should there be any complications her displeasure would be severe.

"The Indian Princes," Lord Austin said, beginning the recitation, "guests of the Queen, and their suites. The Queen of Hawaii and her attendants in gold cloth." Another drink. "The rear carriages containing Princes Francis and Alexander of Teck."

Lord Crittenton sensed a servant at his elbow. The man held a silver saver so that Crittenton could see the envelope addressed to him. He took the envelope from the servant, who backed away from the table, stopping at appropriate intervals to bow to Her Majesty.

Crittenton read the message, fought back a wave of irritation, and slipped the document into his pocket. It benefited one not at all to express emotion in Her Majesty's presence. She viewed such behavior as coarse and unrefined. Crittenton rose in the middle of Lord Austin tedious monologue. "If I may, Your Majesty." Lord Austin, shocked that Crittenton had interrupted him, stumbled to a halt. "My presence is requested by high-ranking police officials, regarding the Irish question."

"Oh? Is there trouble we should be aware of?" Her Majesty asked.

"Indeed, not, Your Majesty," Crittenton said, "a formality, and nothing more."

"But I have just now come to the second procession," Lord Austin said. He was so seldom accorded the limelight; he was reluctant to give up any of his audience. "I have yet to account for the Grand Duke of Mecklenburg-Strelitz."

"You may inform us, Lord Austin," the Queen said. "We would rather have Lord Crittenton address the Irish, in any form or fashion, than be delayed on our behalf."

Crittenton bowed to Queen Victoria and to the committee and backed to the door. It was opened by a servant stationed to prevent awkward exits.

Crittenton waited until the door was closed before turning. Hasselbach lounged at the far end of the long corridor, seemingly unimpressed that he was one of the few civil servants permitted access to Buckingham Castle. Crittenton waved the police superintendent to an anteroom and closed the door behind them. "That was a particularly unfortunate action, asking for me."

Hasselbach was not impressed with Crittenton's pique. "You're my governor, aren't you? Everyone knows the Superintendent reports to His Lordship, Robert, Earl of Crittenton. Everyone knows you can be found, at least once a day, standing before Her Majesty."

Crittenton answered Hasselbach's comments calmly. "You're a vicious man, aren't you, Superintendent? Was it your upbringing? Or is it just your manner? Well, never mind. We'll delve into that subject at another time. You've come for a reason. What is it?"

"Our Irishman has run into difficulties."

Crittenton's tone was unforgiving. "What difficulties?"

Hasselbach looked around the room. "You don't suppose Her Majesty has thought to keep a bottle or two here, do you?"

Crittenton reached for the doorknob. "Look for yourself. I've business elsewhere."

Hasselbach forgot his thirst. "Chamblis has voiced some concerns about Dugan."

"We all have concerns. This is an adventure of concerns, isn't it?" Crittenton turned away. "Good God, man, is he the one Irishman who can't toss a bundle of dynamite?"

Hasselbach said, "I came to you in case we have to make other arrangements."

"At this late date?" Crittenton laughed bitterly. Both men were silent for a moment until Crittenton spoke. "Can he do it? This Irishman. Will he do it?" Hasselbach didn't speak. "Thank you for being succinct," Crittenton said. "So, there is the very real possibility that he will fail."

"We have Chamblis," Hasselbach said. "He'll do it if he's amply rewarded."

"Well, then, give it to him. It doesn't matter who does the deed; we'll blame the Irish anyway."

"Very well," Hasselbach said. "Have you…do you know what we'll do if it fails?"

Crittenton glanced at him with a look akin to pity. "Fail? I do not fail, Superintendent Hasselbach. One way or the other, I am eternally successful. You do not think that my entire plan rests on the shoulders of a filthy Irishman, do you? I have plans beyond those to which you are privy. Your task is to make certain there is a monumental explosion to accompany Her Majesty's Jubilee Procession. Whether it is by Chamblis hands, the Irishman's, or yours is inconsequential."

Hasselbach smiled in appreciation. "You bloody, cold-hearted creature. How many more do you have working for you? How many of us will survive if you succeed?"

"There is liquor in that cabinet," Crittenton said, pointing in the corner. "Fix yourself a drink to stiffen your resolve, and then go and do what must be done. Tomorrow morning, Superintendent Hasselbach, Her Royal Highness, will proceed to her destiny surrounded by the grandest array of royalty ever assembled on one continent. And the following day, when there is a newborn Sun, there will be a new empire. One of vitality and power." He added as he left, "At long last."

"Yes," Hasselbach said without enthusiasm. "Your empire, is it?"

Crittenton straightened. "His Highness the Prince of Wales."

"One and the same, wouldn't you say?" Hasselbach said. "Well, you craft lofty dreams. I will have a stiff drink and go see about murder."

The Times of London
The Queen's Jubilee—Berlin, June 16, 1887. Yesterday Prince William took leave of the Emperor before proceeding to England, and this morning his Royal Highness left for Wilhelmshaven to join his brother, Prince Henry.

CHAPTER 43
SOUTHAMPTON ROW, LONDON

Theodore had never seen a giant before. He was certain the man was going to reach up and pull him from the seat, and there was nothing he could do about it.

He could get in several blows, flattening the man's nose, maybe blacking both eyes. The best he could do was delay the giant's attack. It was a futile hope. His only recourse was to bargain. The giant looked friendly enough. At least he wasn't scowling, although his hand, the size of a small ham, hadn't released the seat rail.

Then, the giant did something that shocked Theodore.

He grinned. "You are, Mr. Roosevelt, ain't you?" The voice still boomed, but he had become benign. "Me brother said come out and find you, and Mr. Abberline."

Abberline appeared on the other side of the carriage, staying close to the vehicle. "By God, Mr. Roosevelt, where did you find Goliath?"

The giant was pleased at Abberline's appearance. "You must be Mr. Abberline?"

"Christy?" Abberline said, spying the little man. "Him I know," he said to the giant. "Who the hell are you?"

"Me, little brother, Big Jonathan," Christy said. "Sorry to startle you, chaps. I was just over there, when you pulled up." He punched Jonathan on the arm. "Didn't I tell you to fetch these gentlemen and bring them into the shop?"

"You did," Jonathan confirmed. "And I was doing just as you asked."

"I saw Mr. Roosevelt's face, and you shocked the poor man into birthing kittens."

Theodore turned on Christy. "He did nothing of the sort. I was planning my play. I suggest we get off the street and find a place we can talk."

Jonathan looked in the cab door. "There's a fellow in here who appears most unhappy."

"He is," Abberline said. He took the opposite door and said to the cabby. "We'll turn you lose, and you can go about your business." He yanked his pocket watch out of his vest pocket and tossed it on the seat next to the cabby. "That'll pay for your troubles. I want you to attend to this mammoth gentleman there. If you say one word about our adventure, he will hunt you down and separate your arms from your body."

Fields was about to protest when Abberline silenced him with a look. "Unless you want to wave good bye with your pickle, I suggest you remain silent. Jonathan, please remove his bonds."

Theodore jumped to the sidewalk, and Christy led them two doors down to a lock and key shop. It was a shop cluttered with key blanks, cutting machines, and padlocks. A thick layer of grime covered everything. The counter was nearly obscured by wooden crates and cardboard boxes.

Theodore knew it would be impossible for anyone on the sidewalk to look in the front window and see anything but darkness. "Where is the owner?"

"Mr. Shaw?" Christy said. "Oh, he's in the back room. He won't bother us."

"You didn't harm him?" Theodore said.

"Not a bit. The old man sleeps twenty hours a day and naps the other four. And, oh, how he loves the bottle." He glanced out the window. "Here's Jonathan now."

The giant closed the door behind him and gave Theodore a satisfied look. "I've never met a Yank before."

"The cabby, Jonathan?" Christy said.

"He's on his way," Christy's brother said. He appraised Theodore. "A real Yank."

Christy remained patient. "Did you see to him? The cabby?"

"I did," Jonathan said. "He won't say a word."

"Well," Christy said. "All we need is Mrs. Roosevelt."

"Edith?" Theodore asked. "Are you saying you saw her?"

"Mr. Roosevelt," Abberline said. "They would have told us if they had."

"Aye, true enough," Christy said. "But I'll tell you, Mr. Roosevelt, she'd do well to keep her distance. I tell you; I kept mine. But…"

"How could you possibly see if she arrived?" Theodore snapped.

"There's nothing to be concerned about, Mr. Roosevelt," Jonathan said. "I was there. I saw all the comings and goings."

"He's a drayman," Christy said. "He's at the hotel twelve hours a day unloading the carts."

"He's not there now," Theodore said.

"Mr. Roosevelt," Abberline cautioned, "let the boys tell their story."

"We just don't know when she will arrive, Mr. Roosevelt," Christy pointed out.

"If we don't," Abberline said, "they don't."

Theodore walked away from the men in thought. "I have an idea. I hope I'm correct."

"That says very little," Abberline pointed out.

"I once carved out a wood duck for my sweetie," Jonathan said. A thought saddened him. "She ran off with another bloke. Took the duck."

"I need a cab and directions," Theodore looked at Jonathan. "You can't go. You'll never pass unnoticed."

"I'm going to stay with my little brother," Christy said.

"Keep this giant out of sight, will you?" Abberline ordered.

"We'll need a place to meet afterwards," Theodore said.

"Here," Abberline said. "We have a drunken owner and a nearly deserted shop."

Theodore wasn't convinced. "The enemy is not a quarter of a mile from here."

"They won't expect us, will they?"

"Then we'll stay," Christy said. "We'll wake Mr. Shaw up every two hours to make sure he ain't dead and give him a drink."

"Come on," Theodore led Abberline through the door and out into the street. Traffic had picked up, and a dozen cabs were parked along the street. Drivers had feed bags out and slipped over their horses' muzzles, while others threaded harnesses through their fingers and tightened buckles.

"You'd better come up with a plan," Abberline said. "Neither one of us has any money. And I had only the one watch."

Theodore looked at Abberline with a broad grin. "I see an old friend who will be more than happy to assist us."

Fields tightened the nut on the front axle, ran the wrench arm over the wheel spokes, listening for the sound of a loose one, and satisfied with the condition of his cab, and slid the tool in the box under the seat.

"God bless a man who cares for his equipment," Abberline said.

Fields straightened slowly. "It can't be."

Theodore slapped the cabby on the back. "Rest assured, sir. It is. Your professionalism so impressed us, that we have returned."

Fields shoulders slumped. "In the cab, I suppose, gentlemen?"

"We wouldn't think of it," Theodore said as Abberline climbed through the door. "We want you to drive us, Mr. Fields." His foot was on the cast iron step when he added, "We can trust you, can't we, Mr. Fields?"

Fields gave Theodore a disgusted look. "You're not going to pinch off my pickle, are you?"

Theodore smiled. "Do you think me that sort of bloke?"

"Small comfort," Fields said. "It hasn't seen the light of day in twenty years. Let us be off."

The Times of London
*The Queen of Hawaii, newly arrived in London for Her Majesty's Jubilee, expressed
confidence that the recent purchase of Pearl Harbor by the United States will
provide both countries with financial opportunities. The Queen of Hawaii and her
attendants in gold cloth will lead the first procession.*

CHAPTER 44
MADAME TUSSAUD'S, MARYLEBONE STREET

Edith regretted dismissing Preston. When they arrived at Madame Tussaud's, the boy seemed ready to stay by her side. Mrs. Norton would expect it, he had said.

"It's for your own good, miss," Preston had argued, although he appeared more motivated by the lurid posters covering the outside walls than his concerns for Edith's safety. She had appreciated his interest, especially when she glanced at the Chamber of Horrors poster. She had tried to look away, but the garish colors and distorted characters seemed to draw her in.

She broke her morbid fascination long enough to tell Preston, "You had better go on now. Your mistress will be concerned for your well-being."

The boy had driven off with a glance over his shoulder. This was none of his business.

Edith stepped to one side of the doorway and wondered if she had made a mistake. Theodore may not remember their conversation. It was just before encountering the Prince of Wales. Before this horrible episode began. She knew he had a remarkable memory. For a man. How could he be expected to remember an obscure conversation? Edith calmed herself. I told him I wanted to visit Madame Tussaud's. He had said yes.

She noticed a wayward thread hanging from her cuff. She examined the sleeve. A shoulder seam was beginning to unravel. Tears welled up and slid down her cheek. Not this, too? I'm kidnapped and lost, and now my dress is falling off me.

She held a small drawstring bag Mrs. Norton had given her. "It's heavy," Edith had said in surprise. "What's in it?"

"A lovely piece of coal," Mrs. Norton had said, patting her on the cheek. "One swipe of this will correct any bloke's intentions."

She remembered Mrs. Norton brushing some life into her hair, and she felt the back of her head with the memory. She felt the soft fabric of a ribbon. "This will give you a bit of color," she had said. "Something to capture your husband's eye."

Edith stepped back against the storefront as the traffic along the side- walk picked up. She noticed a few men glancing at her with interest. She realized why. They think I'm a woman of the streets. Warmth spread over her face. What would mother say? What would Theodore say?

Edith had a horrible thought. What if she was approached? The idea took hold. Well, she thought defiantly, I have a piece of coal to cool their ardor. She swung the bag by its string to test the weight. Let them try.

She watched as a cab slowed past her and pulled to a stop in front of Madame Tussaud's. She stiffened with hope. The passenger door remained closed; the cab unmoving. Perhaps, they were waiting on someone?

Three soldiers wearing pillbox caps and forest green uniforms strolled by, slowing to leer at her. But one, a thin man with a wisp of a mustache, strutted over to her.

"Hello, dearie. Lovely day, ain't it?" The man stank of alcohol.

"I beg your pardon," Edith said. "But I'm waiting for my husband."

The soldier turned to his friends in delight. "See here, chums; the lady's a colonial." He returned to Edith. "This is a pleasant surprise, catching your type all the way out here, but I call myself lucky in the way of love. American, aren't you?"

"I don't care what you call yourself," a man of average height with a red beard said. "Just go elsewhere."

"Now, who are you, and what makes you think this is any of your business?" the soldier asked.

The man pulled back his lapel, revealing a gold badge. "This says it's my business."

One of the other soldiers said, "Come on, Jack. There's other tarts."

"He's right," the other said. "If we get into a row, Higgin's will skin us alive."

The policeman jerked his head, sending them on their way. "Off with you, Jack. There's better hunting elsewhere."

The soldier hesitated but waved to his friends to follow him. "Come on, boys."

Edith watched them leave, relieved, before she said, "Thank you, sir. I really am waiting on my husband."

"And who would your husband be?"

"Theodore Roosevelt," Edith said, and knew the moment the words were out she had made a terrible mistake.

The policeman smiled. "I know your husband. And I know his compatriot Abberline. Small world, ain't it? My names Mackie, and I'm more than pleased to meet you." He pointed to the cab waiting at the curb. "There is our transport, Mrs. Roosevelt." He took her arm before she had a chance to pull away. "Let's not have nonsense about escape." His voice grew cruel. "It'll be the easiest ten quid I ever made."

"I will not go with you," Edith said, trying to pull away from him.

"I've been riding up and down these streets looking for you, so either you come with me, or I'll slap you silly." He jerked on her arm. "Now, get in that vehicle."

The purse swung against her leg.

Mackie sensed her holding back. "Get in there, you bitch, or so help me, I'll club the life out of you."

Edith's fingers wrapped around the string of the draw bag. Her hand tightened on the bag string, and she swung. The bag sailed through the air. It was purely biblical. David and Goliath. Very nearly.

It slammed against Mackie's nose with a dull thud. He cried out, stiffened, dropped her arm, and staggered back several steps.

The door to her right was open, and she dashed into the darkness of Madame Tussaud's, pushing past the crowd. She was nearly blind in the dim lighting of the gallery.

"Miss? Miss?" she heard a young man calling. "You must buy a ticket."

Edith stumbled deeper into the gallery. Gas jets, high on the wall, flickered in the faint drafts. She had no idea where she was or if Mackie was following her. All she knew to do was run.

She found a recess, ducked in, and looked back. Customers moved about the room, shadows in the dim light really, but she did not see Mackie. She couldn't have lost him. Her fingers touched a piece of furniture. She felt the fabric and wood, the arm of a couch. She saw a body. There was a woman lying on her back, her arm thrown over her eyes to shield them. "Wax, you silly woman," Edith told herself.

A couple passed her, chatting softly. They barely glanced at her. Edith watched them walk into a narrow hallway. A man, holding a telescope, dressed in some outlandish costume stood on a platform on one side of the doorway.

She glanced in irritation at the wax figure on the couch. "I hope you end up as a candle."

Mackie. She wasn't safe from him. He could call for assistance. Surround the gallery. She was trapped. Get out, she ordered herself.

Her eyes were slowly becoming adjusted to the darkness. She saw an entrance to another gallery, roped off to prevent access. The sign over the gallery entrance read 'Chamber of Horrors, Temporarily Closed.' No one was likely to enter. She could hide from Mackie in the gallery. She could wait there for Theodore.

Customers glided past. Move now, Edith. You've got to go. Edith slid along the wall, careful to stay out of the light. There were just a few visitors surrounding her, couples mostly. It was warm in the building, and the wax bodies of the subjects emitted a mildly disquieting scent.

She found herself alone, lifted the stanchion rope, ducked under, and hurried into the gallery. There were just a handful of gas lights on the walls, and those were turned to the lowest setting. The deeper she moved into the gallery, losing herself in the darkness, the more alarmed she became. She was annoyed at her fear.

Find a door. A means to escape. The only danger now is Mackie. She knew others would come.

Ten quid, he said. He won't call anyone. Mackie wants the money all to himself. If I stay safely hidden from him, I am in no peril. She knew it wasn't true.

Edith saw a head, lying on the floor, looking up at her with horrified eyes from a deathly white face. Blood pooled around the head, and just a foot from it, sprawled a body. She threw her hands over her mouth to keep from screaming. The body's chest was hacked open. Then she realized the figure was wax. "Oh, for the love of God." She whispered in exasperation, "I shall never mention a word of this to Theodore." She felt a sharp jab in the small of her back.

"If I severe your spine," Mackie said, "you'll have your wish. You can feel the knifepoint, can't you? Yes, you can. We'll walk out of here to my cab without incident."

She tried to force herself to sound brave, but her voice came in a quick rush. "I think not, Mr. Mackie."

"Do as I say, or I'll gut you here and still pocket five quid."

She felt his hand grip her arm as he pushed her forward. The stanchion rope lay on the floor, as they entered the outer gallery.

"Police business," Mackie said to a confused couple.

They moved toward the burst of sunlight that led to the sidewalk and Marylebone Street.

A young man at the front desk erupted in indignation. "That's her, officer. Come rushing in here, like she's too good to pay. We won't have that sort of thing at Madame Tussaud's. We'll press charges, officer."

"No need in that," Mackie said. "She's wanted for other offenses."

Edith felt Mackie's hand tighten. If she made a move to escape or said anything, he would stab her.

They were on the sidewalk, the stench of horse dung and heat somehow reassuring after the heavy air of the museum. The sun's glare made it nearly impossible for Edith to see, and she stumbled on the uneven boards of the sidewalk.

"Over there," Mackie ordered, shoving her to a weighting cab. He jerked her to a stop and, shading his eyes with his knife hand, he looked up at the cabby. "Who are you, and where is Kendell?"

"Sent away by those two pirates," Fields said.

"What two pirates?" Mackie demanded.

"Ask the one behind you."

Mackie turned, and Theodore slammed the pistol into the side of his head.

The Times of London
A great festival gathering is planned in Hyde Park by London's School Children to honor the Queen. Games and attractions will be provided for the school children, whose total is estimated to be 30,000. Sir Henry Irving of the Lyceum Theatre has kindly provided bells that will be rung out at the appropriate time in jubilation.

CHAPTER 45
ON MARYLEBONE STREET

I haven't been exposed to such mayhem since my first marriage," Fields said in appreciation.

Edith locked her arms around Theodore. Her tears mixed with his, as they kissed each other. She felt her heart was about to burst from within, and she could not speak.

"Theodore?" she said. "I never thought I'd see you again."

"Nonsense, Edith. I'm inevitable."

Abberline tapped Theodore on the shoulder. "Congratulations are in order, but you just pistol whipped a man in plain view of fifty or more citizens, so we must be off."

Edith stroked Theodore's face.

"I was in Hell without you," Theodore said. "I would never forgive myself if anything happened to you. Are you hurt? Have you been mistreated?"

Edith smiled and shook her head. "I'm just tired and hungry. And so very, very happy to see you."

Abberline guided them both toward the carriage. "Very touching, indeed. Get in."

"By all means," Fields added. "I've nothing to be but be kidnapped. Climb in, and let's find an orphanage to sack. Better yet, we'll make off with the Crown jewels."

Abberline opened the door. Theodore helped Edith in and sat next to her. The inspector took the seat across from them. The cab pitched as the vehicle began to move.

"You must tell us everything," Abberline said. "We have little time."
Theodore bristled. "For God's sake, man, she's just been rescued."

"He's right, Theodore," Edith said.

"Very well," Theodore relented. "But first we will secure food and drink for Edith. And I can do with some myself."

"My apologies, Mr. Abberline; I thought you were a part of this," she said.

"I am. Apparently, on the side, being hounded. Where were you kept? Did you see anyone but Chamblis?"

"Chamblis?" she asked.

"The scoundrel with the white hair. At the church." Theodore said.

"I was kept in a warder's cottage. I saw Mrs. Sheraton and a dour man named Congreve. I don't know anything else, I'm afraid."

Abberline nodded at Theodore. "Your husband has a remarkable theory that I'm inclined to agree with."

"Theodore?" Edith asked.

"I believe everything centers on the assassination of the Queen," Theodore said.

"What? The Queen?" Edith said. "But how?"

Theodore condensed his explanation into a few sentences. When he finished, he followed it with a shrug. "I'm very sure, that's it. And the entire thing sickens me."

"Who was this Congreve fellow?" Abberline asked.

"A warder. Mr. Congreve," Edith continued, "We never spoke to one another. I hit him with a pitcher and escaped."

"Bully!" Theodore cried. "Bully, for you, Edith."

"Theodore?" Edith said, "We must contact the authorities. We can't let this happen."

"The authorities consist of the very same man that had a knife in your back and most likely the men who hired your kidnappers," Abberline pointed out. "I heartily recommend we avoid them at all costs."

"We must do something," Edith said. She took Theodore's hand in hers. "Theodore, we can't stand by and let this happen."

"Did you see Lord Crittenton?" Theodore asked.

Edith said, puzzled. "No, why should I?"

"He is one of the men behind this," Abberline said. "A wolf in sheep's clothing, if there ever was one. How many more are involved is untold."

Theodore gave Abberline a thin smile. "Is there not one man of position we can count on?"

"Undoubtedly," Abberline returned. "Now, all that remains is to find him, without being shot, stabbed, or kidnapped."

Edith laid her head on Theodore's shoulder. "All I want is a real bath."

"Your department is truly rotten with corruption, isn't it?" Theodore said.

"Mackie is not the department," Abberline pointed out.

"No. But he is Hasselbach's man."

Abberline shook his head. "We're going around and around this endlessly. Who's involved? Who isn't? Is there no one we can trust? Mr. Roosevelt, I don't have an answer. I'm not even certain of the questions. Crittenton appears to be the chief assassin."

"Yes," Theodore agreed." He kissed the back of Edith's hand. "All I care about is Edith. She is out of harm's way. Nothing else matters."

They rode in silence before Edith challenged Theodore. "You know that isn't right, Theodore," she said, brushing his cheek with her fingers. "The Queen. There is more at stake than my wellbeing. Or yours. Or Mr. Abberline's. We must act. We must do something. Even if it puts our lives in jeopardy."

"Edith?" Theodore said. "I will not endanger you again."

She smiled, patting his hand. "My dear, it is not your decision to make. I will do what must be done. As I know you will. As I know, Mr. Abberline will."

"Well," Abberline said. "You know more than I."

"My dear Edith," Theodore said, "I love you so, but never more so than when I am proud of you." He turned to Abberline. "If only we knew more about the Irishmen."

"The Fenians?" Abberline said. "They call themselves patriots. Isn't that enough?"

Theodore nodded. He spoke slowly, lying out what he understood. "They throw bundles of dynamite into passing carriages; is that not so?"

"Single sticks," Abberline said. "Or two or three tied together. But I'll tell you, the man that throws dynamite at the Queen is going to have to have the arm of Zeus. The army lines both sides of the street for some distance."

"Well," Theodore said. "That was a delightful theory while it lasted."

"There are three of us, Theodore," Edith reminded him. "Mr. Abberline? What can we do?"

"Five," Theodore corrected her. "A young cripple named Christy and his very large, younger brother."

She straightened her husband's collar. "Your suit is a mess, Theodore."

"Get some rest, Edith," Theodore said.

"Oh, I'm not resting. I'm listening. Someone has to listen." She nestled her head into his shoulder. "Please continue."

"We have not yet determined the details," Abberline said, "not with any certainty."

"What are you certain about?" Edith asked. "Theodore?"

"I gave some thought to your husband's theory," Abberline said. "Dynamite it is. Now we must determine how and when."

Theodore caught Abberline looking at him curiously. "Well?" he demanded of the policeman.

"Just waiting on your orders."

“Very well,” Theodore said. He kissed Edith on the forehead. “I need a newspaper.”

CHAPTER 46
WESTMINSTER ABBEY

Luzerne County in Pennsylvania had been a dismal blight on the face of the Earth. It was filled with sharp ridges and hidden valleys, and in the winter, all the color was bled out of it. The forests were black, the skies a lifeless gray, and even the snow, which should have been a sparkling white, was covered with a dull coat of coal dust.

In the gallery rooms and long shafts of the deep mines, with steam drills hissing with menace or banging into the coal seams, Benjamin had felt at ease. He should not have, and he knew it. He was deep underground; and if the mine flooded, he would drown, or if the ceiling fell when they were robbing pillars, he would be crushed. Or the gas could come in and silently steal away a man's breath. The worst of it was death could be prolonged. Every miner knew that any talk of rescue was a pitiful ruse.

Benjamin lay on his stomach on the cold dirt floor of the Abbey cellar, inserting blasting caps into the six bundles of twelve sticks of dynamite that lay next to him. His light was a single candle, its base dug into the dirt. The smell of the dry earth beneath him reminded him of Pennsylvania. It was strange that he was carried back to that time. But it was common for him to be completely relaxed when he handled dynamite. It was unforgiving and treacherous, but the explosive and Benjamin had come to an agreement. They shared a mutual respect for each other's power.

Benjamin finished with the blasting caps and examined each bundle, making sure each was securely tied with butcher's twine and the cap was properly seated. He propped his head on his hand, giving himself a moment to enjoy the solitude. He saw Michael in the dark recesses of the cellar. Lingering on the edge of regrets was a dangerous luxury. Thus preoccupied, Benjamin had decided many years ago, a lad was likely to become complacent. Such a lovely word, soft and inoffensive. Complacent.

He noticed a splinter, maybe six inches long, protruding from a ridge of dirt. One edge was cleanly cut, and it looked to have been knocked from a timber. He wiggled it back and forth and pulled it out of the ground. He held it up, catching the feeble light of the candle.

Benjamin smiled. "A piece of the true cross, are you? Are you soaked in Christ's blood?" He examined it. "No. I don't think so. Still, maybe, you can grant me a miracle. Not much of one, mind you." He held the sliver up as if it had the power to grant him what he asked. "Let me get out of this alive, dear Lord, and I promise to go to Mass every day." He threw the piece of wood into the darkness. "And while you're at it, I could use a ham and cheese sandwich and a quart of ale."

He rolled onto his stomach and found the broom handle he had stolen from the caretaker's closet and the first bundle of dynamite. He had laid the primer cord already, six arms from a central line, and planned to attach them to the dynamite blasting cap, then slide the bundle into the window opening that faced the Abbey entrance and push it out under the canopy platform.

He talked to the Almighty as he walked over the uneven, hard packed earth, toward the first window. The dirt crumbled under him, raising a thin cloud. "You see, a fellow has to take care of himself. No disrespect intended, God, but when a lad such as myself learns its best to trust no one, the clergy first and foremost, he can count on a reasonably long life."

Benjamin reached the window, found the primer cord in the near darkness, and began attaching it to the bundle of dynamite. He continued to talk as he worked. "I keep a healthy distrust of everyone. They'll do you false, lie to you, steal from you, and if it benefits them, murder you." He stopped and glanced up. "Call that my Golden Rule." He returned to the work. "Another thing, Your Holiness. Never do what they expect you to do."

He set the bundle on the edge of the windowsill, grabbed the broomstick, and pushed the dynamite, trailing the primer cord out under the platform. When it was five feet from the window, he stopped and pulled the handle back. Satisfied, he swung around and crawled back to the other bundles. He was at peace after speaking to God.

He disappeared into the darkness, the crunch of dry earth following him, the stillness returning to the Abbey cellar.

The Times of London
Westminster Abbey—The Dean of Westminster Abbey has received the Queen's gracious permission, and also the Sanction of Her Majesty's First Superintendent of Works and the Lord Chamberlain to repeat the Jubilee Service in the Abbey on Wednesday, June 23, at 3 p.m.

CHAPTER 47
SHAW'S LOCK AND KEY SHOP, LONDON

Jonathan, surprised at the arrival of a lady, stared at Edith as she entered the shop. The blinds were drawn over the front window and the door glass. Christy had three lamps, sitting on the counter near an array of locks, lit. He was delighted at Edith's presence.

"Ah, Mrs. Roosevelt, a pleasure to meet you. I'm Christy, and this fellow is my little brother, Big Jonathan."

Jonathan couldn't bring himself to say a word at the presence of a woman.

"Yes," Abberline said, "introductions all around, but we haven't time for that, have we?" He glanced around the shop. "Mr. Shaw is still incapacitated?"

Christy's finger came up as if he had remembered a lesson. "Ah, well, I don't know what that word means, but he's safely in the back room with a bottle."

"He's drunk," Jonathan said, pleased with his contribution.

Theodore spread the newspaper on the counter. "Jonathan, stand guard at the front door, if you please. Let no one enter."

"Who'd want a lock this time of morning?" Christy asked.

"The wrong people," Theodore answered, flipping the pages. "Here." He waved Abberline to the counter. "The Jubilee Procession." He tapped the paragraph in bold print. "The Queen's place in her procession is obvious. She arrives last."

Christy thought that obvious. "She is the Queen. Everyone is required to wait on her."

Theodore ignored him. "Do you find the Prince of Wales?" he asked Abberline.

Edith looked over Theodore's shoulder. "There. In the procession of the tenth carriage. 'Grand mounted Guard of Honour of Royal Princes in military uniforms, riding three abreast. Duke of Connaught, Prince of Wales, Duke of Edinburgh.'"

Theodore stepped away from the counter. "Right behind the Queen." "Would that place him in danger as well?" Edith said.

"A good question, Mrs. Roosevelt," Abberline agreed. "A few sticks of explosives will tear a carriage apart. It's not a discriminating way to kill."

"Perhaps," Theodore suggested, "he will not participate in the procession?"

Edith questioned Abberline. "Is that likely?"

"The old girl will insist," Abberline said. "But is it likely? Who's to say?"

"The Irishman?" Theodore posed. The man you saw?"

"Are you asking me what he can do? He was big enough to throw a barrel of the stuff across the Thames," Abberline said. "And a dozen sticks half a block, but I'll tell you, Mr. Roosevelt, I think there is more to it than that."

Christy joined the conversation. "The one I told you about? The brothers, was it, Abberline? The Dynamite Patriots?"

"Yes, thank you," Abberline said. "Feel free to sweep into the conversation when you wish."

"Manners, gentlemen," Edith chided. "Let us be civil, and together we will solve this mystery."

Theodore had been studying the Official Programme while they spoke. "They leave Buckingham Palace at 10:30 a.m. and proceed to Westminster Abbey. They leave the Abbey and return to the palace via a different route."

"There must be a dozen spots along the route to toss a stick of dynamite into the Queen's carriage," Christy said.

"Ten times that," Jonathan added from the door. "I know the streets, big brother."

The room was silent until Edith spoke. "We have no actual recourse, do we, Theodore?"

Theodore was reluctant to admit she was right. "I don't know. What is planned is already in play. It's the how and where of it?"

Edith said, "We must go to the American Embassy, and they must approach the British Government. We should have done that in the beginning. They would believe us, Theodore."

"How far would the words of criminals be trusted?" Abberline pointed out.

Christy concurred. "The very dilemma I've faced my entire life."

The three looked at Christy before Abberline said, "Why don't you trot on back and fix us a spot of tea." "None for me," Jonathan said.

"You told me yourself, Mr. Roosevelt. You assaulted two policemen at the pit. If you did go to the Embassy, what would they do? Lodge a diplomatic protest over your treatment? Ask the British government to launch an investigation? The ceremony goes on; the danger is not postponed."

"Ninety minutes," Theodore mused as he studied the paper. "Time and distance to travel," he allowed.

"A fair distance," Abberline said. "They'll make it easily enough at a cantor."

"Do you hunt, Mr. Abberline?" Edith asked. "The best hunters wait for the appropriate time at the best location. That must be considered."

She had Theodore's interest. "My dear. You do listen to me after all."

"You're more likely to hit a grazing elk, than one who is on the run, aren't you, Theodore?"

He was about to remind her it was far more of a challenge to bring down a speeding animal, when he understood what she was driving at. "Mr. Abberline, is the procession likely to stop along the way?"

"No," Abberline said. "Their lords and ladies would never consent to alter a timetable. Once it is set, Mr. Roosevelt, save for the street collapsing, it remains immutable."

"But, if there were an interruption," Theodore pressed. "The procession might be stopped for a matter of minutes. Or seconds."

"More than enough time," Edith offered.

"In America," Theodore said, "we refer to that as a sitting duck."

Abberline shook his head, walking away. He spoke with conviction.

"The streets are lined with soldiers. There will be hundreds of thousands of people crammed shoulder to shoulder. Even the strongest man, the tallest man, could not overcome that impediment."

Christy appeared with a keg lid bearing a teapot, cups, a sugar bowl, and a tin of tea.

"How is Mr. Shaw?" Jonathan called from his post at the door.

"Right as rain," Christy replied.

"Then the answer is obvious," Edith said. "The only scheduled stop is Westminster Abbey."

Theodore turned to Abberline for confirmation. "Mr. Abberline?" He nodded, but Theodore could see he was not convinced.

"The Prince of Wales becomes King of England, when his mother dies," Edith stated in awe. "It's like snatching a star from the heavens."

"Mr. Roosevelt and I," Abberline said, "suggested the very same thing, but not as poetically."

"As a ward of Lord Crittenton," Theodore said, "judging from my observation of the Prince of Wales, he's as steady as a reed in a hurricane. Crittenton controls the empire."

Abberline continued, "But the Prince in the procession. The likelihood of him being severely injured or killed by dynamite is significant."

"Then it is the indiscriminate murder of the royal family," Edith said.

"Do you have the time, Mr. Roosevelt?" Abberline asked. "I'm afraid my watch has gotten away from me."

Theodore glanced at a clock over the counter. "Just before twelve. If that instrument is correct. In ten hours and a half, the procession will begin. I will have some tea and read the newspaper. Perhaps, something will come to me.”

“If not, Theodore?” Edith said.

“At first light, I shall make my way to the American Embassy and plead my case. Perhaps, they will listen. Perhaps, they can prevent a tragedy.”

“We will go together,” Edith said.

Abberline curled up on the floor, wrapping his arms around himself. “I’m going to Australia. I’ve heard the place is overrun by giant, jumping rats. A man could live off the land forever.”

“That’s the first damned time I heard something logical come from your mouth all day,” Christy said. He realized there was a lady present. “Oh, pardon me, Mrs. Roosevelt. It was only my surprise at Abberline’s encounter with common sense.”

CHAPTER 48
NEAR WESTMINSTER ABBEY

Benjamin's body ached, and he was numb from little sleep, but his mind had never stopped. A steam engine, Benjamin decided, cylinder's stroking, camshafts rotating, and the angry hiss of steam seeping from pipe joints. If only one's mind was an engine of continuous wonder, he decided. A singular device, simple mechanics, a forever instrument that never tormented its operator. What a wondrous, mythical device. Fists were better.

He stopped in the lane, a space between two sagging buildings barely wide enough to allow him to pass. It wouldn't do for a man to be trapped here, Benjamin thought. He stood next to the livery and pressed his ear against the wall slats.

His heart slowed, and all he could hear was the sound of the building settling in the cool of the evening. No light from the streetlamps penetrated the lane, and there were no windows close by to carry voices; but it made no difference. He felt his way through the darkness with outstretched hands, fingertips trailing the surface of the walls. He had a sense that the night was just a state of mind and not a condition of nature. His mother's words, not his.

He heard voices vibrating through the wall, but they were noise without meaning. Two men spoke, one more demanding than the other. They were planning treachery against him. Daniel and Chambliss.

Benjamin drew his knife from its sheath, laid the blade on the back of his wrist so he could feel the cool reassurance of metal. He drew away from the wall, his mind making calculations like the abacus in his pocket. He heard the sharp clop of horse's hooves from somewhere to his left. The sound did not startle him. He'd heard it on the street every day.

He whispered his thoughts only because they were important and should not be contained. "Why do you have to complicate things? Keep it simple, I say. People talk a thing to death without thinking it through." Poor Schiess. His mind had worn down to a fraction of its size, and the powers of logic and analysis that had so amazed

Benjamin twenty years before had been eroded. Schiess was just a pathetic old man who never knew how much he had declined. "Couldn't you have lived another three days, old man?" Benjamin asked.

Well, if Schiess wasn't around to help him, Benjamin would fall back on the old ways. He was more comfortable with what he knew, more dangerous, than was certain. Fuses didn't always do what was expected of them. "Don't give the things too much credit," Benjamin castigated himself. "You talk as if the things have life." They did. For seconds or minutes, and then they disappeared. "I give them life," he said. "I'm God with a quick match. Yes."

Benjamin walked to the front of the livery. There was no lock and chain on the door, but that was so he could open the door and enter with ease. What was it? The fly to the spider?

Never mind. Things would play out as they would.

Benjamin took hold of the handle, jerked open the door, and rushed into the darkness of the livery stable.

The Times of London
Paris—Louis Pasteur's anti-rabies treatment has been
defended in the French Academy of Medicine by Dr. Joseph Grancher. Generally
accepted by knowledgeable physicians in most civilized countries, the vaccine has
been attacked by some despite its creator's reputation.

CHAPTER 49
SHAW LOCK AND KEY, LONDON

Edith awoke and searched for Theodore. Her thoughts were muddled with fatigue, and it took her a moment to locate her husband. He stood by the front door, next to Jonathan's sleeping form, buttoning his coat. It was a studied effort; each button carefully slid into the hole. He has decided, Edith thought.

She stood. "Where are you going, Theodore?"

He kept his voice soft so as not to wake the others. "Go back to sleep, dear. I need to step out, that's all."

Edith moved close to him. She was angry and afraid. "Don't lie to me, Theodore. You're going to do something foolish? Aren't you?"

Theodore took her by the arm and led her to a corner of the shop. She saw him struggle with an answer. She was sick with apprehension.

"I've given this a great deal of thought, Edith," Theodore said. He was being logical. "Too much is at stake and too little time left to us."

"You want to sacrifice yourself," Edith accused. "I won't have it. You're going to turn yourself in, aren't you?"

Theodore tried to soothe her anger. "It's the only way, my dear. Don't you see? I'll go to the American Embassy, explain everything, and the Queen and her party will be saved."

"Theodore," Edith said, "you are innocent. Nothing will come of your action, except your arrest or commitment to an insane asylum."

"We have no resources left to us," Theodore said. He swept the interior. "This is our army. Do you see them?"

Edith wouldn't let her husband sacrifice himself. "Mr. Abberline? Are you awake?"

Abberline stood near the counter. "Here, Mrs. Roosevelt."

"Christy? You as well?"

"I am."

Jonathan rose, towering over them. "I was awakened when Mr. Roosevelt stepped on my hand."

"Do you know this Irishman?" Edith asked Christy. "Have you seen him before?"

"I know what he's *supposed* to look like," Christy said.

"I've seen him," Abberline said. "And you've seen Chamblis, as has Mr. Roosevelt."

"What has this to do with anything?" Theodore asked.

"It is logical to suppose the attempt on the Queen's life will be at the Abbey. The Irishman, perhaps Chamblis, and maybe others will be there. Hidden, of course, but if we get there early, perhaps we can flush them," Edith said. "Theodore, you said it yourself. We are a small army. What if those that oppose us are equally limited in size?"

"But they are not, Edith," Theodore countered. "They have the entire police force at their disposal."

"Suppose they do," Abberline said. "We've eluded them so far. All we need do is continue to do so."

"Yes," Edith said.

"Chamblis and his gang?" Theodore said. "How many do you think?"

"Three or four," Abberline said.

"The Irish brothers are three," Christy continued the count.

"Seven," Jonathan said, totaling the numbers.

"And the police," Christy said. "Let's not forget the Peelers."

"Uniforms and inspectors," Abberline suggested.

"But the others? Crittenton's band? Most of them will be nowhere near the Abbey," Edith said.

"How can you be sure?" Jonathan asked.

Edith turned to Theodore, "Theodore, would you have taken a dozen hunting with you, or three?"

Theodore laughed at the question. "My dear, you are the most intelligent woman I know." He looked at the others. "She's right. Too many will spoil the hunt. Two hunters are ideal, perhaps four. But no more than that. And see here. They must have a line of sight. They may have a lookout or two, but they need to be able to see one another to signal the attack. That is our asset. We know they have to see the Queen's vehicle, so we will locate the vantage points that offer the best view."

"That's the spirit," Edith said. She threw her arms around Theodore. "Don't ever leave me again. The world doesn't need martyrs, Theodore, but I certainly need you."

"No Embassy?" Christy ventured.

"No," Abberline said. "I believe what Mr. Roosevelt is suggesting is that we go on the attack."

"How's that?" Jonathan said.

"We're going after the assassins," Edith said.

The Times of London
The Right Honorable Henry Parson CVO OBE is expected to be named Private Secretary to Her Majesty the Queen. The Private Secretary is charged with communications between Her Majesty the Queen and the Government.

CHAPTER 50
THE LIVERY

Benjamin saw the soft glow of a lantern hung on the corner beam of the farthest stall, as he crouched near the wagon.

Daniel emerged just on the edge of the light. "Benjamin? Is that you?" His voice was calm. His stance was relaxed. "What in the devil are you doing?"

"I heard voices," Benjamin said, standing. "Who's in here with you?"

"Put that knife away, will you?" Daniel said.

Daniel speaking in a soft voice. Friendly. Caring. What was that word again? Complacency. Benjamin had his answer.

"You don't need your knife," Daniel said.

Benjamin felt a twinge of guilt. He was almost beginning to trust Daniel.

"Who's here, Daniel?" Benjamin said. He waved the blade at his brother. "I heard voices. You tell him to come out, and we'll have a chat."

Daniel stopped. The lamp was behind him. He was a faceless figure, his body nearly blending into the darkness. "What is it, Benjamin? For God's Sake, man, put down that knife."

Benjamin studied the darkness, looking for any kind of movement.

"Daniel doesn't know," Chamblis said. He emerged from the deep shadows of a stall. "He doesn't have your gift, Benjamin."

Daniel turned on Chamblis. "I don't need any gift."

"To get along you do," Chamblis answered. "To last as long as me and your brother have, you do. Doesn't he, Benjamin?"

Benjamin saw Chamblis draw a pistol and keep it against his leg as a threat, a reminder that he could just as easily use it and end this nonsensical talk about gifts. Chamblis wasn't ready to throw the die yet. There was more to be done. "You made a fool's bargain this morning," Benjamin said to Daniel.

Chamblis chastised him. "Benjamin, have you so little faith in me?"

"It's my show now," Daniel said, his voice harsh, confrontational. He stepped closer to Benjamin. Daniel wasn't afraid of his brother. "You've treated me like shit for years. No more. You killed Michael, and you would have killed me, too.”

“You’re an evil man, Benjamin,” Chamblis said. “But an inventive one.” He slapped the wagon box. “You and that little consumptive have achieved great things. But now I’m here to take the burden off your shoulders.”

Daniel was bitter. “They don’t think you can do it, Benjamin.” His eyes burned with hatred. “But I can. I know all about the batteries and the wire strung over the telegraph poles. Everything you know, I know.”

Benjamin sunk the knife blade into the wagon’s sideboard, holding both hands out to show he carried no weapon. “Not everything, brother.” He sensed Chamblis moving toward him. “Move up next to Daniel, and we’ll talk. You can still shoot me from there, if you’ve a mind to.”

“He’s lying,” Daniel said as Chamblis joined him.

“Tell me what’s on your mind, Benjamin,” Chamblis said.

“He’s lying!” Daniel barked, sensing the conversation would betray him.

Chamblis looked at Daniel. “Shut up and let him talk.”

“What is it, Daniel?” Benjamin said. “Afraid you’ll lose your twenty pieces of gold?”

Daniel rushed him, hands out for his throat. Benjamin jerked the knife from the board, and, as Daniel’s hands closed around his neck, drove the blade into his brother’s chest. Benjamin felt Daniel stiffen as air escaped his lungs, and he slid to the ground. Daniel clawed at his brother’s coat and vest. Benjamin knew what the man was thinking; in the horror of pain and death, he thought if he could only keep himself on his feet, he would live. Daniel collapsed to his knees and fell backwards.

“You’re Hell on brothers, aren’t you, Benjamin?” Chamblis said. His gun was pointed at Benjamin. “Aren’t you tired of this silliness yet? Why don’t you tell me what you’ve done, and we’ll part chums?” He glanced at the knife. “I never saw a knife that could outrun a bullet.”

Benjamin relaxed. “They are too complicated. The batteries. Without the old man, I don’t know that I can make them work. Let’s keep it simple, I say.”

“Daniel thought otherwise.”

“When Schiess died, I stole a goodly length of fuse from the fireworks men. They should have kept an eye on their wagons. Slow fuse. I used the very same in the mines.”

“Nothing complicated about that, is there?” Chamblis said. “But dangerous? No? A simple fuse? Light it and run. Hardly seems sporting.”

“Sometimes the old ways are the best.”

“You see, Benjamin, Hasselbach was growing concerned. And his boss was growing concerned as well. They don’t have much confidence in men like us, those two.” He nodded at Daniel’s body. “You’re going to light a candle for the poor soul, aren’t you?”

"Why? He'll have more than enough light where he's going."

Chamblis didn't see the humor in Benjamin's observation. "You're not the only one, you know. We've got others standing by in case."

"Maybe. But I'm the best," Benjamin said. "It's a simple thing, Chamblis. A single match. And it's done."

"Where is the fuse wire?"

"I'm disappointed in you, Chamblis. Has loyalty no value in your life?"

Chamblis grew irritated. "Don't play coy, Benjamin. Tell me where, and you can go on your way. I'll even see to your brother's burial. Besides, we've made other arrangements."

"Go back to your café," Benjamin said. He watched Chamblis, his arm tightening at his side, his eyes searching for the right moment. He was done talking; he would have the gun in his hand in an instant, pointing at Benjamin. "Who is he, Chamblis? The other fellow. Another Fenian? Still, it's a good thing not to put all your eggs in one basket."

"You were the lightening rod, you bloody foolish Irishman. Blow up the Abbey? Now what sense would that make? My employers are gentlemen. They like things tidy."

Benjamin understood. He was never meant to succeed. If he wasn't captured by the authorities, it was up to Chamblis to stop him. The abacus. Beads sliding over the brass wires, each action spurring another, and at the end of it, the beads arrayed in mathematical formula. A predetermined arrangement, was it, Benjamin? The gentlemen's agent playing those beads so that no matter what you did, you were lost.

Benjamin saw Chamblis move. Danger slowed everything to a crawl. It was ridiculous, a man's heart beating with such force that it threatened to jump from his chest, while every action of his body was frozen. And his mind racing in a frantic bid to signal the arm and hand to pull the knife clear, while his eyes tracked the man who wanted to kill him.

Chamblis raised the pistol.

Benjamin brought the knife up, clearing his jacket, and his arm came back, muscles as tight as a spring, and then snapped forward, the knife flying through the air.

The air exploded in front of Benjamin, and a mule kicked him in the chest. He crumpled, landing against the rear wheel of the wagon.

He was at Coal Creek #3 in Luzerne County. Benjamin was a boy. The mules they had used to haul coal from the mine were nearly blind, and he should have known better than to come up behind them. A mule kicked, catching him with its hind legs.

He couldn't breathe, and stars floated in front of his eyes; and the strength was shaken from his body, like a dog shakes water from its back.

His mind searched for some explanation and decided the only one that made sense was the one he was afraid to consider. This is what it feels like to be shot, Benjamin thought.

The Times of London
June 21, 1887

In the frustration of that design, history will recognize that most momentous and far reaching political triumph of the Victorian Age, and from it, we trust, will note a new phase of a national development which may make a half-century not unworthy of that which closes with the Jubilee of the Queen.

CHAPTER 51
THE QUEEN'S APARTMENTS

Lady Anne entered the Queen's bedchambers at 4 a.m., leading a platoon of chambermaids, dressers, ladies-in-waiting, and a discreet Lord Manning, who laid the documents necessary for the Queen's review on a table near the royal bed. He quickly backed from the room, giving the Queen time for her morning toilet.

Three ladies-in-waiting fluttered to the Queen's assistance, helped her ease her bulk to the edge of the bed, guided her bloated feet into their slippers, and two, taking the Queen's arms, led her behind a curtain, and waited for the Queen to accomplish her first royal task of the day. She did so in silence, having made it known she felt conversation during such an intimate activity was the height of vulgarity.

She washed her hands in a basin near the screen, dried them, and resumed her position on the bed, this time sitting nearly erect against a wall of pillows. With a modest breath, she transformed herself into Queen Victoria, prepared to govern the empire.

"We are quite vexed to see so many weary faces in our chamber," she said. "Are we to assume that our company is incapable of rising to the occasion?"

"Not at all, Your Majesty," Lady Anne returned. The others were satisfied to let her speak. More than her gray hair had earned her the title of The Iron Duchess. "If Your Majesty recalls, Her Majesty's own willpower and stamina are well-known to be unmatched in the land."

The compliment was a prelude, Victoria realized. It was an argument that had commenced yesterday and was about to be resumed today. "We are not inclined to wear it."

"If Your Majesty permits," Lady Anne replied, "Lord Manning, Lord Howard, and the Duke of Ratliff have conducted extensive research into the matter, establishing a precedent that dates to Her Royal Highness, Queen Elizabeth.

Victoria was unmoved. "It hurts our head. We do not wish to wear it. It is uncomfortable.”

Lord Manning was announced and joined Lady Anne in the argument. “Your Majesty, the crown signifies your power. The power of the throne. On this of all days, the Queen should be seen wearing her crown. The people expect it.”

Queen Victoria’s eyebrow arched. “Do they? Very well, then, let the people don that monstrosity. We will not. We have indicated that we shall wear a plain cap as befits our age. That is our decision, and we expect you to abide by it.”

The assembly bowed, accepting her wish. Manning and Anne's exchanged perturbed glances. She was getting difficult as she aged.

“There is another issue, Your Majesty,” Lord Manning said. “It will prove to be disappointing to you, I’m afraid.”

“What is it?”

“If I may, Your Majesty,” Manning said, removing a note from his coat. “This arrived less than an hour ago.”

Victoria waved her permission to read it.

“‘From Lord Crittenton, Second Earl of Larken, to Her Royal Highness.’”

“You may forgo the formalities, Lord Manning.”

Manning bowed. “As you wish, Your Majesty. ‘It grieves me to inform you that the Prince of Wales has taken ill late last night.’”

“Albert?” Victoria uttered in horror. First her husband, now her son. Could God show her no mercy? She was griped in the cold certainty she was about to lose a child.

“Your Majesty,” Manning’s voice broke in. “Forgive me for startling you, but the Prince is in no danger.”

“What?” She was an old fool. And even worse she had been caught at it.

“Permit me,” Manning said, and read. “‘He enjoys the best of health under my own physician, who pronounces him incapacitated but only temporarily so. I regret to announce that the Prince will be unable to attend the Jubilee Procession, which greatly troubles him. He begs me to convey to Her Majesty his apologies.’” Manning folded the document handed it to a lady-in-waiting, who offered it with a bow to Queen Victoria.

“Leave us,” Victoria commanded. She reconsidered. “We require your presence, Lord Manning.” When the others were gone, Victoria spoke. “We are greatly concerned, Lord Manning, that our son has fallen under the influence of drink, as has been his wont in times past.”

Manning was sympathetic. “Your Majesty, I am entirely convinced that the Prince of Wales has been incapacitated by an illness, nothing more. Such, as I gather from the letter, is Lord Crittenton’s belief as well.”

Queen Victoria calmed herself before replying. An expression of any emotion was the height of poor behavior. “We appreciate your sentiments, Lord Manning, but we are equally convinced that Lord Crittenton butters his bread on both sides." It was a vulgar expression, but she felt it expressed the situation admirably. "The Prince will be absent from the procession. Our subjects will be disappointed."

"If I may, Your Majesty," Manning said. "The world has come to behold you, not the Prince of Wales."

Victoria appreciated the compliment. "You are too kind, Lord Manning. We sincerely hope the Prince does not regret his absence. Such an event, if we may be so bold, is unlikely to be duplicated in the history of the world."

The Times of London
Mr. Thomas Stevens of America claims to be the first man to bicycle around the world. The exact distance he has traveled, and the circumstances of his journey remain unknown. It is known that Mr. Stevens is a veteran of the United States Army Bicycle Corps and was well prepared for the feat.

CHAPTER 52
7:30 AM, JUNE 21, 1887
BIRDCAGE WALK, ST. JAMES SQUARE

The sound of Edith's stomach growling broke the silence. She smiled an embarrassed apology. "Apparently, tea does not suffice."

They were sitting on a bench on the edge of a crowded street, that had been occupied by half a dozen people, until Jonathan cleared it with a menacing look. "He's a soft-hearted fellow," Christy explained as the others found a place on the bench, "but thank God, he's a giant. I didn't fancy standing all day."

They were safe from view, hidden by the solid phalanx of spectators that milled about on the walk, searching for a vantage point. The procession wasn't scheduled to begin for another three hours, but the street was filled with excitement. Hawkers wedged their way through the crowd selling tiny Union Jacks or cardboard placards of the Queen. The vendors were jostled by spectators, anxious to buy a memento of the Jubilee.

The din was overwhelming, not thunderous, but constant; words ground into noise, except for the occasional voice that pierced the racket.

Edith slipped a handkerchief from her cuff and pressed it to her nose, hoping the faint aroma would block the stench of the crowd. It was almost frightening, thousands of wandering souls searching for a place or a purpose. Humanity unleashed.

Theodore pulled the procession schedule from his pocket. "Northumberland Avenue to the Embankment," he read. He looked up as Abberline pointed down the street.

"You can't see it from here," Abberline said, and leaned into him, "and then Bridge Street? Right?"

Theodore nodded.

"You can see the Abbey's spires over Westminster Central Hall," Abberline said. He pointed again, not satisfied Theodore had heard him.

"Yes," Theodore said. He felt a hand grasp his and looked to see Edith's smile.

She spoke but her words were lost. He shook his head, miming that he couldn't hear her, and she tried again. She finally conceded it was a futile effort and brought his hand to her lips for a tender kiss.

Theodore smiled, wanting to tell her how much he loved her and how she had changed his life. There would be time to tell her later, he told himself; but a cruel voice asked, "Are you certain?"

Theodore broke away from the idea, pulling on Abberline's coat sleeve. "We can't stay here," he shouted when Abberline turned to him.

"I'm aware of that, Mr. Roosevelt," Abberline replied tersely. They were all exhausted. Time was drifting away.

"We have to split up," Theodore said. "It will double our chance of finding the Irishman."

"You don't know what he looks like," Abberline said.

"No, but Christy does."

"In a manner of speaking," Christy said. "I've never seen the man, mark you. But I've been told."

"That will do," Theodore said. He offered Abberline, "We've got nothing else to go on."

"You'll go with Mr. Roosevelt," Abberline said to Christy. "Jonathan? Stay with Mrs. Roosevelt and remain here."

"No, he will not!" Edith said. Theodore tried to argue, but she cut him off. "I was the one carried off by scoundrels, if you'll be so kind as to remember, Mr. Abberline."

"Edith? Please!"

"Theodore, you will not win this argument. If I can escape my captors, I certainly deserve to see the thing through."

Abberline saw they were attracting interest from the passing crowd. "Let us not forget our situation, shall we?"

"I will go with Mr. Abberline," Edith said. "Jonathan, please be so good as to accompany your brother and my husband."

Abberline looked to Theodore to solve the problem his wife had created, "Mr. Roosevelt?"

"Well," Theodore said, "you said she has spunk. Let's play this out her way."

"Spunk," Abberline said sarcastically, "just the sort of commodity I desire in women. Very well then, this is what we shall do. Mrs. Roosevelt and I will stroll down Great George Street, turn onto Margaret Street, and look for the Irishman. We'll return by Old Palace Yard, through the Poet's Corner, and across the Cloisters. That will put us directly at the west entrance."

"The Queen's entrance?" Edith said. "How will we pass?"

Abberline ignored the question. "You three will make your way down Tothill and into St. Margaret's Church Yard. We'll meet there."

"We've agreed then?" Theodore said. He didn't want any confusion about the mission. "The quarry is close to Westminster Abbey."

"We'd better bloody hope that he is," Abberline said.

Theodore said, "Up to this point, we've assumed he's just one man. If we find him, Mr. Abberline?"

"Subdue him," Edith volunteered, but she realized as she spoke that they had a pitifully slim chance of doing so. They would need reinforcements of some kind.

Abberline's answer was unexpected. "The one thing that won't be lacking around the Abbey is the London Metropolitan Police Department."

Christy gave him an alarmed look. "Now just a bloody moment, Inspector. We've been doing our best to stay out of the Peeler's clutches."

"Find the Irishman. He'll have to have a clear view of the entrance. Mr. Roosevelt is a gentleman, let him do the talking."

"No!" Christy said. "Throw myself into Newgate for a hundred years? I did my bit for Queen and country, when I agreed to help you, Abberline."

"Keep your voice down, Christy," Jonathan said. "People are looking at you."

"Christy?" Theodore said. "All you need do is locate the fiend. Point him out, and I'll take care of the rest. You have my word." He held out his hand.

Christy, helpless, looked at Jonathan, and then Theodore. He took the hand but dropped it abruptly. "I'll find him, but you get the cops. And don't expect me to stay around." He looked at Jonathan. "You listen to your big brother, you great slab of goodness; when you see me run, you run with me."

"Yes, Christy."

"Don't yes me with that hang dog look," Christy snapped. "You do just as I do."

Theodore wanted to be clear about something. "Mr. Abberline," he said, "I must have your word, as a gentleman…" He didn't realize how frightened he was for Edith until now. Every hour she was gone had been like a knife through his heart; and now that he had her back, he knew he could just as quickly lose her again. "You will see that no harm comes to Edith. Can I have your word on that?"

It was Edith who spoke first. "You needn't ask that of Mr. Abberline, Theodore."

"You have my word, Mr. Roosevelt," Abberline said.

Theodore realized how worn the policeman looked. His cloths were wrinkled and stained, his face was haggard, and his eyes were red and swollen. It came to Theodore that he was as weary as Abberline.

He smiled at Edith, hoping to allay her fear. "Well, my dear. It is time once more to embark on an adventure." The words sounded hollow. He could not have chosen anything worse.

Edith moved to Theodore, throwing herself in his arms. She held him, and said,

“You must take care of yourself, Theodore. Nothing brave, you understand. And don’t be rash. No charges without the proper support.” She pulled back, kissed him, and joined Abberline. “We must be on our way, Mr. Abberline.”

Theodore waved to Christy and Jonathan. “Gentleman, we must be off.”

The Times of London
A troubled young woman has thrown herself off of the Vauxhall Bridge in full view
of a number of witnesses. The police have determined the woman to be
approximately 25 years old, with blonde hair. No other identification is available at
this time.

CHAPTER 53
BUCKINGHAM PALACE
9:14 A.M.

Queen Victoria felt overwhelmed in the Music Room, although compared to most of the other rooms in this wing, it was modest. She circled the floor in a casual walk, dressed in her typical mourning clothes, topped off by a simple white cap.

There were one hundred and fifty-eight royals of various countries, islands, houses, kingdoms, and empires, as well as their parties, in the Ball Room, White Drawing Room, East Gallery, and Cross Gallery waited for the procession to begin. Clamoring for an audience with her, Queen Victoria thought. Bees in a hive, each centered on an audience with the Queen.

Victoria had instructed Hopewell, Major Domo of the palace, she was not to be disturbed. Hopewell, diplomatic, calm, and patient, would see she was not. Even Lord Manning deferred to Hopewell. The Major Domo was her gatekeeper.

Victoria avoided glancing at the mirrors strategically placed on the wall to add dimension to the room. Years and childbirth had robbed her of her once petite body. She carried a silk handkerchief to add grace to her movements, but it was a silly affectation.

She continued to stroll, enjoying her privacy. The room's three crystal chandeliers captured light from tall windows bordered by forest green curtains. The parquet floor was a wild pattern that seemed on the verge of continuous movement.

Her footsteps were soft. She dropped her eyes and watched her tiny black shoes sneak from the hem of her dress and disappear, like kittens at play.

She felt someone at her side.

Albert had joined her, dressed in his splendid uniform, a red sash draped across his broad chest, his eyes deep, and commanding, but a playful smile tugging at the corners of his mouth.

"You are a naughty girl," he whispered to her. "All here have gathered to see the Young Victoria." He took her by the arms and gently turned her, so she faced the mirror. A beautiful girl wearing a look of amazement stared at her.

"Oh," she gasped in surprise. "How young I look?" She turned to Albert. "How handsome you are."

He scolded her with a fatherly look. "You are very distracted, my dear. Upon seeing you, one might even suggest you are in love."

"With you," she said. "You are my life." She saw that chairs filled the room in long rows. A quartet sat on a low stage, tuning their instruments. In the front to the right, slightly removed from the other chairs, were two for Albert and herself.

People were milling about, talking, laughing, and behaving as if she were not there. She was vexed at their shameful behavior and was about to complain to Albert, when she noticed he had somehow aged and seemed troubled. His side whiskers were shaded with gray and his pallor unhealthy.

"This affair with Albert Edward," Albert said. "I find it most unsettling."

She was startled by her husband's appearance. "Affair?" Was he speaking of the women? Poor Alexandra. How horrified her son's wife must be. But this was nothing new. It began virtually after their honeymoon.

"He has fallen under the spell of others," Prince Albert said. "He dishonors you by failing to attend the procession. He should take his place in the Guard of Honor of Royal Princes."

Victoria tried to understand. How did Albert know about this? She received notice just this morning of the Prince of Wales' illness. What has happened? Am I going mad? I am too old for this nonsense. I have come too far, given too much. Lost too much. Dear Albert, why did you have to leave me?

She considered the mirror. The beautiful young lady was gone, replaced by a matronly old woman dressed in black. She turned away before she became lost in the image.

"It was a dream," she said to the empty room. She made sure she was alone. To be overheard would be too embarrassing to consider.

I have given everything. She heard voices through the door, but the noise passed. "I wish you were here, my love. The years were too few."

There was a quick knock on the door. The door opened, and Hopewell appeared with a bow. "Your Majesty, it is time."

Victoria gathered herself and became the Queen. "We are at your service, Hopewell. Let us proceed."

*H.M.S. Baltic, one of the Royal Navy's newest monitor
class vessels was reportedly engaged in action with pirates in the Red Sea. The
pirates, severely underestimating the Baltic's armaments were wiped out to a man.
There were no casualties inflicted on the ship's complement.*

CHAPTER 54
9:28 AM STOREYS GATE

Jonathan led the way, parting the thick crowd like Moses and the Red Sea. Theodore followed, with Christy a reluctant third.

They were soon immersed in a swirling mass of people, the crowd buzzing with excitement. The sun's heat spurred them on.

For a moment, Theodore was convinced their search was futile. How could one find a single person in this mass of humanity? He pulled Christy next to him. He had to shout to make himself heard, but he knew there was no danger in someone overhearing him. The only voice the crowd had was an indistinguishable roar. "Don't lose sight of Jonathan. How close are we to the Abbey?"

Christy said, "There is the Abbey, right enough." He pointed to the right, over the heads of the crowd at the Abbey's twin spires in the distance. "If that big blockhead would step to one side, you could see it." He reached out, pulling on Jonathan's shirt. "Don't get so far ahead," he instructed his brother.

Jonathan nodded a reply.

Theodore said, "Well done. With any luck, we'll be there in a few minutes."

Christy gave him an incredulous look. "At this pace? We're better off to walk on the tops of their heads. This is a fool's errand."

Theodore gripped Christy's arm. "I know you're frightened, young man. As we all are. But you must take heart." It was obvious that Christy had had too much time to think about the situation.

"What do you care, Mr. Roosevelt? When this is done, you get on your boat and go home. Jonathan and me will get the gallows. You think because we're talking to one another, we've become chums? I know you don't give a bloody damn about what happens to me and my brother."

Theodore ignored Christy. "Jonathan?" Theodore shouted. "We need to pick up the pace. Can you do that for us?"

Jonathan glanced over his shoulder with a smile. It was a challenge, and it was obvious that he liked any opportunity to use his strength. "Stay close by, Mr.

Roosevelt. We'll be through this lot in no time."

Theodore leaned close to Christy. "I have no time to bargain, Christy, so I'll be clear. I have a gun. Find the Irishman for me, and you'll have your freedom. Impede me, and I won't hesitate to shoot you." It was a hollow threat. But as Jonathan cleared a pathway, he realized there was nothing idle about his words. It was his life, and Edith's life, and the chance to stop a murder.

He heard Jonathan's voice booming ahead, ordering people to one side. It was a game for him, Theodore realized. He was a child at play.

Theodore looked at Christy. The man was frightened, but of Theodore or the circumstances, he wasn't sure.

Now, at least, Christy would help Theodore find the Irishman.

CHAPTER 55
9:34 AM, GREAT GEORGE STREET AT BRIDGE STREET

Edith took Abberline's arm, as he led her through the crowd. She felt trapped, drowning in an ocean of people trying to reach Whitehall. She could not get her breath. She tasted sweat and filth, and she remembered the cool interior of the warder's cottage. The Queen's Jubilee. It was nothing but a carnival of madness; voices rolling over the people's heads. I want to go home, Edith thought, but felt ashamed.

A small army of boys waved dozens of placards in the air, hawking pictures of the Queen and the Royal Family. Others offered crudely printed Crosses of St. George. The street had turned into a torrent of people, swelling and rolling, until Edith felt herself being bumped from body to body.

"Mind your footing," Abberline shouted, pulling Edith to one side.

A large mound of fresh horse dung lay in front of her. Other pedestrians had not been as fortunate. The green pile was marred by their footsteps. "I must have fresh air, Mr. Abberline," Edith said. "I can scarcely breathe."

"This way, Mrs. Roosevelt," Abberline said. "We're on Old Margaret Street."

A regiment of soldiers, wearing gleaming white cork helmets and bright red coats, split the crowd in the street. The formation halted with a shout, peeled off two companies, and sent them to either side of the street. They formed a cordon, creating a pathway between the celebrants and the pavement.

Edith remembered that she hadn't properly apologized. "Mr. Abberline, I'm afraid that I have been unkind to you." She was afraid time would pass, and she would never have the chance. She wanted to tell Abberline.

"Unkind?" Abberline said. His interest was on the crowd, not on what she said.

"We believed, I should have said, I believed that you sent the message sending us, Theodore and myself, to St. Martins-in-the-Fields. I believe you led us into a trap. For that, I heartily apologize."

"I did not, Mrs. Roosevelt."

"Yes," Edith said. "Regardless, I beg you to accept my apology."

"Mrs. Roosevelt," Abberline said, "let it go."

"That's hardly the thing to do when one finds oneself in error."

"Wait a moment," Abberline said, pulling Edith into the recess of one of the stands. "Are you ill?"

Edith coughed. She fanned her face with her hand. The air was so heavy she couldn't breathe. "I can't …"

He pushed her farther under the stands. "Here. Get in the shade. Do you feel faint?"

"No," she lied. Her head felt as if it would split open, and she swept her long hair off her neck. It felt grimy in her hand. She heard a band approaching, the sparkling sound of fifes and drums filling the air. She thought of Theodore. He loved the military. She was being silly. Someone had a hold of her, and she struggled. It was the man with the white streak, but her alarm disappeared when he spoke with Abberline's voice.

"Come with me, if you please, Mrs. Roosevelt." He fought his way through the crowd, cursing them, elbowing them, until he found a space near a pile of discarded lumber. A round man holding half a meat pie in one hand and a soiled napkin, shouted at him.

"Here now! Who gave you permission to take my place? Imagine the gall of this chap," he complained to the crowd around them. "Come here with his bird, just because he thinks he can."

Edith slumped against the mound of scrap lumber. "Go away, won't you?" she said, exhausted. "I have to rest."

"Well, we all have to rest," the man said. "But you and your man ought to go someplace else."

"For a moment," Abberline said, "just give us a moment."

A short man shouldered his way next to the man with the half-eaten sandwich. "That's it. Give them a bit now, and what'll they take later?"

The big man drew on the speaker's indignation. "That's it. You've got it right, there. Now you two love birds, you up and fly away so Charlie Lester can see the Queen."

Abberline lifted Edith to her feet. "Come on. We've got to be going. There's nothing here but loud, fat men." He made a path for her through the crowd, as Charlie Lester watched in triumph.

He turned to the crowd. "See? See how it's done? Don't give up what's yours, I say. Fight for your rights." He noticed all that remained of his sandwich was a piece of greasy wrapping paper. He looked at the crowd with a hurt look. "Someone made off with my breakfast."

Edith pulled Abberline to a stop. "This way," she shouted. She was surrounded by madness, drums echoing off the fronts of buildings, the continuous roar of crowds as they cheered the appearance of carriages, and the knowledge, fear really, that they would fail.

They ducked through the uprights of viewing seats, coming out of the structure on the north side of the Abbey.

"We can't see anything," Edith shouted. "How are we going to find the assassin?" She saw Abberline ready to begin his arguments and then realized they were defeated. "There are too many people," she continued. "We must find Theodore and the others."

"I don't know where they are," Abberline said. "I can't see a bloody thing. No! Wait. Wait. We can go around the Abbey and come up on the other side."

"How can we?"

"It's our only chance. Your husband …" A battery of cannons fired a salute. "He's bound to have had as much trouble as we have. He might have to cut through Little George and slip through Little Sanctuary Streets. Both are too small for the crowds. If he does, I don't know if we can find him."

"We don't have time to track him down," Edith said.

"Yes, yes, I know," Abberline said. He made his decision. "We need your husband. We must find him and combine our forces. See here. We'll drop through Poet's Corner and across the Cloisters."

"Yes," Edith agreed. There was nothing else they could do. It was impossible to see anything over the heads of the crowds; the noise was so disconcerting she couldn't think straight; and she knew Abberline was just as frustrated as she. "Do you have the time?" she asked.

"I have no watch." Abberline said it with such a sense of loss, that he sounded like a little boy forsaken by his friends once knew he meant that the Queen's procession had probably left Buckingham Palace and was enroute to the Abbey. What he meant, was, they were out of time.

They pushed their way through the people crowding the sidewalk. They were under the white and red striped canvas awning that curved along the broad lawn of Westminster Abbey. A spray of flags topped an elaborate portico of streamers with banners and bunting. They made their way under the awning, nothing more than a way to mask a narrow lane that separated the south side of the Abbey from a cluster of decrepit buildings. Poets Corner was a humble strip of flagstones dotted with statues and bronze plaques.

Edith took Abberline's hand. "I don't like this place, Mr. Abberline. It feels as if it belongs to the dead."

"It might as well be a graveyard," Abberline agreed.

Edith craned her neck, looking over the towering wall of the Abbey "We'll never find the Irishman," Edith said. "He could be anywhere." The idea struck her. "Inside?

Can he be inside? We must find a way?”

“We can’t chance it,” Abberline said. “There must be a hundred policemen surrounding the Abbey. Let’s go through the Cloisters and find your husband.”

Edith ignored him, looking up. Above her were hundreds of wires strung from pole to pole, hanging from cross T’s. Telegraph wires, of course. Telephone wires as well, but not the thousands that cluttered New York’s streets. She stepped back, tracing the wires with her eyes, looking for an answer. It was a fantastic spider web, but with no pattern, no reason, no sense of symmetry to it.

“Mrs. Roosevelt? Is something the matter?”

Come now, girl, she heard Theodore’s voice; you can reason it out.

Abberline followed her gaze.

Edith could not take her eyes from the sight. “Mr. Abberline? Where would you hide a fuse if you didn’t want it found?”

“It’s not that simple,” Abberline said. “It can’t be.”

“No?” Edith said. “You see how one crosses the others,” she pointed to the wire, tracing its path with her finger, “and drops down into that tiny window at the base of the Abbey?”

Abberline looked up again, followed the wire with his eyes, and took several steps away from the building for a better view. “Bloody hell.”

“It comes from that building, there,” Edith said. “The livery.”

“Right,” Abberline said. He took Edith by the shoulders. “See here, Mrs. Roosevelt, I hate to do this to you, but you must find your husband. I’ll need his help.” He pointed to a modest lawn nearly overgrown with bushes and trees. “Go straight there. Turn right at the west end of the building. You’ll be on Tothill Street and then Church Yard. Mr. Roosevelt ought to be coming towards you. Find him. I don’t know what’s at the end of that wire. You must go. Now.”

“I’ll find him,” Edith assured Abberline. She threw her arms around Abberline’s neck and kissed him on the cheek. “For luck.”

CHAPTER 56
LITTLE SANCTUARY STREET

The crash of church bells from across the city filled the air, each trying to outdo the other, none able to silence the increasing thunder of the mob. The narrow street bound by tall buildings did nothing to protect Theodore from the thunderous noise.

Little Sanctuary lived up to its name. The crowd had rolled down George Street or onto the stunted King Street, to form up on Sanctuary Street before crashing into St. Margaret's Church Yard. Theodore, Jonathan, and Christy kept close to the buildings to keep a better view of the Abbey. The only way they could move closer was to force themselves into the crowd. That would have been madness.

They stopped in the doorway of a dressmaker's shop. "Now what?" Theodore asked.

Christy took his bowler off and slid his forearm over his brow. He gave Theodore a sour glance. "I don't know how to get any closer to the Abbey. Walk on these fools' heads if you must; we can't seem to go through them."

"I can," Jonathan said.

"Right," Christy said. "You take Mr. Roosevelt here and make for the Abbey." He dropped to the stoop and hung his hat on his knee. "I'll wait right here, until the circus passes on."

"Get up," Theodore said. "We need you."

Jonathan stepped between Theodore and Christy. "Leave him, Mr. Roosevelt. He's afraid."

Theodore looked at the big man. "What about you? Do you think we've lost?"

Jonathan smiled broadly in return.

"Well, then, stick with me." He caught his bearings. "How do we get to the Abbey's west end?"

"Follow me," Jonathan said. He pushed into the crowd with Theodore behind him. "Don't think ill of Christy. He's a first-rate chap, but he's always had that strange turn of mind."

"I know all about brothers," Theodore said.

Little George Street was a twin to Little Sanctuary Street, a slim ribbon of paved street bordered on either side by two- or three-story brick buildings. Jonathan and Theodore melted into a thin stream of people, making their way down Little George Street.

They stopped. In front of them stood Westminster Abbey. Its mass filled the sky. The only thing that separated them from their destination was a narrow field of merchant's tents and tables.

"St. Margaret's Church Yard," Jonathan pointed. "I believe we can cross there."

Theodore saw the flash of armor above the heads of the crowd. Cavalry. Lances, swords or helmets, gleaming in the sunlight as the troops formed for escort.

"Mr. Roosevelt," Jonathan said. "There are two policemen coming towards us."

"Look at this, will you, Earl?" Phil said to his partner. The two constables had no difficulty making their way through the crowd. They were given a wide berth.

"They said a big fellow," Earl said, circling Theodore and Jonathan. The two remained still, waiting.

Phil stopped in front of Jonathan. "A freak, Earl. That's what he is."

That was too much for Theodore. "Now, wait a minute. This man is my friend. You have no reason to accost us."

Phil turned to Theodore, eying him with contempt. "A gentleman, are you?" He closed on Theodore. "An American. This is the other one, Earl." His face was inches from Theodore's, and the man's breath stank of beer and sausage. "What have you done with Abberline and your wife, Mr. Yankee? Roosevelt, isn't it? A Jew. Come all the way across the ocean to make trouble for good, God-fearing Christians. You know what you've gone and done? You've bumped me and Earl there up to sergeant."

Jonathan started to speak.

"Shut your filthy hole," Phil ordered. "You know Earl came prepared, don't you? He's got a fine little Belgian revolver." He pulled a nickel whistle from the tunic jacket. "One toot on this, and we'll have the boys here before you can say Dick Worthington. This means a knighthood, for certain, doesn't it, Earl?"

Theodore felt the muzzle of a pistol pushed into his chest. Earl smiled at him. "One mistaken move, and you'll die. Let us all go for a walk, shall we?"

"Don't forget," Phil warned Jonathan. "He can shoot a big man easier than a small one."

"Do as they say, Jonathan," Theodore said.

Phil led the way, shoving his way through the crowd. Jonathan was behind him, and Earl was behind Theodore.

Theodore's mind was racing. He could break free, but fighting his way through the crowd would be almost impossible. He felt the gun in his back. When did they emerge from the crowd? Perhaps, then. But would that be too late?

He didn't come this close to failure. Think of something, Theodore. Find a way.

Christy crashed into Earl. The pistol spun into the air as Christy cried, "Get him, Jonathan!"

Jonathan spun, driving his huge fist into Phil's chin. The bobby's arms flew up, sending the day stick whirling through the air; and Phil fell against two surprised men.

Christy rose, picking up the gun. "What's the world coming to that Peelers go about armed?" He pointed the pistol at Earl, who was just climbing to his feet. "Take your friend and be off with you. And don't ever insult my friend, Mr. Roosevelt, again."

"This is a hanging offense," Earl said, helping Phil up. "You'll get yours."

"Go on," Christy said. "I'll have nothing more to do with you today." After they pushed their way through the crowd, Christy smiled at Theodore. "Leave you alone for five minutes and look how you end up?"

"Yes," Theodore agreed. "Come on." He darted into the crowd. It was thinning out a bit, melting into clusters, floating across the square. He was almost at a run. He saw a line of stands ahead to his right. Vendors in flimsy shacks selling cakes, pies, roast beef sandwiches, ginger ale, anything to part a person from his money.

Theodore glanced over his shoulder, looking for police. Christy and Jonathan were close behind.

Theodore slowed, moving behind the line of stalls. He removed his coat and threw it over his shoulder. The heat was stifling. He stopped, and the brothers came up to him. "Let's split up," he suggested. "You two go there and circle around the Abbey. I'll go in that direction."

"Do you think that wise, Mr. Roosevelt?" Christy questioned.

Theodore wiped the sweat from his forehead. "I don't know. Maybe it isn't, but we can cover more territory." The brothers appeared reluctant to leave him. "Go on, now," he said. "Christy? That took courage."

"Courage?" Christy smiled and shook his head. "Not a bit of it. I was too much of a coward to abandon you, Mr. Roosevelt. Good luck to you."

The brothers departed, and Theodore broke into a run, staying clear of the vendors. He had to find the Irishman. He saw nothing along the north side of the Abbey. The crowd had shifted, thinning out for some reason. He moved along the line of stalls, using them to block his movement. He had a clear view now.

He trotted out of the rank of shacks, keeping his eyes on the Abbey. Nothing was out of place along the side of the building. The dowager was untouched, settled virtuously in place, unyielding in grandeur.

Theodore found himself at the back of the immense bank of scaffolding covered by red and white striped canvas awning. He ducked under the framing and bent down.

He could see through the slits in the planking. There was a line of red-coated soldiers spaced along the street. He shifted position and saw a company of sailors drawn up in front of the Abbey.

The spectators on the scaffold above broke into a thundering ovation, and Theodore made his way forward through the bracing until he could see the street. They were cheering a company of Indian Princes mounted on beautiful black stallions. The riders wore silk turbans, anchored with shining gems, and tight-fitting jackets of red, green, and dark blue. They were magnificent and the spectators honored them with a boisterous applause.

Theodore stepped to a more secluded place. He remembered the schedule of The Royal Procession. It started at 10:30 a.m., with fifteen minutes between each station. There would be no variation, no delay. The Queen was the last to reach the Abbey; that made perfect sense. Were the Indians in the first or second procession? He tried to picture the schedule, but he realized he was sure of only one thing. The Queen was just minutes away.

Theodore moved closer to the front of the scaffold. It became nearly impossible to see anything. The soldiers lining the street were ten to fifteen feet apart, and Theodore had found a vantage point from which he could see through a gentleman's legs; but the procession blocked his view up and down the street. He had to take up a site closer to the Abbey. The only way to find the Irishman, Theodore decided, was to find something out of order.

He saw it on the third floor, the end window. The farthest on the right facing the street. Every window in the buildings was crowded with spectators, straining to see the parade. Every window save one. It stood, a single empty, dark eye, facing the street.

He felt his blood drain away. He'd been wrong. Abberline had been wrong. He knew a lair when he saw one. Theodore remembered the long black procession of Lincoln's funeral parade passing his grandfather's house. He could see everything from high above the street.

A superb location for a man with a bundle of dynamite. Or a rifle.

CHAPTER 57
TOTHILL STREET

She had run past the Little Cloisters, across a poorly kept lawn, found a natural pass between two hedges on the west end of the Great Cloisters, waited for grooms to lead mounts from the procession to a holding area, and then stepped onto Dean's Street. They had created a vast open-air corral, closing off the street for the procession's horses.

"Hold there, young lady," an imposing sergeant major ordered. He approached her trailing two privates. His size and manner made them look like children.

Edith did as she was told.

"What are you doing back here, young lady?" His tone was sharp. "Account for herself, if you please?"

Edith feigned confusion, stepping so close to him that she was practically hidden from the soldier's view. "Oh, please forgive me, won't you, sergeant major, but I'm turned around."

He was impressed that she knew his rank. He softened. "You know the army, then? Well, good for you, young lady, but you still haven't answered my question. There's to be nobody back here, except the groomsmen."

"Oh, I know, blast my silliness," Edith purred. "But I've become separated from my brother. We were in the crowd, and then he disappeared." She felt exhilarated concocting a lie and telling it with so little effort. "Perhaps, you've seen him. He walks with the use of a cane. I'm afraid he has a great difficulty getting about."

"You're lost, is that it?" the sergeant major said. He spun at the privates, voice booming. "What the Devil are you doing hanging about here? Go back to your post and stay there until I dismiss you." The two men were double timing away from the sergeant major, when he gave Edith a warm smile. "If you don't mind me saying, you're a charming creature. That red hair suits you splendidly. What may your name be?"

"Miss Carow," Edith said. It was disquieting to say her maiden name. It was almost as if her marriage had not happened. "Please? I feel dreadful, but I must find Theodore. He's such a fragile man. His leg, I mean."

"We can't have the poor sod staggering about the streets, can we? But before we set off in search of your brother, where may I reach you after this silliness?”

Edith flushed. “Aren’t you bold? Is it true what they say about British soldiers? I’ve heard you’re scoundrels. Get me to the other side of the Abbey, will you? If you do, sergeant major.” She lifted on her toes and kissed the sergeant major on the cheek. “You’ll have my address and my undying adoration.”

“Splendid. Now, where would you like to go, exactly?”

“The north side of the Abbey, if you please. St. Margaret’s Yard,” Edith said. She did her best to appear disconsolate and added, “Theodore vowed to meet me at that exact location.”

The sergeant major grew hesitant. “The Queen’s horse and several regiments of infantry are between us and your brother. Several thousand citizens as well. I can’t just walk you to the Yard without a good many questions being asked of me.”

“Please. It’s critical.”

“Yes. Yes,” the sergeant major brushed aside her pleas. He thought over the situation and snapped his fingers in triumph. “Never let it be said that Sergeant Majors John Rogers didn’t have an answer to every problem. We’ll go through the Abbey, Miss Carow. We’ll brass it out, and the Devil to anyone who tries to stop us.”

“You are wonderful,” Edith said.

Rogers offered his right arm. “Grab a hold, miss, and let us take a stroll. Remember, not a word to a soul when we get in the Abbey. You’ll be at your brother’s side before Her Majesty herself makes an appearance.”

The Governors of Northumberland Gardens have petitioned the Lord Mayor for funds to expand the Gardens into Greater Scotland Yard. Several blocks of buildings will be demolished to make way for the intended growth.

CHAPTER 58
ST. MARY'S CHURCH YARD

The window could be for either purpose. A lookout to signal the arrival of the Queen's party. Yes, beyond a doubt.

Or a sharpshooter. Which?

Theodore turned both options over in his mind. It was a fine location for a look out. Above the crowds, a good field of vision over to Bridge Street and the Abbey's west entrance just three hundred feet away.

But better yet for a sharpshooter.

Either way, Theodore, he told himself. You've got to get up there.

The shrill shriek of a constable's whistle startled Theodore, and he slipped deeper beneath the scaffold. He watched as three policemen wrestled a man to the ground, as they fought to keep a woman from kicking him. A pickpocket. He chose the wrong target this time.

Theodore returned to the vacant window. Don't be impetuous, Theodore, he warned himself. An open window could mean nothing more than an unoccupied room.

"Theodore!"

Edith rushed at him and threw herself in his arms.

He drew her close, squeezing her as if he might never see her again. "That's not a brotherly embrace," Sergeant Major Rogers said.

Edith felt Theodore tense. "No, Theodore. Wait." She took Roger's hand. "I owe you an apology, Sergeant Major. This is my husband, Theodore. I hope one day you will find a woman who loves you as much as I love Theodore."

Rogers snorted. "Love. What do I need with love? I've got the army." Edith watched him perform a crisp about face and marched away.

"Edith? What…?"

"Theodore," Edith cut him off, "Mr. Abberline has found them. There is a fuse of some sort leading into the Abbey. He sent me to find you." She stopped, surprised. "Where are they? Christy and Jonathan?"

"Circling the Abbey," Theodore said. "What about the fuse?"

"It's run from a building, over the cross trees of telegraph poles, and into the

Abbey. Mr. Abberline is waiting for our return.”

“Is he certain?” Theodore asked.

“Yes,” Edith said. “Mr. Abberline needs us.”

He hesitated.

“Theodore,” Edith said. “What is it?”

It was the window. Its dark eye called to him. “There is a problem,” Theodore said.

“What?”

“A window across the street. On the third floor of a building. There’s no one in it. Not a soul. If I were going to shoot a Queen, that’s where I’d set up.”

“But the explosives?” Edith pleaded. “Oh, Theodore, are you certain?”

“There is only one way to know,” Theodore said.

He was right, she knew he was right. “We need more time,” she said. “We have to delay the Queen’s procession somehow so you can get into the building, and for Abberline to find the bomb.”

Theodore nodded. Delay the Queen. But how?

“I can do it,” Edith said.

“Edith?”

“I saw horses on the other side of the Abbey. I can steal one and ride into the procession.”

Theodore was stunned. “Steal a horse? It’s far too dangerous.”

“We are out of time, Theodore. Get to that window. I’ll stop the procession.”

“I can’t …” Theodore started, and hesitated. “I can’t lose you.”

She kissed him deeply and said. “Don’t you realize, dear Theodore? Nothing unfortunate will happen. We’ve just now found each other.”

“Yes, of course,” Theodore said. “You must hurry. Stop the Queen as far from that building as you can.”

Edith smiled. “I will, Theodore.”

The Times of London
Mr. Morris King of the United States Meteorological Service will speak at the July
meeting of the Royal Meteorological Service on the subject of the extraordinary
snowflakes encountered this last winter at Fort Keogh, in the state of Montana, USA.
The largest snowflakes were 15 inches wide and 8 inches thick.

CHAPTER 59
POET'S CORNER

"I wish I had a time piece," Abberline said, peering around the corner of a dry goods store into Old Palace Yard. It was quiet on this side of the Abbey, and even the crowds that had been filtering toward the west end of the building had dwindled to virtually nothing. That meant that the Queen would arrive soon, and he had to act now.

He eased back up Poet's Corner, until he came to the livery. He had no weapons; the Roosevelts had disappeared; and Christy and Jonathan had probably abandoned the cause. "Well," Abberline decided, "that shows good sense."

The large twin doors of the livery were parted leaving a space no more than two feet wide between them. Darkness seemed to seep from the interior, and stillness filled the livery. Abberline approached the doors. The noise from the procession, cheering spectators, marches, and the crash of drums beating out a cadence reminded him he must hurry.

Instinct warned him there was danger inside. Keep your mind on the game at hand, he thought. A wandering mind was a fine way to shake the undertaker's hand.

Abberline crouched down, making himself less of a target, tightened his hands around the door, and jerked it open. Make it quick, old man, he advised himself.

Sunlight flooded the interior of the livery. Abberline dove in, rolled under the wagon. A dead man was watching him. Eyes slightly open, mouth gaping, and a feast for a hundred hungry flies. He'd seen worse. It didn't matter.

He lay under the wagon, looking at the body. Abberline was stunned when he saw the other man, flat on his back, with a large knife sticking out of its chest. He found an odd comfort in familiarity. "Chamblis."

Abberline crawled out from under the wagon, quickly searched the interior of the livery, and walked over to the body. Chamblis had a surprised look on his face, something that would have been comical, if it wasn't for the blood that had oozed down his chest and soaked the ground around him black. Abberline pulled the knife out of the dead man, happy to have a weapon. He knelt and searched the body, finding a wallet holding thirty pounds, a procession schedule, and two pieces of peppermint candy. Abberline threw the candy into the corner and slipped the wallet into his pocket. He stood, stepped around the unknown dead man, and examined the wagon bed. He didn't know what he was looking at. The wagon was loaded with huge glass jars, filled with liquid, with devices of some sort attached to the edge of the jars. A single, thick wire, fed in through the hayloft was coiled around the bed stakes. But it was not connected to the jars.

He could smell metal, copper he thought, maybe something else; and he noticed a wire leading from the contents of each jar, draped over its edge.

He returned to the thick wire, uncoiled it, and examined the end. It was electrical, for as much as he knew; and those jars were meant to create electricity. It wasn't attached, making it useless. Then, why was it here?

There were two men dead. Who killed them? Abberline knew Chamblis, but he'd never seen the other, younger man. He knew for certain the body wasn't the big Irishman with the red beard. He dropped the coil in disgust.

Where was Mr. Red Beard, he thought?

"Dear Heavenly Father, could you not see your way clear to grant me one bloody day where no one shovels shit on me?"

He walked out of the livery, shaded his eyes with his hand, and followed the wire from the loft and over the telegraph wires. It dropped alongside the Abbey and disappeared into a ground-level window. A window far too small for a man to crawl into. He surveyed the Abbey foundation along the Poet's Corner and saw what he was looking for. No matter the Abbey's grandeur, its stories of kings and conquests, or the coronations held under its massive cathedral roof, it was a building. Buildings in London during the stifling heat of summer should be avoided. In the cold, dank, winter, where frigid winds sneak into the best of these buildings, heat must be provided for the occupants. It was accepted. Buildings needed coal.

Abberline jogged toward the coal shuttle in the Abbey's shadow, he reasoned he had a fair chance of getting down through the shuttle and into the cellar unnoticed. He had no idea what he expected to find, but he had a knife and at least one criminal unaccounted for.

Where were the others? The Roosevelts? Jonathan and Christy? Was he the only one left? He shrugged. "So be it."

Abberline pulled back the shuttle door and was overwhelmed by the sharp stench of coal. His eyes began to burn as coal dust floated out of the chute, surrounding him, escaping into the sunlight. He pulled his coat over his mouth, placing his foot carefully on the slick chute. He felt a rough board along the wall, took a step, tentatively, and searched for another. The noise of celebration from behind him gradually faded. It could be hell into which he was descending, deep into the bowels of the Abbey that towered over him. One and the same, Abberline decided, and continued, carefully setting each foot firmly before advancing. His right foot dropped on solid ground, startling him. He hadn't expected to be in the cellar that quickly and knew he wasn't paying attention. He pulled the knife from his jacket pocket, reminding himself to be more careful. He didn't know how many conspirators he faced, or how they were armed. Roosevelt could still arrive and see the shuttle doors open and draw his own conclusion. But Abberline did not have confidence in happy endings.

He listened for the sounds of men moving about, but the Abbey's cellar was silent, stripped of any signs of life. He moved forward, his eyes adjusting to the gloom.

Abberline was clear of the coal bin, used a stone pillar to shield him, and maneuvered as quietly as he could for the base of another pillar.

Light flared up in the darkness, as a match hissed angrily.

Abberline froze. He saw a man sitting against the base of the pillar. A large man lighting a lantern. He stood, wincing. A huge man with a twisted smile.

The man with a red beard, the man from the Chamblis Cafe, held a pistol on him. A dark stain covered his chest. He was wounded. He raised the lantern, throwing more light over Abberline.

"I know you," Benjamin Dugan said.

"Abberline."

"I don't know the name." He drew in a breath but reacted with pain. "But I know the face."

"At the cafe. I saw you there."

"Right," Benjamin said. He waved the pistol. "Sit down, Mr. Abberline. All we have to do now is wait for Mrs. Brown."

The *Times of London*
In that design, history will recognize the most momentous and far-reaching political triumph of the Victorian Age, and from it, we trust, will note a new phase of a national development.

CHAPTER 60
GREAT CLOISTERS

Edith was frightened. She'd experienced that emotion so often in the last week it had become strangely familiar. As she followed the cleaners swarming in and out of the Abbey, dusting pews, setting candles, and sweeping up piles of dust, she was amazed to find the feeling that overwhelmed her now was anger.

She followed three excited servants out of the Abbey and into the Great Cloisters. They disappeared around a wagon filled with cleaning materials, and Edith headed for the street that had been blocked for the horses. Bored horse holders, each holding the reins of several horses, waited as mounted grooms led other animals to them.

Edith scanned the corral and the squad of horse holders. Their mounts, properly saddled and awaiting riders, were indifferent to the turmoil around them.

She was shocked to see there wasn't a sidesaddle in sight. Well, she thought, what did you expect? She walked to the edge of the corral. The horse holders were too busy to pay attention to her, as the grooms rushed back and forth, delivering mounts.

When Edith saw the bay, she almost cheered. He looked like her uncle's mare, Lexington, nearly 16 hands high, with two white socks and a bald face. Lexi, she was called.

The horse holder that held her, and three other mounts, was a slight boy in a uniform that hung from his slender frame. The bay was well-behaved, while the other horses tried to pull away.

Edith walked to the corral, ducked between the upper and mid-rails, and worked her way back to the boy.

"Hey!" one of the grooms shouted. "What are you doing there?"

Edith disappeared into the herd, gently pushing the horses aside as she made her way to her target. She heard shouting. Grooms were making their way over the fence and into the corral. She had to hurry.

The groom shouted at the horse holders, trying to point out Edith. Several other grooms joined him and stood in their stirrups to see into the mass of swirling horses.

Now the horse holders were shouting curses at the grooms, telling them to back away. The noise excited the horses. They fought their holders, trying to pull loose, whirling against one another, whinnying in fright. The corral became obscured in dust.

Edith covered her mouth, choking back a cough.

The bay was in front of her, ignoring the chaos around her. Edith held out her hand and touched the bays rump, patting it reassuringly. She slid her hand forward over its flank, felt the soft surface of the blanket, and then the smooth leather of the cantle.

The poor boy holding Lexi was shouting at the groom who had first raised the alarm.

"Where is she? Do you see her? What the bloody Hell is going on?" One of the men called from outside of the corral.

"Shut up, will you?" another said.

"I don't see anyone."

Edith patted Lexi's left flank. She was out of time.

She hooked her left foot into the stirrup, wrapped her hand around the pommel, and swung into the saddle. She reached down, jerked the rein from the horse holder's hand, and kicked the bay in the side. Lexi sprang forward out of surprise, barreled through a line of horses, and through a line of grooms.

A dozen horses, startled by the bay's flight to freedom, pulled away from the horse holders, and running through the corral's gate, added to the confusion. Edith draped herself over Lexi's neck, spun her around to clear a path, and dug her heels into the flanks. The horse lunged ahead, breaking through the phalanx of grooms, footmen, and led horses. It was like someone dropped a cannon shell into the mass, animals scattered, bowling over horse holders, grooms fought to keep control of their mounts, and Edith saw a pathway to the street open.

Edith felt hands grabbing at her. A soldier reached for Lexi's bridle.

"Now!" Edith shouted, and the horse tore through the crowd of soldiers trying to trap her. Edith felt herself floating in air as Lexi jumped the corral fence. The mare landed on the cobblestone, slipped but regained her footing, and bolted down the lane. She was on the street in an instant, and Edith guided her clear of the soldiers lining each side of the route.

Edith saw a string of carriages, surrounded by outriders, and cavalry straight ahead. The Queen's carriage was drawn by matched creams, and she was probably escorted by Life Guards. She shouldn't be difficult to find.

"There! Get her." A detachment of Native Indian Cavalry spilled out of a cross street, thundered through an opening in the crowd, and headed straight for her.

The exotic uniforms and fierce glare of the bearded Indians stunned Edith. Lexi, sensing the danger, bolted forward so quickly that Edith was almost thrown out of the saddle. She recovered and laced her fingers through Lexi's mane.

They raced down the middle of the street, passing between two rows of soldiers more preoccupied with keeping the crowd on the sidewalk than Edith's ride. She glanced over her shoulder and saw the Indian cavalry a good distance behind them. They were big men, wearing breastplates, riding big horses, chasing a slight woman on a spirited animal. Edith never knew she could enjoy excitement quite as much as she did now.

Edith saw the Queen's carriage. But guarding it were a dozen lancers, gold helmets shimmering in the sunlight, behind a solid wall of steel-tipped lances.

The Times of London
Jubilee Procession officials have taken every precaution to forestall any attempt by anarchists to interfere with Her Majesty's Jubilee. Scotland Yard, members of the Queen's Household Guard, and special units of the army have assured the public that they need not worry.

CHAPTER 61
ALONG THE PROCESSION ROUTE

Theodore kept a firm grip on his fear. Not for himself, he was certain what he was going to do, but for Edith. She was the one who was exposed to danger. He edged along the stands, squeezing between the structure and a building's wall. There was enough room for him to pass unnoticed until he got to the lower seats. There he would have to rely on brute strength, but he would have to be quick. If he delayed, Edith's efforts were wasted, and the Queen would almost certainly be killed. His timing had to be perfect.

He heard cries to his left, followed by screams; and in a bizarre choreography, everyone's head turned in the direction of the disturbance. The lines of soldiers who were drilled to remain at attention, turned their heads to follow the noise.

The spectators on the sidewalk in front of him did as he hoped they would, they shifted to the edge of the street for a better view. He pushed behind, and then through the crowd, as Edith raced by, low on the neck of a bay. Her skirt flew out behind her, and her red hair whipped the air with excitement. He heard a thunder of hooves and watched as a squad of Indian cavalry raced after Edith.

Theodore had no time to think about Edith or her situation, if he didn't act quickly, he would lose his chance. Lowering his shoulder, he rammed into the back of a thin man, shoving him out of the way. Theodore was in the street and raced between two soldiers. He heard shouting and more screams, and the whole world exploded in pandemonium.

He had another rank of soldiers to breach, and then the crowd. He looked up, locating the window, and then broke through the red line.

"Make way!" Theodore shouted at the people packed on the sidewalk. They parted, falling back. He found the doorway he knew had to lead to the room. A sign above it advertised vantage points available for the Queen's Jubilee at reasonable prices. Theodore went through the door and into a hall with a narrow stairway on the right. A plump woman, fanning herself vigorously, sat on a rocking chair, guarding the steps.

"Sorry, dearie," she said. "Every rooms let. If you want to see Her Majesty, you've got to take your chances on the street."

"The third floor," Theodore said, gasping for air, "did a single man rent the room?"

The woman increased the fervor of her fanning. "I'm sure I don't know; but, in any place, we've nothing for you. Now don't block the doorway. I'd like to see the celebration."

"As you wish," Theodore said. He sprinted past her and was halfway up the stairs before she knew it.

The Times f London
The London Dock Authority has announced the tempo-
rary closing of Wool Quay, Galley Dock Quay, Chester's Quay, and Brewers Quay
for repair and improvement.

CHAPTER 62
WESTMINSTER ABBEY

Abberline heard trumpets. A royal fanfare. The Queen's entourage was near. Benjamin slumped against the pillar, weakened by his wound. He kept the pistol pointed at Abberline.

"You ought to have that cared for," Abberline said. He had only minutes left.

Benjamin nodded to the knife. "You found that in Chamblis, then? I traded it for the pistol. I'll get it back from you when this business is done."

"You'll bleed to death before too long."

Benjamin swung his eyes to the fuse running across the cellar floor. "Two hundred feet a second, once it's lit. A might faster if the weather is right." He swung the lantern door open, exposing the flame.

Abberline watched Benjamin closely, waiting for an unguarded moment. The man was weak. He had to force himself to remain upright. But he was a big man with the strength to fight his wounds and enough to aim the pistol and pull the trigger. The only light in the cellar came from the lantern, but that might be to Abberline's advantage. If he rushed Benjamin, there was a chance the wounded man would overturn the lantern. It would be nothing for him to light the fuse. Drop the lantern, that's all.

He listened, more trumpets, but Benjamin didn't react. He was dying, Abberline knew.

Benjamin's head bobbed, before he focused on Abberline. When he spoke, his voice was faint, robbed of energy. "You're waiting on me to die, aren't you?" He laughed. The sound was as dry as an August field. "Well, God and the Devil can fight over my soul, but I ain't ready to go yet."

"Who hired you?"

Benjamin reached into his coat pocket, pulled out the abacus, and threw it to Abberline. "I want you to count the dead for me, Peeler. Those that died for or against a thing." He set the lantern next to the fuse.

Abberline said, "Don't do it."

Benjamin aimed the pistol at Abberline. "I'll kill you without a thought, if you move again." He swayed, caught himself, and slid down the column to a sitting position. He set the butt of the pistol on his knee to steady it.

Abberline could wait but not for long.

Benjamin looked up, as if he had heard his name called. "There? Did you hear that?"

Abberline watched Benjamin reach for the lantern, pawing at it, like a drunk reaching for a doorknob. He sprang forward. Benjamin fumbled for the pistol, pointed it at Abberline, and fired.

The Times of London
A Mr. Gottlieb Daimler of Germany is said to have in-
vented a carriage that requires the use of an engine only to move it about.
Experiments on such devices have been undertaken in this country, the United
States, and France with mediocre results.

CHAPTER 63
IN THE QUEEN'S PROCESSION

Edith saw the lancers walk their mounts steadily forward, a solid wall between her and the Queen.

She pulled Lexi to a stop and looked over her shoulder to see the Indian cavalry slow to a cantor and form in line to block the street. She leaned over Lexi's neck. The horse, sensing the trap, slipped sideways in excitement. "You have pluck," Edith said. "It's well you do. We've got to buy Theodore as much time as possible. We'll walk up to those lancers like we haven't a care in the world; but when you feel my heels, I want you to whirl like a Dervish." She patted Lexi's neck and tapped her on the shoulder with the reins. Lexi sprinted forward but slowed to a steady pace, matching the advance of the lancers. Edith heard the clack of horseshoes on cobblestones behind her.

The Queen's carriage, attended by driver and footmen in scarlet, remained still, waiting for the street to be cleared.

They were close enough now, Edith thought. She twisted the reins in her hand, jammed her feet in the stirrups, and leaned over Lexi's mane. "One, two," she counted, "three," she shouted, kicking Lexi.

The mare bolted forward as Edith jerked her reins to the right. Edith caught the lancers by surprise; but they reacted quickly, spurring their horses to catch her. Lexi was fast and four hundred pounds lighter than the lancers' mounts; and when she raced for the gutter, she had the advantage.

The line of soldiers arraigned along the sidewalk scattered, and Edith knew she had a chance of slipping past the lancers and reaching the Queen's carriage. She would have just seconds, but she had to warn the Queen.

A lance point struck Lexi across the shoulder, and the horse screamed in pain. Lexi reared, twisting away, and lost her balance. The sidewalk cleared in a frantic rush, people shouting and screaming as the wounded horse and the red-haired woman, fighting to stay in the saddle, fell into the leg of an arch welcoming the Queen.

Edith felt as if she were in the grips of a tornado. She screamed when she saw the lances rushing at her and felt herself losing control of Lexi. She was tossed in the air. The world passed before her eyes in flashes of color, and then she was engulfed in darkness.

The Times of London
Mr. Chester Greenwood announces the opening of his
General Merchandise Store by Appointment to the Queen, located on the corners of
Oxford and Vigo Streets. Goods offered include country clothes and waterproofs,
tartan cloth, and hosiery.

CHAPTER 64
WESTMINSTER ABBEY

Abberline ducked, but slipped and fell to the ground, rolling to his feet. The pistol shot sounded like a cannon going off, as the crash echoed off the stone walls. He rushed Benjamin, watching as the man pulled the hammer back on the pistol.

He had the knife out and tried to drive it into Benjamin's chest, as the pistol came up and filled his vision. He grabbed Benjamin's hand, jerking the pistol to one side. It exploded again; the noise so violent that Abberline felt as if his ears had been pierced by needles.

Benjamin forced Abberline's arm down, his strength overwhelming the inspector. Abberline fought back, driving the knife at Benjamin, whose hand clamped around the inspector's wrist like a vice.

Benjamin roared in pain, bringing his weight against Abberline. He kicked at the lantern, trying to send it onto the fuse.

The lantern rolled across the dirt floor, catching against a rock. The two men struggled. Abberline felt his arm being forced back, and he knew the gun was drawing closer to his head. Abberline twisted to one side, hoping to drive the knife into Benjamin's chest with the weight of his body. But Benjamin flung him around, slamming his body into the pillar. Now the fight grew even more desperate, Benjamin towering over Abberline.

Abberline was losing the duel. He felt his hand slipping, and the strength draining from his arms. Sweat rolled down his face, burning his eyes, and he tasted the salt. He was going to die.

Not yet. Not yet.

Abberline sunk his teeth into Benjamin's nose, feeling cartilage crunch. The iron taste of blood filled his mouth, and he felt Benjamin's hot breath wash over his face as the big man screamed. Benjamin tried to pull away; and when he did, Abberline felt him shift. That was all he needed. Abberline threw his weight behind the knife, driving it into Benjamin's body.

Benjamin staggered back, sagging. The pistol fell from his hand, landing with a thud on the ground. He looked down at the knife, reached to draw it from his body, and then saw the lantern just inches from the fuse. He stumbled toward it. Abberline forced himself upright, using the pillar for support.

Benjamin took a step, then another toward the lantern, and then sunk to his knees, gazing dully at the knife protruding from his chest. His eyes were fixed on Abberline, giving the inspector a crooked smile. "That's irony, all right, killed by my own knife."

Abberline picked up the lantern, closed the door, and set the lantern at his feet.

Benjamin licked his lips and sought Abberline out. "Would you be kind enough to light a candle for me when you leave this dreadful place?"

"I'm not Catholic," Abberline said.

"I'm not much of one, myself," Benjamin said. He fell forward in the dirt and lay still.

Abberline sat back, breathing heavily. His arms trembled from exertion. He knew fear would hold off until later, and then it would claim its payment, shaking his body as a reminder that death had been so close he could smell the foul stench of its breath. "Mr. Roosevelt," Abberline said. "I hope you have a bloody good excuse for missing this party."

CHAPTER 65
ON THE PROCESSION ROUTE

Theodore heard shouting below. The old woman had probably sent for the police to retrieve him.

He ran faster, taking the stairs two steps at a time. He stumbled on the third-floor landing, crashing against a door frame. He felt a sharp pain race up his right arm as he staggered to his feet. He drew the revolver from his pocket. He snapped open the cylinder and ejected the cartridges into his palm. Three were spent, three were good. He loaded those into the cylinder, closed it, and started down the hallway.

He heard the mangled sounds of talking and a few scattered cheers coming from the rooms facing the street. Every door to every room would be open to create a draft.

Even a current of hot air was preferable to the fetid atmosphere of a closed room. Every door was open except one.

The hall was a good four feet wide, a generous space for a boarding house. A row of double-set windows, each sash flung open, was on his left, with the rooms on his right.

He forced himself to move slowly, trading caution for the impulse to run down the hall and burst into the room. This was no time for a charge.

He faced the closed door, listened carefully for any hint of its occupant, tightened his grip on the pistol, and threw himself against the door.

It crashed open, slamming back against the wall, as Theodore burst into the room and hit the floor in a ball. He rolled to his feet, bringing the pistol up, ready for the assassin.

The room was empty.

Theodore stood in the center of the room, his arms and shoulder burning from the collision with the heavy wooden door, confused. There was an iron bedstead against one wall, a wardrobe on the other, a dresser topped by a washbasin, pitcher and towel rack behind him, and a small table and chair by the window overlooking the Abbey.

"Look at this!" a man shouted behind Theodore. "Look what this chap has done."

Theodore looked at the doorway. The hallway was filled with people fighting to see into the room.

"What is it, Terry?" a tiny woman immersed in the crowd asked. "Is it a bomb?"

"Bloody hell!" another man shouted. "It's a bloke with a gun."

Theodore waved them away with the pistol. "Stand aside, please." He turned back to the room as the hallway emptied in cries of confusion. It didn't make any sense. This was the perfect location for a sniper's lair. He couldn't have been wrong.

The window overlooked the Abbey. Theodore saw a stool turned upside -down next to the chair. It was out of place. Everything in the room was where it should have been, bed firmly against wall, pitcher within convenient distance of washbasin. The stool, a ready-made shooter's bench.

He went to the window and looked out. A band of streamers running across the street blew back and forth, blocking his vision.

Theodore looked down the street. The procession had stopped some distance from the Abbey. There was a mass of cavalry milling about the street, but he could still make out the distinctive horses of Queen Victoria's team.

Edith had done it. She had stopped the procession and given him the time he needed. He could not see her in the confusion; but he knew the Queen's escort was reforming, and the parade would continue its journey to the Abbey. If I had a better position, I might be able to see Edith.

Then he knew. The shooter. The best location. The idea sent him speeding out the door, scattering the crowd. Theodore raced back down the hall to the stairs. That's it. That's why. The assassin had gone for position, abandoning the window.

The roof. Far above the street, a complete view. A perfect place for murder.

Theodore ran up the stairs, stopping at the door that led to the roof. The door was opened a crack letting a sliver of sunlight into the stairwell. He eased the door back, crouching.

This was no time to be rash, but he knew the shooter would have a glorious shot at his target. Theodore realized that Edith's plan had worked too well. She had stopped the procession for Theodore to get to the shooter. But with the procession stopped and the streamers blocking his view, the assassin had been forced to seek another location.

Theodore stepped into the sunlight. The heat on the roof sucked the breath from his lungs. The tarred surface pulled at his boots, a thousand tiny fingers. He stopped, surveying the scene.

There were three chimney blocks, each a brick fortress with a dozen cast iron tubes jutting from them. There was no room on the blocks for a shooter to position himself for a good view of the street. Theodore decided to move around to the left. Hopefully, that would bring him behind the shooter.

Theodore stepped carefully. The tar sucked at his shoes. He twisted his foot before lifting it to move. He made it to the first chimney block. He kept close to the brick wall, pistol up, ready. He squatted down, listening, trying to balance on the slippery surface. He set his right foot carefully, settled himself in position, and then peered around the block.

A rifle butt rushed toward him. He threw his arm up, blocking the blow, crying out with pain. He stumbled, landing on his back. He nearly had the pistol up, when he saw the rifle pointed at him.

A tall man holding a Mauser action rifle had it aimed at Theodore's chest.

"Drop the pistol," the shooter said.

"Drop the rifle," Theodore ordered.

The man shook his head. "Whatever you think you're going to do, won't matter. It's all done. Lower your pistol, and you might get out of this."

He had no play. The man would kill him before he moved the pistol. Theodore tossed the revolver aside and climbed to his feet, holding his hands in the air.

"Who the Hell are you?" the man demanded.

"Theodore Roosevelt."

"Roosevelt? You're that woman's man?"

Theodore knew who he was. Congreve, the warder. "You can't shoot me. The authorities will hear the shot."

Congreve growled contemptuously, "They wouldn't hear a cannon firing in all this noise. Turn around."

Theodore shook his head defiantly. "No."

"I'll shoot you here."

Theodore didn't move. "You'll be found out my friend; and when you are, it's the gallows for you." He inched feet back.

"Why the hell didn't you stay in America?" Congreve swung the butt of the rifle. Theodore ducked, heard Congreve cuss, and saw him pivot. His boots were stuck to the roof. He was thrown off balance.

Theodore threw a fierce right hook that caught Congreve on the corner of the eye. The shooter staggered to one side but slipped in the molten tar, dropping his rifle. He struggled to remain upright.

Theodore threw another punch, catching Congreve on the chin; but the man shook it off and rushed at Theodore. He barreled into Theodore, trapping him in a bear hug, and threw him on the roof.

Congreve glanced around frantically, trying to locate his rifle. Theodore pushed himself up and charged Congreve. He rammed the warder in the chest, knocking him off his feet.

A fanfare split the air, and Theodore knew the Queen was just arriving at Westminster Abbey. But where was the rifle? Had it fallen off the roof? He saw Congreve rolling to his knees, his shadow falling over the rifle. Theodore had knocked the man onto the weapon.

Congreve rose, the rifle in his hand, bringing it up.

Theodore raced at Congreve, hitting him high on the shoulder and chest. A rifle shot cracked in the air about Theodore's head, as he and Congreve fell back. He slipped in the tar, tried to regain his footing, slipped again, and grabbed Theodore's coat, pulling him.

They tumbled off the roof. Theodore grabbed the brick edging. Congreve's weight was too much. He heard a rip and saw surprise on Congreve's face as Theodore's coat tore away. There was a scream that ended in a crash and the sound of wood splintering.

The iron top cap burned into his hands. Theodore kicked his leg up over the top cap and managed to pull himself up. He fell on the roof and climbed slowly to his feet. He looked below. Congreve's body splayed in the wreckage of an outhouse.

He collected the Mauser and pistol. Now, his only concern was Edith.

CHAPTER 66
CRITTENTON'S ESTATE, 12 MILES FROM LONDON

L ord Crittenton received the delegation from the Prince of Wales in his library. He was surprised to see that Inspector Frederick Abberline led the group, but he had prepared himself for any eventuality. He recognized the others: Colonel Banks, Lord Arnett, Brigadier General Marsham, and young Major Charleston, a favorite of the Prince's.

"Gentlemen," Lord Crittenton said. "What an unexpected pleasure."

"You can hardly call it that," Abberline said. "I'll wager it was expected, but I'm certain it won't be a pleasure."

"General Marsham," Crittenton said. "why are you letting this policeman speak for this august group?"

"Because, Lord Crittenton, it is the Prince of Wales' wish, and this gentleman risked his life to foil a plot to murder the Queen."

Crittenton said, "Yes, I heard about that treacherous event, but I have no idea what brings you gentlemen here."

"The Prince of Wales," Abberline said, "recognizing your good service to the royal family, and to himself, in particular, is certain that you will undertake yet another task that will assure your loyalty."

Major Charleston laid a box on Crittenton's desk and opened the lid. An Adam's revolver was nestled in the red velvet interior.

Crittenton looked at the group. "You can't be serious."

"I think the expression," Abberline said, "is dead serious."

"Now see here…" Crittenton began.

"Crittenton," Lord Arnett stopped him, "the whole distasteful charade is over. We know about Hasselbach, your man Congreve, and the Irish connection. You wanted to stop the Home Rule Bill. You wanted to eliminate the Queen and replace Her Royal Majesty with the Prince of Wales, in hopes you could control him."

"You poisoned him," Abberline continued, "so he would be too ill to attend the procession. You couldn't take the chance he would be injured or killed. And as far as this suggestion goes," he waved at the pistol, "I would much prefer you be hanged."

"It's this," General Marsham said, "or your lands seized, your fortune confiscated, your peerage revoked, and your family turned out."

"Why not a trial?" Crittenton asked. "Why not let me tell all I know and watch the monarchy topple? I'm not the sort to give in to threats. Come, gentlemen, let's play this out in a court of law for everyone to see."

Abberline dismissed the others with a glance. He waited until the door closed behind him before he spoke. "I am a policeman. I serve justice as best I know how."

"How quaint," Crittenton said. "So, you would like me to take my own life? There's no justice in that, is there?"

A moment passed before Abberline replied. "I suppose it's all up to the bloke holding the gun." He pulled a revolver from his coat and pointed it at Crittenton's head. He pulled the hammer back and watched a flicker of horror cross the other man's face.

"I don't see you playing the murderer," Crittenton said calmly.

"You could be wrong," Abberline said. He squeezed the trigger. The room exploded.

Gun smoke hung in the air as Abberline sidestepped Crittenton's body, placed his pistol next to the dead man, swept up the box containing the other pistol, and left.

The Times of London
Parliament announced the increase of the Public Bills
Committee, from 12 and to16 members. The members of this committee consist of
representatives of both houses who are selected for a specific term of service.

CHAPTER 67
THE PERSONAGE WAITING ROOM, BUCKINGHAM PALACE

Theodore paced in front of Lord Manning, who decided it was more appropriate to read from a dossier than to discuss the matter with the American. Mr. Roosevelt, whose wife was under a doctor's care in the bedchamber next door, hardly seemed the patient type. Manning, feeling that good breeding required him to engage the American, decided to offer Roosevelt a bit of comfort in his own way.

"Are you Americans all an energetic lot?" he asked. "Or are you an aberration?"

Theodore stopped and glared at Manning. "My wife is injured. I am not concerned with your opinion of my countrymen."

"Your wife," Manning returned calmly, "is in excellent hands. Lord Callaud, despite his Gallic heritage, is Her Majesty's Own Physician and very competent. And you, sir, are a hero." He held up the dossier. "This report tells me so."

"Edith is the hero," Theodore said. "Abberline is the hero. I was lucky."

Manning gave Theodore a wry glance. "Yes. Is that not the case with all live heroes? Touching on this matter of heroics, Her Majesty has made the unprecedented and remarkable decision, despite my misgivings, to visit you and your wife; here, in this suite. Are you familiar with the proper etiquette?"

"Of course," Theodore snapped. "For God's sake, man, I'm not a provincial."

Manning was barely convinced. "Of course not."

The bedchamber door opened, and Doctor Callaud, a small man with a round torso, followed by two nurses in gleaming white and blue uniforms, appeared. He crooked his finger at Theodore. "Your wife would like to see you now, Mr. Roosevelt. Please be so kind as to limit your visit."

Theodore rushed by them before the doctor finished his directions, slamming the door behind him.

Callaud looked at Manning to explain this unusual behavior. Manning shrugged before returning to the dossier. "Americans."

Edith sat in a wheelchair as a nurse tucked a blanket over her lap. A bandage covered her forehead, and her right arm was in a sling; but, to Theodore, she was the most beautiful creature he had ever seen.

"Theodore!" she said, her face breaking into a smile. Her red hair, carefully combed and falling to below her shoulders, glowed in the light streaming through the windows.

He rushed to her but stopped, unsure of what to do. The nurse, hardly more than a child, stood to one side, hands properly cupped over her waist. Theodore's situation amused her. "Shall I wheel you to the Waiting Room, Mrs. Roosevelt?" she asked Edith.

"No, thank you," Edith replied. "My husband will assist me."

The nurse curtsied. "You have a most remarkable wife, Mr. Roosevelt," she said.

The sentiment embarrassed Theodore. "I know that. I wouldn't have married her otherwise." After the nurse left, Theodore turned to Edith. "Remarkable, indeed. How many times have I expressed the very same thought?"

"Do I warrant an embrace?" Edith said.

Theodore looked at Edith in exasperation. "I don't want to hurt you."

"Kiss me then," Edith ordered.

Theodore leaned over, wrapped his arms awkwardly around her waist and kissed Edith deeply. He held her, rapidly kissed her cheeks and neck, and returned to her lips. He stood, grinning broadly.

"I want to go home immediately," Theodore said, "as soon as you are well."

"I am well now," Edith said. She stroked Theodore's arm with her free hand. "But we are not going home just yet. You owe me a real honeymoon."

"But you're injured."

"Bumps, and bruises, and a sprained wrist. I want to see Italy and France. I want to see everything."

Theodore laughed. "Why, my dear girl. What's gotten into you? I couldn't pry you away from your books, and now you've become an adventuress."

"Yes," Edith said. "It was an unexpected conversion."

"Well, that sort of thing happens," Theodore agreed.

Edith suddenly remembered. "What about Abberline? And Johnny? And Christy? What's happened to them?"

Theodore took Edith's hand in his and kissed it. "Safe. Every one of them. Johnny and Christy were released and compensated by the Metropolitan Police. I haven't seen Abberline, but I was told he would be well taken care of." He looked at Edith, "France?"

"Italy, first," she said. "There are too many intrigues in France at present."

"Indeed," Theodore said. "Unlike England."

They were interrupted by a soft knock at the door. Lord Manning appeared, announcing himself by coughing delicately into the back of his hand. "I hate to disturb this romantic reunion, but I've been informed the Queen will arrive shortly. It would be indelicate for Her Royal Majesty to hold an audience in this bed chamber, regardless of Mrs. Roosevelt's injuries."

Edith tugged on Theodore's sleeve. "He's right, Theodore, wheel me into the Waiting Room. Quickly, now."

Theodore took hold of the cane back of the chair and pushed. "I hope Her Majesty doesn't expect you to curtsy."

"Unlikely," Lord Manning answered for Edith. "But she may be required to tilt the chair forward in deference."

Queen Victoria entered the waiting room. A little black crow with white lace cuffs and a sad, round face, Edith thought.

"Your Majesty," Lord Manning said. "May I present Mr. Theodore Roosevelt and his wife, Mrs. Edith Roosevelt, of America."

Edith sensed Theodore, who stood close to the chair, bowing. She inclined her head as a poor substitute for rising.

Queen Victoria settled into a chair, smiling permission at Manning to begin.

"Her Royal Majesty wishes me to express her appreciation for the service rendered by both of you, in the late unpleasantness visited on Her Majesty's Jubilee Procession."

"My pleasure," Theodore said.

Edith responded to the shocked look on Queen Victoria's face. "What Mr. Roosevelt means is that it was our honor and privilege to serve you in your time of need."

Victoria glanced at Manning. "She must be the politician."

"What my wife means to say …" Theodore began.

Victoria raised a thin, white-gloved hand to silence him. "We are not interested in your interpretation, Mr. Roosevelt. And as for you, Mrs. Roosevelt, we are most impressed with your spirited ride into the lances of our guards." She waved Manning to carry on.

"While Her Majesty has taken precious time from her various Jubilee Celebrations to thank you, there is an entirely practical consideration for this audience."

"There is?" Edith said.

"Due to the delicacy of the recent events," Manning continued, "Her Majesty feels it necessary that neither of you speak of this incident. Mrs. Roosevelt, your heroic ride will be explained as that of a maddened suffragette intent on embarrassing the government. The poor woman was killed in a fall from her horse. Mr. Roosevelt, your confrontation with the villain Congreve is reduced to a drunken encounter, the late Mr. Congreve, falling to his death."

Theodore, disappointed, replied with a simple, "Oh."

"It is a shame, is it not, Mr. Roosevelt," Her Majesty said, "that one's efforts are often reduced to afterthoughts? You may be assured we are familiar with that same dilemma and have learned to accept it. Your efforts, both of you, are to be lauded, but they will also be denied." She held her hand up, seeking Manning's arm for assistance to rise. She spoke to Theodore and Edith. "We envy you, your youth, and life together. We pray your years are free of toil and pain."

Manning led her to the door, opened it with a bow, and followed her out.

It was a moment before Edith spoke. "How sad she seemed. I could just cry, Theodore."

"Not for her or us either," Theodore said. "We have countries to see and a home to build." He grinned at her. "That Abberline fellow impressed me."

"Oh?" Edith said.

"I think I would make a splendid policeman. Do you think I would make a splendid policeman?"

"Not at all. You haven't the temperament," Edith said.

"Well, I must set my sights on something."

"Why not, president?" Edith said.

"That, too," Theodore said, hooking his thumbs into his vest pockets. "First a policeman, then president. What do you think?"

"Bully, Theodore," Edith said, "just bully."

www.ingramcontent.com/pod-product-compliance
Lightning Source LLC
Chambersburg PA
CBHW042103160726
48295CB00017B/968